NO WAY IN HELL

A STEEL CORPS & TRIDENT SECURITY CROSSOVER

J.B. HAVENS & SAMANTHA A. COLE

USA Today Bestselling Author

To our readers and loyal fans.
Without you, this book would never have been a thought in our minds.

AUTHORS' NOTE

Any information regarding persons or places has been used with creative literary license so there may be discrepancies between fiction and reality. The Navy SEALs and other US military branch's missions and personal qualities within have been created to enhance the story and, again, may be exaggerated and not coincide with reality.

The authors have full respect for the members of the United States military and the varied members of law enforcement and thank them for their continuing service in making this country as safe and free as possible.

The room stank of vomit and piss. Seriously? The police department couldn't pay someone to clean their fucking interrogation room? Carter sat in silence, his knee jiggling like crazy almost on its own accord. He'd fucked up—big time. At eighteen, just when he thought he could turn his life around, his past had come back to bite him in the ass. And now, his life was over. Kaput.

The only reason he'd gone back to his foster father's house after completing his boot camp training in the Marine Corps was because of Vicki Sanders, another foster child Roland and Marion Osbourne had taken in. While some kids came and went, Carter and Vicki had been with the Osbourne's for three and two years, respectively. They'd both learned over the years not to get too attached to anyone because it was only a matter of time before they'd be shipped off to another foster home. Carter had been in the system since his birth mother had abandoned him at a Walmart when he was six. Vicki's parents had been killed in a car accident when she was ten, and no relatives stepped forward to take her in.

Despite his resistance to the younger girl's charm, Carter had come to love her like the sister he'd never had. When he'd reached his eighteenth birthday, he'd enlisted—not just for a better life for himself, but a better life for her. She was sweet, pretty, and smart as a whip. While it wasn't for him, he wanted to help pay for her college when she graduated high school in two years. The Osbournes were more interested in gambling away the stipends they got from the state for fostering than helping the kids. Once the fosters reached eighteen and were no longer moneymakers, the couple kicked them out, not giving a crap where they went or what happened to them after that.

After the boot camp graduation ceremony, Carter had been given three days leave before he was supposed to ship out to Hawaii, so he'd hitchhiked from San Diego to Temecula, an hour's drive away. He'd wanted to show off his uniform and new muscles to his foster sister. She'd always teased him that about his skinny arms and legs, but in a loving way. It was far from the teasing and bullying he'd been subject to over the years, constantly being the "new kid" at school after bouncing from one district to the next.

The Osbournes lived on a street that bordered both the low and middle class areas of the city. But one look at its peeling paint, curling roof tiles, and brown grass and shrubs, you knew exactly what income level it favored.

When he'd arrived at the house, the first thing he'd noticed was the Osbournes' old Ford was in the driveway. That was nothing new. Neither of them worked, relying on their combined disability and the foster checks. But on Thursdays, Marion took the bus to go visit her mother in a nursing home. She couldn't care less about the woman other than the small inheritance she was supposed to get whenever her mother finally croaked.

The next thing Carter had become aware of when he

entered the house was Roland wasn't sitting in his recliner, chain smoking, and burping up lunch. The TV was blasting and Carter had grabbed the remote, lowering the volume. That was when he'd heard it. A soft cry of pain, followed by begging. "P-please. Stop."

And then another voice. Harsher. Deeper. "Shut up, you little bitch. You fucking owe me."

Cold ice had run through his veins. No. No way was that bastard doing what Carter thought he was doing. He didn't even remember taking the steps down the hall. Finding Vicki's door locked, he'd kicked it in. The scene before him had had him seeing red. Fury had pulsed through him, as Roland jumped from the bed he'd just been raping Vicki in and tried to stuff his dick back in his pants.

"What the fuck are you doing here, boy? You don't live here no more!"

Vicki stared at Carter in horror. Her clothes were torn, her face red, swollen, and wet with tears. She'd grabbed a blanket to cover herself up, but he was no longer looking at her. His focus had been all on the man he was about to kill.

Carter had very little recollection of what had happened after that. All he knew was his fists were now raw and bloody, he was under arrest, and Vicki and Roland had been transported to the hospital in different ambulances. He had no idea if the bastard was dead or alive and didn't care. All he cared about was finding out if Vicki was okay, but no one would answer his questions.

He'd been placed in this interrogation room almost two hours ago. The door was locked with a police officer standing guard outside. Carter knew this because the cop had escorted him to the bathroom and back about a half hour ago. No one had come to interview him, to get his side of the story. He wondered if anyone was behind what had to be a two-way mirror watching him, waiting for him to break down and confess. Not that it mattered, they had him dead to rights. The patrol officers had needed to physically haul him off Roland's unconscious body. No matter what happened, his life in the military was over before it had barely begun.

The clock on the wall continued to tick off the minutes until, finally, the door opened and a man in his forties walked in, wearing a navy blue suit, white shirt, and red tie. He was about six feet tall and two hundred pounds. His dark brown eyes matched his dark hair which was a little longer than a crewcut. Without saying a word, he tossed a thick folder on the table and sat down across from Carter.

They stared at each other for several minutes. Carter felt like a lab rat being analyzed, and he fought the urge to squirm. Soon, the younger man couldn't take the silence anymore. "Who are you? A detective? Can you at least tell me if Vicki is okay before you send me to county?" The local lockup was probably his first stop on the way to state prison.

Instead of answering the questions, the man sat forward and opened the manila folder. Carter was shocked to see the photo that'd been taken of him for his military ID weeks earlier. He really had changed since then, adding at least thirty pounds of muscle to his formerly lank frame. Even his face appeared different.

"Private First Class Carter, my name is Gene McDaniel, and I work for the United States government. I'm here to offer you the choice of two options. Number one—I walk back out that door, you never see me again, and probably spend the next few years in prison for attempted murder." Carter's mouth gaped. Well, that told him the bastard was still alive. "Option number two—you come work for me. Now, before you answer that, let me explain a few things. If you come work for me, it means as far as everyone who knows you is concerned, you're dead—killed in a prison fight. Your Marine Corps record, as short as it is, will disappear. You will become a ghost in the world of black ops. You will belong to Uncle Sam and defend this country until your dying breath. So, what's it going to be? Door number one or door number two? You have ten seconds to decide."

Carter continued to stare open-mouthed at the man, certain this was all a dream or he was being punked. He blinked several times, unable to formulate an answer. His hands ached as he stretched his fingers out. *What the hell is going on?*

Without warning, the other man stood and strode to the door.

"Wait!" Carter yelled.

McDaniel turned on his heel to face him but remained silent.

"Wh-what about Vicki?"

"What about Ms. Sanders? She's being treated for her injuries at the emergency room. Roland Osbourne will go to trial for raping and assaulting a minor, if and when he wakes up from the beating you gave him."

Carter stood, his mind racing. He knew a little about black ops. Ever since he'd made the decision to enlist about two years ago, he'd been reading everything he could get his hands on to decide which branch of the military to choose. It had been a tossup between the Navy and their SEAL program and the Marines' Special Forces. "If I take option two and go with you, I want two things."

"You're hardly in the position—"

Carter slammed his hand on the table, the sound echoing in the small room. "This is not negotiable—two things and I sign my fucking life over to you."

With one eyebrow raised, McDaniel gestured with his hand for him to continue.

Licking his lips, he prayed to God he was doing the right

thing. "Vicki is taken care of . . . for the rest of her life. The Witness Protection Program or whatever—I don't care if she doesn't qualify. She gets whatever she needs to get through this, a shrink, counselor. And her college is paid for when she's ready. If you're who you say you are, then you can get all of that done."

The older man paused and then nodded. "And the second thing?"

"Osbourne never steps one foot out of prison for the rest of his life. If he does, I *will* come back and kill him."

Seconds ticked by, and Carter wondered if he'd asked for too much. His gut clenched when McDaniel turned, reached for the knob, and pulled the door open. But instead of walking out, he let another man, dressed in a police uniform, enter. McDaniel stared intently at Carter as he spoke. "Captain, any photos and papers you have concerning Mr. Carter here are now classified by the United States government. He's coming with me."

Eight years later . . .

I SAT IN THE HEAT, pulling at the stupid, maroon, nylon gown. The hard wooden chair beneath me was uncomfortable, to put it mildly. It was sticking to my sweaty skin, but as soon as I pulled it one way, it stuck fast somewhere else. The only thing I liked about it was it covered the bruises. Like a dumb ass, I'd gone to my father's house last night. I'd left some stuff behind and thought I could sneak in and out without him noticing me.

Usually, he was passed out cold by two a.m. I should have known better . . .

I waited impatiently for my name to be called. I was

smashed between a jock whose name I could never remember and a peppy cheerleader with bows in her hair.

Ugh . . . kill me now. Was this day ever going to be fucking over?

The jock next to me was announced, and I stood, waiting my turn to get this empty ceremony over with. I was only here today because Aunt Beatrice made me come. She was a few rows back, wiping her eyes with a tissue, camera in hand, ready to snap some pictures.

"Bea Michaels . . ."

That was me. I walked up a few stairs, then across the small stage. After shaking hands with a few teachers and the principal, I finally accepted my diploma from the superintendent. I looked out into the audience and saw Aunt Beatrice clapping, and when I caught her eye, she put her fingers in her mouth and whistled shrilly.

I smiled despite myself. As much as I hated being here today, I knew it meant a lot to her. I hadn't told her yet that I'd gone to my father's house last night. She would see the bruises on my arms, legs, and back soon enough. This day was more for her than for me—I didn't want to ruin it.

I walked back down the rows of chairs to my seat, where I'd been forced to sit and listen to speeches by what seemed like every single person in town. Before I sat, I gave a small wave to the man standing near the last row. His uniform set him apart from the crowd, and he wore it well. The dark green fit him like a glove, complimenting his dark hair and eyes. Clean shaven and handsome, he was getting a lot of stares from the females in the crowd—and a few males, I noticed with amusement. He smiled back and returned my wave.

His name was Alex Mitchell—Sergeant Alex Mitchell to be exact—and he was a recruiter for the United States Army.

I'd signed papers with him yesterday, and I ship out for basic in four days.

I was going to be free. Free from my father and his beatings. Free to choose the life I wanted. I'd scored off the charts on my ASFABs, the entrance exams for the military. The Air Force chased me hard, but I signed up with the Army instead. After my initial training, I'll go to work with military intelligence. All I really knew was I would be assisting Special Forces operations on mission's around the world—and I'd be well beyond my father's reach. They wouldn't tell me anything more.

Before I knew it, the ceremony was over, and I was walking into Aunt Beatrice's waiting arms. She held me tight, feeling cool and soft even in this heat. Chanel No. 5 surrounded us in a scented cloud. I knew I wouldn't be seeing her for a while and wanted to hold her close, wrap her scent around me, and carry it with me.

"Oh, Bea, I'm so proud of you." She kissed my cheek and squeezed me tighter.

Her arms bumped and pressed against my sore back. I winced but then pushed the pain aside. There would be time enough for that later.

Laughing, I tried to pull away, but she held on. "Aunt Beatrice, it's like a thousand degrees. Hug me again in the air conditioning."

She released me, and stepping back, I met Sergeant Mitchell's eyes. He eyed me carefully, noticing I was wearing long sleeves under my gown even though it was pushing ninety degrees. Crossing his arms across his massive chest, he frowned severely.

"What?" I dared him to say something. I had great respect for him, but this wasn't something I was going to get into with him. Not here and not now.

He glared at me. "It's 'sir.' Get used to addressing people

by sir, right now. In a few days, you won't be able to speak without it. Try again."

"Sir, what you are staring at, sir?"

"Better, but can the attitude," he grumbled.

"No, Sergeant," Aunt Beatrice said. "She's not in the army, yet. And have you met her? She's nothing *but* attitude." She put her arm around my shoulders, pulling me close against her side. This time, I couldn't hold back the wince.

"Bea? What's wrong?" Her laser eyes looked me over—I swear she had x-ray vision.

"Can we go now? I'm hot as hell, and I want to get out of this stupid outfit." I walked away, heading to the parking lot, not waiting for their either one of them to respond. They were taking me out for an early dinner, and I'd insisted on something low-key. I hadn't wanted a party—didn't really have anyone to invite anyhow. I was somewhat confused as to why my recruiter was even coming, I mean, he'd gotten my signature, wasn't his job done?

They caught up with me at the car. Aunt Beatrice was giving me the stink-eye all moms seemed to have. Guilt rushed through my gut, tightening my muscles, as she frowned. "You have something you want to tell me, young lady?"

Instead of answering her, I opened the back door of her little sedan and stripped off my gown. Under it, I had on a long-sleeved, black shirt and green cargo pants with heavy, black boots. I pulled off the hot shirt, revealing the white tank I wore underneath.

My arms were covered in finger marks and bruises. A few scratches from his nails were also scattered around. Giving them both my back, I raised the tank up, nearly to my bra, so they could see the large, purple marks along my spine and ribs. His boots had been heavy, and I was lucky to have escaped with just bruises and not broken bones this time.

Aunt Beatrice gasped.

"Motherfucker!" Sergeant Mitchell pulled my shirt down and spun me to face him. "What happened, and where is that fucking cocksucker? I know people who can get this done. No one will find the body. Ever." His face was red with fury, cords stood out on his neck, and he fought to rein himself in.

"Wow, chill, dude. If you turn green, I'm running the fuck away." Meeting his eyes, my false humor fled. "Don't worry about it. I'm fine. Nothing that won't heal. It's my own fault."

A sob escaped Aunt Beatrice as tears ran down her face. "Bea . . . wh-what happened?" Spinning me toward her, she cradled my face in her hands, staring into my eyes. Her soft, brown ones were full of so much guilt and sorrow. I was the cause of her pain, always. It didn't matter that my asshole of a sperm donor was the one who dealt the blows. By sharing it with my aunt, I broke her heart a little more. If I could ship out this very second I would—taking myself and my shit storm of a life with me.

I shrugged, trying to make it seem as if it was no big deal. "I wanted to get the last of my stuff. I forgot some of Mom's things in the attic and thought he'd be passed out. He was at first, but he woke up when I was trying to leave." Staring at my boots, I rubbed my left one back and forth in the gravel, making a small hole that I wish would swallow me up any second.

Sergeant Mitchell was pacing back and forth, muttering obscenities under his breath as the crowd from the graduation passed us by on the way to their vehicles. "This ends now, do you hear me?" Fury darkened his face and tightened his fists. "Did you get your stuff?"

"No. He . . . uh . . . took it and threw it aside, then starting in on me. I didn't get a chance to grab it."

"You two go to the restaurant. I'll go get your stuff."

Sergeant Mitchell strode away, cracking his knuckles and not giving us a chance to respond.

"What do you think he's going to do?"

Aunt Beatrice looked sideways at me. "I think he's going to deliver the beating your father deserves."

2

Alex pulled up to the run-down, two-bedroom house where Bea had spent most of her life. A few years ago, her aunt found out about the abuse and stepped in, moving her niece into her place. But up until that point, this small house, with its falling-down porch and weed-choked lawn, had been Bea's Hell.

A rusted out Chevy sat in the gravel driveway, along with piles of other unidentifiable junk. There was a stale smell wafting out from the open door of the house. Sickened by what he was seeing, he slipped off his jacket and left it in his car, along with his cover, it was too hot for the damn hat anyway. What he was about to do could end his career, but he wasn't sure if he cared. For any man to treat their own flesh and blood, their child, this way was deplorable. He was anxious to see how this bastard handled someone his own size.

The porch sagged and swayed a bit when he stepped onto it, with dust and dirt thick as a carpet on the boards. He could see Bea's small footprints in the dirt from the night before. They were straight and even on the way in, but on the way out, they were scuffed and staggered—as if she'd stumbled out, unable to walk properly. That tends to happen when you've been kicked to the ground like a dog.

The stench intensified as he pulled open the squeaky screen door. Stepping into the living room, Alex gave his eyes a moment to adjust to the dim light. As his vision cleared, he was disgusted by what he saw. Empty beer cans, bottles, and trash littered the house. Pizza boxes with flies gathered on top, and plates with blue mold growing were on nearly every surface.

The worst was the man sprawled on the threadbare, sagging couch in nothing but dingy, yellowed briefs. Overweight, un-showered, and repulsive, the man he assumed was Bea's father was snoring openmouthed, showing tobacco-stained teeth and a bit of dried vomit on the corner of his lips.

Gliding forward on silent feet, Alex kicked the man in the side with every ounce of strength and rage he could muster.

The bastard rolled off the couch onto the disgusting floor with a grunt. Glassy, red-rimmed eyes popped open in pain and confusion. It was easy enough to tell by his expression and the smell coming from him he was still drunk.

"Who the . . . fuck are you?" he choked out between gasps for air. A livid red mark was popping up on his ribs.

Oh, I've only just begun . . .

"Get your fat, fucking ass up, you worthless piece of shit." Alex grabbed him by the arm as he stood and dragged him to the bathroom. The small room was just as filthy as the rest of the house. Shoving Bea's father into the shower stall, he flipped the lever all the way to cold and turned it on. The man squealed in shock as the water hit him full on in the face.

"Fuck . . . dammit . . ." He was stuttering and trying in vain to escape the spray.

"Sober the fuck up, asshole. I don't want you to forget the beating you're about to receive."

"Who are you?" His eyes were clearing, and he was coming around. His expression becoming a mix of fear and anger.

"I'm your worst, fucking nightmare come to life." Alex took a fistful of the man's wet hair and dragged him sputtering, thrashing, and yelling out of the shower back to the living room. Releasing him, he pushed the bastard back onto the couch.

"I-I don't know what this is about, but . . . but get the fuck out of my house. I don't have any money—go rob someone else."

The drunken fool really had no fucking clue.

"On your feet."

"Fuck off."

"Stand the fuck up and take your beating like a man, or I'll kick you to death like the dog you are." Alex snarled in his face, sickened by the sour stench coming from the drunk's mouth. The bastard refused to move, so true to his word, Alex flung him down onto the dirty carpet.

"Not so tough now, are you? How does it feel getting kicked like an animal?" Over and over, Alex planted his boot into the bastards face, sides, and stomach.

Bea's father twisted away, vomiting bile onto the carpet.

"P-please . . . stop," he begged.

"Is that what Bea said last night when you were beating her?" Alex kicked him in the back, bowing the man out in an arch. "Is it?" Jerking him up, he dealt out blows to the bastard's face. The man's nose cracked, and he howled in pain. His lips and gums were bleeding from the beating.

Alex's arms were heavy and tired from the vicious ass kicking he was handing out.

"S-stop." He was crying now, sobbing like a baby, tears mixed with the snot, blood, and vomit already on his face.

Delivering one last, vicious kick to his ribs, the satisfying crack of a bone breaking was music to Alex's ears. "If you ever, and I fucking mean *ever*, go near Bea again, I'll come back and kill you. Got it?"

The man curled up, sobbing in pain and shame. Leaving him to it, Alex glanced around and saw a small pile of boxes tossed to the side—photos and trinkets spilling out of them. He gathered them up and carried them out to his car.

Bea's life was about to start a new chapter, and the only thing he wanted her taking was these small boxes.

BEATRICE STARED out her bay window, her fingers with a white-knuckled grip on her elbows. Her mind flashed back to all the times her beloved niece had come over colored with new bruises. She blamed herself for all of it. She should have seen how her brother had spiraled down after his wife's death. He blamed Bea for it, even though there was no way that precious baby had been responsible. Her brother was a weak man, always had been. Bea's mother was a saint for putting up with him, but she saw something in him that no one else did. Beatrice couldn't help but wonder how different things would be if Jessica had lived.

Bea was escaping him, joining the Army, and leaving all this behind. Her heart was breaking for her niece, that something like this was even necessary.

A knock on the front door startled her out of her woolgathering. "I'm coming, just a minute."

Opening the door, she found a disheveled looking Alex

holding an old cardboard box. "What did you do?" Not waiting for his reply, she pulled him inside and into the kitchen. Setting aside the box he held, she gripped his hands and examined his bruised and bloodied knuckles.

"I did what should have been done years ago." Unapologetic and maybe a little self-righteous, the bruises and Alex's expression told the story.

"I see." Pausing, she grabbed a large metal bowl and filled it with water and Epsom salt. "Here, stick your hands in."

"You're not pissed?" Hissing at the liquid, he tried to pull his hands out, but she just shoved them back in.

"I'm sad. Not angry. Bea deserves a better life than this one. She's been dealt a shitty hand, through no fault of her own. I won't say that my brother didn't deserve a beating— Lord knows he's handed out enough—but it also solves nothing. It might even come back onto my niece. Though I suppose you didn't think of that, did you?"

"No, ma'am. I didn't. She's leaving in four days. What can he do to her now?" Shrugging and cleaning off his hands, Alex pointed to a box she hadn't bothered to inquire about. "That's what she was trying to get last night."

Beatrice sighed. "You're a good man, Alex. You and the Army are saving my niece's life. I hope you understand that. If she stayed here, one of them would end up dead."

"The Army is just a means to an end for her—she's saving her own life. I'll make some calls and make sure she's watched over, keep tabs on her as best as I'm able." Slipping his jacket back on, he added, "Let's go eat, I'm starving. Where's she at?"

"In her room, changing I think." Walking down the hallway, she knocked softly on the second door on the left. "Bea?" Twisting the handle, she got an eyeful of her niece's bruised back before Bea jerked her shirt down to cover them again. "Are you ready to go?"

"Yeah, I'm ready. Why is he coming to dinner anyway?" she asked, obviously having heard Bea and Alex talking in the kitchen. "I mean, I get it now, since he beat the shit out of the asshole, but even before that he wanted to come. Why?"

"Is it so hard for you to understand that maybe, just maybe, someone likes you and wants to spend time with you?"

Confusion twisted her face. "Wait, you mean like *like*? As in, *likes* me? How is that possible?"

"No dear. He's twice your age and your superior now, sort of. He isn't interested in getting into those ridiculous ripped jeans of yours. Really? We're going out. Can you please wear pants that don't have holes in them? And don't roll your eyes at me, young lady!" Sighing heavily, she continued, ignoring Bea grumbling under her breath. "You're brilliant, you know that, right? And strong—I wish you haven't had to be so strong. But it's part of what makes you who you are, and I wouldn't change anything about you."

"That's quite the speech, Aunt Beatrice." Buttoning her fresh pair of jeans, Bea sat to pull on her shoes.

"Don't belittle it. Alex is a good man and he sees something in you. He also knows that you're going to do great things and wants to at least be a part of your beginning."

"Okay, let's go eat. And I'm totally going to play the graduation card. I want a root beer float with whipped cream." Giving her an uncharacteristic hug, Bea walked down the hallway showing no signs of the pain she was in. Beatrice's heart broke a little more—her baby girl was a woman, grown up far too early. Forced too soon to hide her pain within the depths of herself. Shouldering her burdens and forging ahead each day. There was something unique about Bea—a rigidity in her spine and soul that was going to allow her to carve out her place in this world. Even at eighteen, her niece had a warrior's heart. The Army was going to be her proving ground. Beatrice had faith they would draw every ounce of her potential out and shape her into who she was supposed to be. She just hoped it wasn't too painful for her niece who'd already known a lifetime of heartbreak.

3

Six years later . . .

L eaning against the hood of a run-down jeep in the bowels of Iraq, US government, black-ops agent T. Carter waited for someone to answer his secure satellite phone call. It was hotter than Hades, but he didn't dare remove the flack vest he wore over his T-shirt, even though he was within the confines of Abu Ghraib, the US prison and detention center in this hell-hole. On one of the military bases, it would be fine, but not here. He was taking a break from an interrogation and calling in to the US Army's intelligence division to verify some information the prisoner had finally given him. Usually, someone from the division would be present for the interrogation, but due to a combination of circumstances, which included an emergency appendectomy, they were doing without on-site intel for the moment. Carter hadn't wanted to wait for a replacement, especially since he could get someone on the sat phone.

JB HAVENS & SAMANTHA A. COLE

A clicking came over the line followed by a female voice. "Code number, please."

While she didn't identify herself, he knew her name was Corporal Bea Michaels, but everyone at intelligence called her "Mic." "Hey there, sweetheart. Always a pleasure to hear your voice. Code number 009-859SRU."

"Hello, 009-859SRU. The voice verification system confirms your identity and that you are not under stress. What can I do for you today? And don't call me sweetheart."

Chuckling at her annoyance over the endearment, he wiped his sweaty brow with the back of his hand, ignoring the bruised knuckles, then gave her the three names he needed checks on. If the information was good, he would let the guards take the prisoner to the medical ward for treatment for the beating he'd been subjected to.

The clattering of a keyboard being used came over the phone. A pause and then more keys being struck. "I can confirm the first two names as being part of the cell we've been watching in the Kirkuk region—low-level runners from what I see here. However, I'm not finding any information on Rifaah Khalaf, unless he's twelve years old."

Carter snorted. "What the fuck do you have a twelve-year-old kid in the system for . . . never mind, this is Iraq. I can figure that one out for myself. Shit. No, the Rifaah Khalaf I'm looking for is in his late thirties or early forties."

"Sorry, that's all I've got. I tried a few variations of the spelling, but nothing else is coming up. It's either someone we haven't come across yet or a false name."

And Carter had a pretty good idea it was the latter. *Fuck.* He really didn't want to go back in there and start torturing the guy again. Shit like this sat in his gut for days afterward. "I'll see what else I can get for you and then call you back. Thanks, sweetheart." He quickly disconnected the call before she could yell at him.

There was something about Mic that niggled at him. She was intelligent as hell, but he was starting to think her skills were being wasted behind a desk. Quick to put two-and-two together, she also had a tough-as-nails attitude. There were only two female interrogators over here, but Mic had the same instincts that were needed to be one—the question was, did she have the guts? Maybe he'd talk to her superiors. With her smarts, and the right training, she could be an integral part of the war against terror.

He ran a hand through his sweat-soaked hair, glad he'd been able to trim it a few days ago for the first time months. At the sound of his name being called, he glanced over his shoulder to see Lieutenant Ian Sawyer walking toward him, along with Master Chief Jake Donovan. The two were part of SEAL Team Four, which had found the prisoner, that Carter was currently dealing with, in a cave and transported him here. It wasn't the first time he'd worked with these men and the rest of their team, but it had been a good seven months since he'd last seen them in the party city of Rio de Janeiro.

That mission had been a lot nicer than hanging out in this fucking sandbox though. Team Four had been stateside at the time and had been sent down to Colombia to gather intel on the head of a drug cartel, Ernesto Diaz, who had also been dabbling in arms dealing and white slavery. They'd followed the man to Brazil which is where Carter had run into them . . . well, technically he'd only run into Devon "Devil Dog" Sawyer, Ian's brother, who'd drawn the short straw. The SEAL had ended up renting a tuxedo and going to the black-tie event where another cartel leader Carter had been tailing was set to have a meeting with Diaz. Team Four and the US spy had been attacking the arms exchange pipeline from both ends, only Carter's end had come from the Middle East. A few months later, Diaz had been killed during a joint raid by Team Four, the DEA, and the Colombian authorities.

Unfortunately, his brother Emmanuel was now trying to rebuild the fallen empire.

After wiping his sweaty palm on his cargo pants, he extended the hand for them to shake. "How's it going, Sawyer? Reverend?" Ian rarely had a nickname that stuck for more than a week or two, although not for lack of trying on his teammates' part. But the team sniper had earned the moniker "Reverend" for sending his targets straight to Hell—do not pass go, do not collect your seventy-two vestal virgins.

"Here. Thought you could use this." Ian handed him a cold bottle of water which he gratefully accepted. "Get anything from him yet?"

Carter nodded while downing the whole bottle, the cool liquid was heaven against his parched throat. Why anyone would willingly live in a desert was beyond him. When he was done, he wiped his mouth with the back of his hand. "Shit, that was good. Thanks. Yeah, he started talking after I convinced him he wasn't walking out of there without giving me something. Unfortunately, the asshole underestimated our intelligence department. He gave me two low-level pieces of shit and either a false name or someone we haven't had the pleasure of meeting yet."

"My bet is on a false name."

"Mine, too. Where's the rest of the team?"

Tilting his head toward the military personnel mess hall, Reverend answered, "Taking a load off for a few. Babs had an engine light come on in the bird right before we were about to take off for the base and didn't want to risk it. She's checking it out."

Tempest "Babs" Van Buren was an Air Force chopper pilot who was often assigned to ferry the SEAL teams around. Her nickname stood for "bad-ass bitch" and referred to her remarkable flying and ironclad guts. While it was normally the Army helo pilots who flew the special-ops teams around, Bab's skills in combat flying were incredible and in high demand. With a lot of convincing, and probably a little bribery, her superiors had put her on loan to the SEALs. If she said the bird was grounded, then there had to be a good reason for it. She did everything she could to make sure everyone got back to base safely and in one piece.

The door to the interrogation bunker opened, and Fisher Jackson stuck his head out. Without speaking, the Army Master Sergeant raised a questioning eyebrow at Carter, who just shook his head in response. With a mumbled "fuck," the tall Black man ducked back inside.

Tossing the empty water bottle into a nearby trashcan, Carter said his goodbyes to the two SEALs, then headed back into the bunker, pulling on the black, balaclava mask to hide his identity. It made him sweat like hell, but the alternative of letting the man see and possibly memorize his face was out of the question. He stopped outside the room where the prisoner sat in a lone chair with his arms tied behind his back. Akram Latif's face and bare torso were covered in fresh bruises and two incisions Carter had made across his chest with a knife before the guy had broken down and started talking. Two prison guards, who had been trained to assist during the intense interrogations, stood on either side of the door, awaiting their next orders. Their faces were also hidden by masks. Jackson was watching the action from another room, via a camera feed.

Taking a deep breath, Carter barked, "Fill the tub."

Without question, the men entered the room and turned on the hose which had been run through a small hole in the outside wall—the prison's version of indoor plumbing. An old cast-iron tub, with most of its white paint peeled off, sat in the corner. Carter stepped into the room, grabbed the prisoner's chair, and spun it around to face the tub.

At first, the man eyed it in confusion, but as the water level began to rise, he realized what it was for—and it wasn't a bubble bath. Panic set in. "No! No! I told you all I know! Please, do not do this! Please, I beg of you! In the name of Allah! Please!"

The black-ops spy ignored him and removed his flack vest—it would just be in his way. His watch was next—he stuck it in his front pants pocket. He'd already locked his 9mm sidearm, backup ankle pistol, a KA-BAR, and two other knives from various hiding places on his body in a weapon locker outside the door. The fewer weapons, the less chance of the prisoner getting his hands on them—and there were plenty of torture implements around the room already. He doubted the man would ever get the drop on him or the guards, but it was better to be safe than sorry, as the saying went. Too much cockiness could get you killed.

When the water level was high enough, he nodded at the guard holding the hose to shut it off. Using a small utility knife, Carter sliced through the duct tape keeping the man's legs attached to the chair. Grabbing the prisoner by the hair, he hauled him off across the room, disregarding the screams and begging. Struggling was useless with Akram's arms tied behind his back. The operative threw the man's upper torso over the edge of the tub and plunged his head under water. He held him there for a count of ten, then lifted him high enough that he could take a single gulp of air before being shoved back under again. After another count of ten, Carter let the man breath oxygen once more. Getting in the man's face, he snarled, "You fucking lied to me, Akram. And you'll find I'm not a man you want to lie to."

Not waiting for an answer, he thrust the man's head back into the water and counted to twelve this time. A count of eighteen was usually fatal.

Yanking on Akram's scalp, he pulled him out and let him

drop unceremoniously to the dirty floor. Carter squatted next to the gasping, soaking-wet man whose eyes were now wide with the fear of impending death. This time, he spoke in fluent Arabic, the most common language in Iraq, so there would be no misinterpretation. "I want to know all about Rifaah Khalaf, starting with his real name. You may be stupid enough to lie to me, but Khalaf has to be based on someone you really know. Now, unless you want me to castrate you before sending you off to the seventy-two vestal virgins you won't be able to fuck in the afterlife, you better start talking."

And talk the man did.

An hour later, Carter was back on the sat phone with Corporal Michaels. "Ramzi Khatib."

"Oh, fuck," was the response he got, not that he'd expected anything different. His blood had run cold when Akram had finally spilled his guts and given him what he'd asked for. Ramzi Khatib was a man with no soul. He killed for sport—men, women, children—it didn't matter to the bastard. In a different part of the world, the man would be a hunted serial killer. Here, he was a psychotic leader to a bunch of radical lemmings. And now the US military knew where to find him.

After giving Michaels all the information he had, he disconnected the call. She would take it from there. Before morning, the info would be verified. If all of it was true, then the Navy SEAL team, who'd gone back to base sometime within the past hour, would be on their way to take out one of the top five most wanted al Qaeda leaders. And Carter would be on a plane out of this hell-hole. Paris sounded good right about now. There was a private BDSM club there with a pretty little submissive named Alayna, who loved when Master Carter came to town.

"GOD-FUCKING-DAMN-IT!" Ian Sawyer's team was just as pissed as he was, but most of them were on watch for tangos or any other threat, while Curt "Elmer" Bannerman, Eric "Wabbit" Prichard, and he searched the now-abandoned bunker. Their interpreter, Rashaad, stood nearby in silence, eyeing him warily.

This was the second time Ramzi Khatib had slipped through their fingers. The first time was three months ago, after Carter—the team only knew the spy by one name—had gotten the information from the prisoner at Abu Ghraib. As soon as the Intelligence commanders had given them the go-ahead to helo into Khatib's location and take him dead or alive, they'd been on their way . . . and had arrived twelve hours too late. This time, however, it looked as if the bastard had only gotten a three- or four-hour head start.

Once they were done searching the bunker, they'd start interviewing the remaining occupants of the little, goat-herding village just north of Tikrit. It sat at the base of a hillside which was too low in elevation to be considered a mountain but came close.

"Anything?" Ian barked at the two men under his command. Unfortunately, the answers he received were "negative." Kicking a decrepit wooden chair across the dirt floor, he tapped the mic connected to his headset. "Are we clear out there?"

Marco "Polo" DeAngelis, Brody "Egghead" Evans, and Ben "Boomer" Michaelson were keeping an eye on things from inside a hut across the dirt expanse. Reverend and Devon, were on watch from a few hundred yards up the hill. Steve "Urkel" Romanelli and Pete "Robin Hood" Archer were in the bunker with Ian and the others but had their gazes out two glassless windows. This was their first time back in the sandbox without Ian's best friend, Jeff Mullins, and he still wasn't used to not hearing the man's voice over the headsets.

Jeff's retirement, though, had been due to a rheumatoid arthritis induced medical discharge, instead of being KIA or wounded in combat. He was otherwise alive and well, at home with his wife and daughter, Jennifer, who also happened to be Ian's goddaughter. The fourteen-year-old had been affectionately dubbed "Baby-girl" by Team Four, and she, in turn, called them all "uncle."

It was Polo who answered him. "All clear. Just watch where you step. The herd of fucking goats that just went past took some nasty-ass shits not far from your door."

"Fucking peachy—if it's not IEDs, then it's nasty-ass goats. Let's start chatting up the locals."

Most of the people in the village seemed to know very little information which could help the team locate Khatib, but there was one man in his thirties whose actions were raising all kinds of alarms for Ian. This was someone who knew more than he was admitting to . . . but not for long. Standing in the man's three-room hut, Ian snapped his fingers toward the interpreter. While the SEALs all knew Arabic, the different regional dialects were a problem sometimes, so it was easier to have an interpreter to sort things out. "Ask him his fucking name and if he speaks English."

Rashaad spoke in Farsi to the man who answered, "Bakar Azizi. Some English."

"Good," Ian spat. "Tell me where Ramzi Khatib is."

Glancing at his wife and two children, who were under the watchful eyes of Urkel and Robin Hood, Azizi shook his head. "No. I know not who that is."

"Bullshit!" He upended their small, wooden dinner table, eliciting a startled shriek from the woman. The young children began crying, but Ian wasn't in the mood to be lied to. Too many lives were at stake. "Search the fucking place! Egghead, get the fuck in here!"

"Copy that."

While Devon, Jake, Marco, and Boomer were watching their six from outside, Elmer and Wabbit started tearing the place apart, looking for anything that would lead them to their target. Azizi's shouts for them to stop were ignored. As the two teammates moved the search into one of the smaller rooms, the Iraqi stood in the doorway, pleading with them. Brody came jogging in the front entrance, and Ian indicated for him to follow into the third room. They began moving everything, searching for what they suspected was there—a cache of weapons. Rugs were kicked aside, mattresses were flipped, and furniture moved. Suddenly, they heard Prichard yell, "No!"

Before they could react, a small explosion rocked the hut. It hadn't been enough to knock down the walls, but everything had rattled something fierce. Ian and Brody ran from their room, shocked at what they saw. Their interpreter was dead with a larger piece of wood through his left eye. Azizi was pinned to the outer wall with an even larger, splintered piece through his upper chest in the area of the heart. He was in pain but alive—for now. Urkel, Robin Hood, and Azizi's screaming wife and children had not been in the line of fire from the explosion and had escaped without a scratch. Urkel began to tend to the injured Iraqi. They would need to get as much info from him as possible before he died.

Ian ducked his head into the room where the blast had occurred, relieved to see his men alive on the floor. Aside from some minor injuries from the splintering wood, they would be fine—thank God.

Ian stared at what had once been a large wooden armoire-type closet. "What the fuck happened?"

Bannerman stood, then reached down to give his best friend a hand up. "Fucking Wabbit just save my life, that's what fucking happened." He was yelling without realizing it.

His ears were probably still ringing from the blast and would be for a while.

Brushing the dirt and splinters off himself and talking almost as loud, Prichard added, "The fucking thing was booby trapped. As Elmer was about to open it, I saw that fucking rag-head start to panic. Just knew something other than us finding his stash was about to happen. Dana would have kicked my ass if anything happened to this fucking dude. My wife is determined to marry him off one of these days."

"Like that'll ever fucking happen."

They stepped over to the now ruined piece of furniture. There hadn't been anything other than the bomb and a few blankets and rags in it. Pushing the smoldering remnants out of the way, they found a trap door underneath. Not taking chances, Ian turned to Brody. "Go swap out with Boomer. I want him checking this thing for more booby traps before we open it."

Within minutes, their EOD—Explosives Ordinance Detonation—specialist declared it safe. Boomer lifted the trap door, lit up the space with his Maglite, and whistled loudly. "Ho-ly shit! We hit the fucking mother lode, boys!"

Ian peeked into the underground bunker. It was filled with weapons of all kinds, lots of paperwork, money in different currencies, some computers, video equipment, and who knew what else. "Son-of-a-bitch."

4

I'd gotten a report this morning from my commander that in the hour before sunrise SEAL Team Four had failed in their second attempt to capture Ramzi Khatib. What they did have, however, was a rag-head pinned to a wall teetering on the brink of death. I needed to get intel from him before he died.

My orders were simple, get my ass to the village on the double and try to ferret out any information I could from the bastard. My bag of toys was resting near my feet. I had considered getting a car battery from one of the guys in the motor pool, but I would need to be more creative than that. Electrocution was brutal and effective but, movements would jar his wound and possibly kill him before I was ready. I'd spent the last two months in interrogation rooms in Abu Ghraib, learning the tricks of the trade, so to speak. I'd been shocked when my commander had called me in and given me my new orders—I'd been requesting to be a field interrogator for almost a year before it had been approved. Apparently, after helping track down some difficult intel for operative 009-859SRU, he had recommended me for interrogation training. I'm not sure why because I hadn't had the chance to speak to him in the months since but I'd be forever grateful for the opportunity.

Three months ago, when I had given the higher-ups Khatib's location, I thought it would be taken care of right away. These al Qaeda fuckers always proved more elusive than we bargained for. It had taken two months of questioning and water-filled bathtubs to get a new lead on his whereabouts. Sitting at my desk in HQ, I went over all the information again—his known contacts, previous sightings, and everything else we'd been able to find out about him.

Now, because I knew this guy backward and forward, I was being sent in with one of Uncle Sam's "private contractors"—aka an undercover CIA operative—to interrogate a possible associate in a village Khatib had been in less than five hours ago. Hopefully, this would be the break we needed to track the bastard down. It wouldn't be easy—many of these fuckers had no fear of death. My major advantage was that I was a woman—they don't know how to handle a woman willing to kill *them*, even though they had no problem turning their own women into suicide bombers. Their religion was playing into my favor here.

Clutching the handle of my bag tightly, I ran out as I heard the Blackhawk start up. Army Specialist McCoy was waiting on the edge of the field where the chopper was. He dressed like a specialist and talked like one, but he was all CIA. I was one of the few people on base right now who knew he was undercover. He was there to watch over my first official interrogation and step in if needed. I had been the assistant up until now.

"Ready for this, Mic?" McCoy shouted over his shoulder as he climbed aboard, the words almost drowned out by the accelerating rotors.

"Yeah. He's dying anyway. I'm just going to make his death take a little longer." In truth, I was nervous as hell—my palms were sticky with sweat, and my stomach was flipping. We strapped in and rose smoothly into the air. The engine and wind noise made it impossible to talk—I was grateful for the excuse. Even with a headset on the noise was a constant thrum in the background. Losing myself in my thoughts, I mentally prepared for what I was about to do. On the flight there, I slipped on a tactical hood, covering my face from the nose down. My helmet covered my hair. I was still unmistakably a woman, but interrogators were always targets, and it was best to keep your identity concealed.

It seemed like seconds later we were landing about a hundred yards from the edge of a small village—if you could call the dozen or so huts a village. Dust flew into the air from the rotors, and I saw Lieutenant Sawyer ducking out of the nearest primitive structure, heading our way.

"You've got this, Mic." McCoy handed me my bag, following behind as we ran to meet the SEAL.

"I'm aware of that."

There was a young woman with two small children huddled outside the hut, tears streaking down their dirty faces. Only the woman's eyes showed—she was wearing a traditional *niqab* which covered her to mid-chest, the rest of her body covered by a *jilbab*. It was a loose fitting outer garment, similar to a robe, which disguised her body shape. Her eyes were bloodshot and resigned to what was coming. I figured she knew her husband was almost dead, and that I, and the man behind me, might make his death much worse.

"Corporal Michaels!"

"Yes, sir." I stood rigidly in front of Sawyer. His men were spread out around the perimeter, covering our asses. The heat was vicious, beating down on our covered heads. Sweat rolled down my spine under my uniform, settling uncomfortably on the small of my back. *Fucking Iraq.*

He glared at me, but I knew his anger had nothing to do with me. "You're going to do whatever it fucking takes to get me my intel, because if you don't, your ass is on shit detail until I decide otherwise. Copy?"

"Yes, sir, I copy. Don't worry, I'm not leaving here without that fucker's location. I want this bastard planted in the sand as much as you do, sir."

While he was Navy and I was Army, he was a fucking SEAL. Their very presence demanded respect from anyone in a uniform, and the branch didn't matter. From what I knew of him, he was a good man, took care of his men, and that was enough for me.

He eyed me curiously. I knew he was trying to imagine my petite body frame in the role of an interrogator who had the guts to torture someone for information. "How the hell did you end up in this job, Michaels? Don't take this the wrong way, this isn't a sexual harassment issue, but with your intelligence and looks, you should be sitting in a comfy office at the Pentagon, not out here in the fucking sandbox."

"Sometimes, sir, playing in the sand is a lot more fun."

I OBSERVED what was in front of me, thrown and unsure where to begin. Azizi was impaled through the fucking chest —stuck fast to the wall like some sort of grotesque, modern art piece. He was panting heavily, but that seemed more from fear than anything else. There wasn't much blood either, but that would change if the wood was pulled from the wound. Sawyer's man, Romanelli, had stabilized the large shard with gauze so it wouldn't move around.

The shack was small and dark, the heat hanging heavily

inside. The shadowed half-light in here made the room seem to shrink in on me. A few deep breaths into my belly moved the walls back to where they belonged as I prepared to begin.

Standing in the doorway, Sawyer's arms cradled his rifle casually against his chest. He would be the only other person present for this. If the medic, Romanelli, was needed, he would be brought back in.

"McCoy, ideas?" I dropped my bag on the floor with a heavy thunk. Kneeling down, I opened a side pocket and handed him latex gloves, then donned my own with a snap.

McCoy was opening his own bag, pulling out and then discarding most of the equipment. "Get the wife in here for starters."

Sawyer spoke into his radio and moments later Azizi's wife was pushed inside the hut, her screaming children outside begging for their mother. Due to my intelligence training, I'd been required to become fluent in Farsi, so I knew exactly what was being said. Good thing, too, since the interpreter was dead.

I stood close to Azizi, making sure he got a good view of me in the low-light. I pulled down my hood, not concerned he would get a description of me. I don't think the people in Hell he'd be joining in a few moments were much of a threat to me.

"You're going to answer my questions, or I'll inflict pain on you, the likes of which you've never imagined. Then, if you still don't talk . . ." I jerked his wife close to me by the arm. Reaching up, I ripped her shroud-like *niqab* off. He was screaming at me in anger, and she was crying, twisting in my grip, trying to get her headdress back. Looking at her, what I saw had me clenching my jaw in rage. She was young, very young. If she was sixteen I would have been shocked—her *husband* was at least three times her age, and her children were around three and five years old. Finger-shaped bruises covered her neck like a horrifying necklace, her jaw was black and purple, her lip, swollen heavily and split.

Sawyer got a look at her, and foul curses flew from his mouth. McCoy was silent beside me, but his face was nearly purple with rage.

"Take her out. She's had enough pain already." I handed back her covering and pushed her toward Sawyer. She was shaking and crying, but I didn't miss the look of hate, rage, and, not surprisingly, relief she shot over her shoulder at her worthless husband. Sawyer gently passed her off to someone outside the hut.

My hands still shook, but not with fear or anxiety. Now, it was anger. I fought to control it and not just put a bullet in this piece of shit. Selecting a heavy hammer from my bag, I had a better idea.

"McCoy, Lieutenant, hold his hand flat against the wall, stretch his arm out straight." My voice was guttural and sounded strange even to my ears. I'd thought the first time I tortured someone would be hard, but this was easy. Maybe too easy. I'd worry about my sanity later.

I kicked through the debris on the floor and found what I was looking for. Sturdy pieces of metal, a little twisted from the blast but they would work just fine. They'd been part of the hinges or handles.

Azizi was pale and quivering. I showed him what was in my hands and let him figure out what I was going to do.

Speaking in Farsi, I clarified my intent. "I'm going to nail your hands to the wall and your feet to the floor. That way, you can't thrash around and kill yourself. There will be no escaping this."

I moved between McCoy and Sawyer, my gloved hands gripping the sharp metal firmly. The bastard tried to struggle, but they held him tightly, not letting him kill himself before we had our chance to force him to spill his guts. Careful not to jar the wooden shard in his chest, I placed the end of the makeshift spike on this palm and brought the hammer down with all the force I could muster.

A meaty *thunk*, which I felt more than heard, rang up my arm. Azizi's screams drowned out any noise. The metal wasn't through his hand yet, so I hit it again as blood ran down his wrist and arm, onto the wall and floor, flowing over Sawyer and McCoy's protected hands along the way. Another strike and the metal began to pierce the old and crumbling plaster wall. He was howling in pain, long and loud. Snot and tears were running down his face, mingling with his beard. One last solid hit drove the metal through the side of the shack.

"I know you're a Muslim and all, but does this seem familiar to you?" Bending down, I picked up another chunk of metal. This one was bigger than the other, wider. It would take more force to drive it through his palm.

He'd stopped screaming—now he was just moaning in pain. Sweat poured from him as shock began to set in. McCoy reached forward and took his pulse, nodding at me to proceed. If Sawyer was surprised with my actions, it didn't show.

"Hold his other hand." I'd slipped into command easily, it felt oddly natural. I counted each beat of his heart in his wrist, his skin was slimy, and he stank of piss and the musty reek of goat. Looking down, I saw the front of his robe was sopping wet. He'd pissed himself in terror. My mouth stretched into a wicked smile, and I brought the hammer down. Metal ringing out loudly, the vibrations of the strike flowed through the hammer like a tuning fork. He didn't scream this time, just groaned and gasped. Blood poured from the wound as I drove the spike through his hand and into the wall behind him.

Stepping back, I dropped the hammer at my feet with a

hollow *thud* and crossed my arms over my chest. "Now that I have your attention. Are you ready to answer my questions?"

Fifteen minutes later, Sawyer had every ounce of intel his little heart could ever hope for. Azizi had sung like a canary, spilling his guts, both figuratively and literally onto the dirt floor. I stayed in the shack with Sawyer, filling in as an interpreter. McCoy had gathered our things and gone outside to radio the convoy that they'd have two extra passengers. The SEALs would be taking the helo to go get Khatib before he had a chance to change locations again. Several Humvees full of soldiers were on their way to clear out the cache of weapons and other items found in the bunker.

"Got everything you need?" I asked the stoic SEAL. He hadn't said much of anything during the torture. I wasn't sure if he was sickened or surprised—if I had to guess though, I'd go with the latter. I knew I had shocked myself with the ease with which I had tortured this man. If it didn't bother me—well, good. I'd see how I felt about this later. Adrenaline was still pumping through my veins, making me hyperaware of my surroundings. Even my breathing was loud to my ears right now.

"Yeah. Let's put this fucker out of his misery." Sawyer reached for the wooden shard in Azizi's chest.

"Wait." I stopped him with a hand on his bicep. He looked down at me, arching one eyebrow in question. "I'll finish what I started."

"Be my guest." With a flash of respect in his eyes, the lieutenant stepped back out of the way, giving me space to work in.

Grasping the wood with both hands, I fought to find the leverage I needed to pull it out. It was slick with blood, wedged tightly in his chest and the wall behind him. Lacking the correct position to pull it out, I picked up my hammer, instead.

I briefly met Azizi's eyes—they were wide with fear, rolling in their sockets with shock and terror. "See you in Hell." I swung the hammer two-handed, smacking solidly on the side of the shard, driving it toward the center of his chest, puncturing his heart and killing him instantly.

"Remind me never to piss you off, Michaels." Sawyer extended his hand for me to shake.

"Likewise, sir."

We left his body hanging on the wall, already drawing flies. A fitting end to the husband of a child bride, wife-beating bastard, and terrorist that he had been.

5

Heading back to the base, I gripped the seat in front of me in the M114 Humvee the best I could. We were bouncing over ruts big enough to swallow a small car. The mountain pass was narrow and dangerous. Staff Sergeant Montez was in the front, with Private Ruez driving. The radio crackled, static breaking up the transmission.

"Sergeant, what the fuck was that?" I leaned forward and shouted to be heard over the engine noise, my M16 wedged tightly between my legs. I fucking hated Humvees—their sub-par suspensions were blown out almost immediately upon arrival to Iraq.

"No idea, but it didn't fucking sound good." Twisting a knob, he tried to clean up the reception. "Ironman Two Six, this is Punisher One Nine. Over."

He was attempting to check in with the other company that was just over a mile in front of us. The narrow twisting road made it impossible to keep them in sight. Besides my staff sergeant and Private Ruez, I was in the back with

Private Anderson, Specialist McCoy, and our gunner, Corporal DeSalvo.

The Humvee in front of us held the rest of Staff Sergeant Montez's squad. It had taken them very little time to load the weapons and electronics into the Humvees, and we were on our way back to base.

A squawk on the radio grabbed our attention again. "Punisher One Nine, Ironman Two Six. Over." Heavy gunfire came across the radio loud and clear. Without being told, we double checked our weapons, preparing for a battle.

"Go ahead, Ironman Two Six, over."

"Punisher One Nine, Proceed north with caution, taking heavy fire." The radio crackled again, interference breaking up his words. "Do . . . ambush . . . turn . . . base. Over."

"Say again, Ironman Two Six?"

The radio fell silent.

"Ironman Two Six, say again. Over."

"If your fucking foot isn't on the floor, make it happen right fucking now, Ruez!" Staff Sergeant Montez yelled the order, and the Humvee shot forward. They weren't fast, but Ruez was going to get every single bit of horsepower up and running. "Lock and load, ladies. We've got a rescue to do. Corporal Michaels?"

"Yes, Sergeant?"

"I know you're one of those smart fuckers over there in intelligence, but I expect you to pull your fucking weight. Got me?

"Got it, Sergeant!" My already sweating palms dampened further. I gripped my weapon and patted my MOLLE vest, double and triple checking my extra magazines were in place. I'd been in the Army for six years, stationed in some of the nastiest hellholes on the planet, but I'd yet to see much combat. A few skirmishes here and there, but no casualties on my side—thank God.

We smelled the smoke first, then we saw the black pillars of smoke and flames reaching for the sky. Not a soul was in sight from this distance.

"This doesn't look good, Sarge." Ruez's voice cracked with fear. He was nineteen if he was a day. Poor kid had only been here for two weeks.

"No, Private, it does not. Roll up as close as you can." Twisting in the seat slightly, Montez shouted to DeSalvo, "Keep your fucking eyes peeled! Be ready to light up some rag-head fuck-wads on my command!"

"Roger, Sergeant!"

I could barely hear him over the wind that was picking up. We pulled up to the wreckage behind our lead Humvee, and the sight greeting us was burned into my brain—I knew I would never forget that day.

Bodies were strewn all over, legs and arms spread several feet away from the torsos they'd once been attached to. Blood soaked the sand, black and thick. It was a massacre, unlike anything I had ever imagined.

"You know the fucking drill, people. I want five meters, then twenty-five," Montez ordered. Speaking into his radio, he ordered the lead Humvee to set up a security position.

I scanned the area, the ground, ditches—everywhere my eyes could see five meters out around the vehicle before getting out. "Clear, Sarge!" The others all responded the same. Which didn't mean there was nothing there, only that we couldn't see it.

As one, we opened our doors and stepped out onto the loose soil and hot wind. The unmistakable stench of death hit us in the face like a hammer blow. Private Anderson was bent at the waist, puking his guts out into the dirt.

"Knock it the fuck off, you pussy. Check twenty-five before you get us all killed," McCoy shouted from the cover of his door.

Anderson wiped his mouth and stood, rifle to his shoulder as he scanned the surrounding hills. Seeing nothing, we stepped away from the M114.

"Stay the fuck together—I don't like this," Staff Sergeant Montez commanded. "Watch your fucking six. I want eyes everywhere."

"Copy that, Sergeant." I turned to the left, towards the half dead excuses for plants this fucking sandbox had. None of the little bushes were big enough to hide anything, which meant my section was clear of tangos. All I saw were the dead, blood, and sand.

A pop to my right had me pivoting on my heel, weapon up, searching for a target. Private Ruez was on the ground, his gloved hand clutching his throat, which was pouring a river of blood.

"Man down! Ruez is hit!" I barked, grabbing their attention. Men from our lead Humvee set up defensive positions around us. They were firing up into the hills, the cracks of rifle shots and explosions from grenades shook the ground at our feet. The enemy was using the hills and rocks for cover, popping up to fire and toss grenades, before ducking back down out of sight.

I fell to my knees beside the injured man, jerking his hands off his throat. Arterial spray slapped me hotly in the face, the metallic flavor of pennies hitting my tongue. Spitting his blood from my mouth, I pressed my hands tightly to his neck. My actions were in vain, Ruez was pale and limp. He'd bled out in seconds. With a swipe of my hand, I closed his now vacant eyes. He was old enough to die for his country and brothers, but he'd never be old enough to buy a drink.

Pop-pop! Another two men from the first Humvee fell.

"Sniper above us! Get your fucking asses to cover!" Montez was screaming and waving his arms, getting us to move backward, behind the cover of the Humvees. We returned fire, the cracks of our rifles adding to the chaos. DeSalvo had climbed back into the Humvee and was manning the fifty-cal. Hot brass fell down like rain as speeding lead flew up the hillside.

The firing of the fifty-cal ceased, and I looked back to see DeSalvo gone. I jerked the rear door open to find his dead body laying awkwardly over the seats, most of his face rendered to red meat.

"We need to move! Do you want to die today, soldiers? Get your asses into the Humvees—bug the fuck out!" Montez pointed wildly, spurring us into action.

The unmistakable whistle of an RPG had us all diving for cover. The lead Humvee was engulfed in fire and was slowly turning into a pile of molten metal and burning rubber.

"Incoming!" I screamed, seeing the trail of a second round headed our way from a nearby ridge. I grabbed Anderson by his flak vest and hauled him after me. We dove into a ditch as our Humvee was hit, the explosion throwing sand and fire into the air. The shock-wave hit us, knocking us down further into the ground.

"We have to fucking move!" I hauled the stunned Anderson up, jerking him after me as I ran down the road, trying to find cover. "Keep fucking going!"

I checked back over my shoulder to see some of the men from the lead Humvee were following us, chasing us down. Montez was in the rear, the last man, making sure no one was left behind. My ears were ringing sharply, I couldn't hear fuck-all, but my eyes worked fine. I was firing, trying to cover us, my weapon heavy and hot in my hands.

Taking another glance back, I saw Montez's body freeze . . . and then dance. Bullets ripped through his body, shredding him. Blood flew out of his chest in a red mist. His mouth opened in a silent scream as he began to fall. Time slowed and then stopped altogether. He hit his knees, clutching his chest and stomach with shaking hands.

His lips opened and closed as blood poured from his mouth. "Go," he said. I couldn't hear him, but I knew what he meant as sure as if he were standing next to me. He was giving me his men to command—to save. They were *my* men now. Somehow in the last few minutes, I'd become the ranking NCO on scene.

I nodded to him and turned away as time sped back up to normal. The screams of the dying and the crackling and sparking of fires filled my ears.

A whistle and a whoosh flew past our heads. "RPG!" I screamed, diving into the dirt. A split-second later, I heard a second round fly by, the smoke trail headed right for us. The heat and percussion from the blast slammed into my body. I looked back, the men from the lead Humvee were in pieces, ripped apart by shrapnel.

Scrambling to my feet, I hauled Anderson up and pushed him forward. We ran. When McCoy fell in beside me, I pushed even harder. Grit flew into our faces and still we ran —heading for a second ridge where we could hopefully find cover. We gasped for air, and our legs were weak, but still I pressed them. I wasn't going to die today, and neither were my men.

Minutes and hours blurred together. For two days, we ran and fought, being forced deeper into the countryside with every mile. The only radio we still had between us had taken a hit—we had no comms, no food, and very little water. Exhaustion pulled at us—we were all wounded at least once. I'd been grazed on the upper arm, the searing pain ripping through my flesh. I didn't bother with a bandage, our med kits were nearly empty. The little we had left I wanted to save only for the most serious wounds among my men.

I consulted my map again. We were deep behind the wire,

in enemy territory, with no way to call for rescue. We were dangerously low on ammunition, each of us only had one full magazine left. Thirty rounds apiece, we couldn't afford to stop and fight—we'd be slaughtered.

"Mic, where are we?" Anderson was panting beside me, his face red with sunburn.

"We're about a fifteen klicks from the ambush site. They're gaining on us again, too. I'm trying to circle us around and back. We've only got one more day of food and less than that in water. The best I can hope for is that HQ hasn't given up on us and will keep sending out search and rescue until we're found. We have to keep moving, get as close to the ambush site as possible if we have a chance in hell of surviving this." Thirty miles on foot, most of it in the dark while being pursued by the enemy . . . *fuck, fuckity, fuck*.

"Copy that." McCoy stood next to Anderson, their eyes searching for tangos, as they waited for my command. I wished I'd had enough time to collect Montez's dog tags, along with those from the others who'd died. His family back home would never know he'd died saving us—our mission in that fucking goat village had been deemed classified. I knew, later, I would grieve. Right then, I had to focus on getting us out of there alive.

SITTING BEHIND HIS MACHINE GUN, gunner Marco DeAngelis kept his eyes peeled from the open door of the Blackhawk helicopter they were flying around in. After a shootout with Ramzi Khatib and his men, which had made the OK Corral sound like a BB gun fight, it had been dark when they'd returned to base to find out the convoy was missing. It had never reached the base, and there had been no communication or mayday from them. It wasn't the first time the desert conditions had fucked with allied radios, and he doubted it would be the last.

The burnt out vehicles and dead soldiers had been found at an ambush site about halfway from the village to the base. The deceased had been retrieved by the Army and loaded up into choppers to be sent home by plane to their loved ones. Because many of them had been unidentifiable, at first, due to facial wounds, and others had been blown apart, it had taken a few more hours to realize that three people were still unaccounted for—Corporal Michaels, Specialist McCoy, and Private Anderson. It was unknown if they had been captured, killed in another location, or were still out there somewhere, so there were four helos out searching the area surrounding the ambush site. The search had been hampered by a sand storm and the fact they weren't getting any signals from their personal locator beacons.

At the moment, two of the helos were taking the northern sectors, while the others covered the southern ones. Darkness was fast approaching again as the sun had almost set, and they still hadn't been able to determine where the missing were. Over the headset comms, Marco heard Ian order the two pilots to fly over another southern section of the desert, not wanting to admit defeat and return them to base. They would rescue or recover their own no matter how long it took—no way in hell were they leaving them behind.

Marco thought about his sister, Nina. She was the only blood family he had left since their grandmother had passed away. But even when the crotchety old woman was alive, there had been no love lost between them. She'd been an alcoholic and a gambler who hadn't been thrilled when her grandchildren ended up living with her after their mother died of a drug overdose.

Nina was the lone person who would be notified if something ever happened to him. The only other people who mattered to him were here with him—his team . . . his brothers. Following Ian and Dev to Tampa was ideal for him when he opted out of the Navy. Nina's best friend Harper was from the area, and his sister had relocated there after graduating from college with her teaching degree. She'd started a new job this past September in one of the Tampa elementary schools. In their last Skype chat, she'd said she would be able to start paying him back for his financial support over the past four years, and he'd basically told her to fuck off. He wouldn't take one cent from his kid sister. He was happy he'd been in the position to help her, since he just knew Nina was destined for great things, despite their crappy upbringing. He couldn't wait to get back to the base because one of her care packages had just arrived, and he hadn't had time to open it yet. She was always sending the team all sorts of goodies, along with letters from her students, which always brightened their day. And after the past forty-eight hours, they could all use some love and cheer from the US of A.

As they scanned the new sector, behind Marco, looking out from the other side, Boomer shouted he saw a bunch of Iraqis. Their weapons were raised, and they appeared to be firing at an unknown target. The pilot banked in that direction for a closer look. The Blackhawk helicopter Babs was flying, with Dev, Brody, and Ian aboard, followed on their tail. Suddenly a flare snaked up from the ground and illuminated the dimly lit sky in bright red. Marco couldn't believe it. *Holy fuck, that had to be them!*

As they flew closer to where the flare had originated, they saw the tangos had obviously seen it, too, and were firing on the three individuals they were closing in on.

"Incoming!" their pilot yelled, pulling up fast and hard, while the rest of them held on tight, and the RPG flew harmlessly past them. Thank God for the onboard radar alerting him to the threat before anyone actually saw it. The pilot then quickly got them in range, and Marco and Boomer started laying down hot lead with the big guns. Brody and Dev were doing the same from the other Blackhawk as they took out the asshole with the rocket-propelled grenade launcher. In the doorway, next to Marco, Jake was using his sniper rifle to fire on the targets. The enemy started dropping left and right.

Marco saw one of the US soldiers go down after being hit in the leg, and he let loose a volley of ammo from the M60 at the bastard who'd climbed out of a ditch and fired the shot. The man's body spun around as it was ripped apart, and Marco felt no remorse for sending him to Hell. "Fucking hooyah!"

When it appeared the insurgents were all either dead or dying, Ian ordered Babs to land the Blackhawk to pick up the trio. Now that the Marco's helo was hovering over them, making sure no other tangos popped up from anywhere, he could see it was McCoy who had been hit and was lying on the ground. Anderson and Michaels were standing over him, back to back, watching each other's six. They were covered in sand, dirt, and blood, but they were alive.

How the fuck had this motley crew survived until now?

6

Darkness fell in the desert and with it came the cold. People always forget, it may be hot as the surface of the sun during the day in this barren wasteland, but at night there is nothing to hold the heat. While it didn't get below freezing, the drastic temperature change played hell with our bodies.

We had made good progress today, we were within ten klicks of the ambush site. If we weren't picked up tonight or in the morning, we'd die. We were out of water—all of us had split and chapped lips from the wind and vicious sun. Our skin was blistered with sunburn, and gritty sand was in every crack and crevice of our bodies. I wanted to lay in a tub of cold water for a month.

I studied my ragtag team as we stayed low and hopefully out of sight. "We wait here. This is a decent, defensible position. I want watches rotated every two hours. If these fuckers pin us down, we're toast." There was a rocky outcrop behind us on an elevated slope. We had cover on one side and the high ground on the other. This was as good as it was going to get. Checking my personal locator beacon, I popped out the battery and touched it to my tongue. Nothing, no tingle, no slight buzz, dead. "Dammit. My PLB is toast."

"I don't even have mine, no fucking idea where I lost it." McCoy was patting his pockets, looking to no avail.

"Mine is dead too." Anderson weakly said. The fire and drive were seeping out of us with every step and drop of sweat.

"Keep your eyes open. If they send a search party, they should find us here. If you hear a chopper, wait until it's close and set off a star-cluster flare. And don't fuck it up, we only have one. Then stay fucking frosty, boys. If our rescue can see us, so can those hadji motherfuckers."

"Copy that, Corporal." McCoy raised his hand. "I'll take first watch." He'd kept his cover perfectly and let me take command, never letting on that he was a senior CIA interrogator, not that he had any more combat experience than me to begin with.

I'd just settled in for a quick nap, using my pack as a pillow, when the air was broken by the thumping of rotors. A few tense moments passed before we saw the unmistakable light formation of two choppers in the distance—one was an Apache attack helicopter, and the other was a Blackhawk.

"Friendlies incoming!" Anderson shouted in excitement, forgetting to keep his voice down.

"Pop the flare! Take up defensive positions! Make every fucking round count!" I barked the orders, instantly alert. McCoy smacked the bottom of the flare with his palm and it arched up in the sky, exploding into red light, just like fireworks only much brighter—highlighting our position.

Within seconds, we began taking fire from the south. The birds were on approach from the east. Anderson threw his last grenade toward a band of advancing tangos, the boom shaking the earth, and the flying shrapnel sending men screaming in pain. We stood close together but gave ourselves room to fight.

"Lay down suppressing fire! Only shoot at what you can fucking see!"

"I can't see shit!" McCoy shouted in rage, firing back. Green and red tracers marked our lines of fire. I knew the birds would see us from the air.

We fought for what felt like hours, but I knew, in reality, it was only minutes. The bolt in my rifle clicked empty. I dropped the M16 and pulled my sidearm. I had two magazines for the M9, and I hoped like hell they lasted until our rescue arrived. I waited as the bastards got closer and into range. They were running towards us, screaming "*Allahu ackbar!*" I didn't have time to be afraid, I just reacted—my training long since taking over any thought process my adrenaline saturated mind could fire up.

"Bring it, fuckers! Expressway to hell coming right up!" Anderson shouted back in response.

We were firing nearly nonstop, pausing only to reload. In the moonlight, I could see white-robed figures advancing in the darkness. They knew we were close to done. Pressing their advantage, they increased their rate of fire.

"Hold your positions! Neither of you moves, you hear me, you sons of bitches!"

"Hooah!" Their war cries barreled through the night.

I clicked empty, both magazines spent. Re-holstering my weapon, I pulled my KA-BAR, preparing to gut these fuckers with my bare hands if I needed to. "It's a good, fucking day to die. It's been an honor fighting by your side, gentlemen." I didn't want to die tonight, but the enemy was going to breach our defensive line before the birds got here.

Anderson was by my side, his own KA-BAR steady.

I could see the faces of the enemy as they crested the hill, screaming their own war cry, which we answered. I watched them as time slowed more, skipping a beat as their robes flapped behind them like wings.

More gunfire rang out, and McCoy fell to the ground screaming in pain, blood pouring from his knee where he'd been hit.

"McCoy is down!" With no time to see to his injuries, I stood in front of him, ready to fight to the death to protect him. Anderson closed the short distance to my side, we stood back to back over McCoy's body as he struggled to stop the blood flowing from his leg. The al Qaeda fuckers had spread out, using the terrain to flank us.

Buurrr . . . the unmistakable sound of the M60 door-gun firing on the insurgents in front of us was sweet music. Their bodies were torn apart by the screaming lead.

In seconds, the men who had been chasing us for two days lay in a pile of tangled limbs and blood.

Anderson fell to his knees beside me, tears running down his dirty cheeks, washing a path clean. I considered joining him, but instead, I turned and watched our rescuers land and step off the Apache.

"About fucking time!" I slung an arm around McCoy, helping him limp over to the bird, where they pulled him inside and immediately began working on his leg. I turned to Lieutenant Sawyer. "I'd just about given up on you finding our asses."

His nose wrinkled as he got a whiff of us. "Jesus fucking Christ, woman, you stink. I don't know if I want you and your dirty ass crew in my chopper."

"Just try and stop me. SEAL or not, I'm getting on that bird with my men, and I'm getting the fuck out of Iraq. I'm done with this shit." Not waiting for his reply or expecting him to stop me, I ordered Anderson to board. I high-fived the man on the door gun, thanking him for saving us.

Sawyer climbed in after us. "Babs, get this can in the air before their stench ruins it for the rest of us."

As the SEAL corpsman tended to McCoy, Sawyer handed me a bottle of water, and his grin and nod of respect lifted my spirits. I'd saved my men—it was a good end to a horrendous battle. We were wounded and banged up, but we'd made it out. I knew if Sawyer and his men hadn't shown up, we wouldn't have survived the night. We owed them our lives.

———

DEVON SAWYER DROPPED his mess tray on the table and sat between his brother and Boomer. "Someone pass the salt, pepper, hot sauce, ketchup, and anything else that'll make these fucking eggs edible."

It was 0800 hours, and already the heat index outside the air conditioned building in Camp Bucca was at a 113 degrees. It would be closer to 130 by the afternoon—hot enough to fry an egg on the ground and possibly the whole damn chicken. He glanced around the table. Prichard was reading a new letter from his wife, and next to him, his best friend, Elmer, was flipping through the latest issue of *Sports Illustrated*. Urkel and Archer had a backgammon game spread out between them as they sat across from each other. A few of the guys were talking about the new security business Ian and Dev were opening next year when they finally opted out of the Navy. Marco, Jake, and Brody had already made plans to come work for them after they finished up whatever time they had left before retirement. Boomer was interested in joining them, too, but he had about three more years to go before that happened.

"So you still haven't decided on a name for the business yet, have you?" Jake asked.

Devon shook his head while he seasoned his eggs. "No. Whatever I like, big brother hates, and vice versa."

"What about Sawyer Security?"

After swallowing his last piece of burnt toast, Ian answered, "We thought of that, but decided with Dad being the big real estate mogul he is, we don't want people thinking we're trying to ride on his coat-tails—" He stopped abruptly, then raised his booming voice. "Michaels!"

Looking where his brother's gaze was aimed, Devon saw Corporal Michaels walking toward an empty table with her breakfast. She paused, trying to figure out who had called her name, and Ian waved her over. Even though she'd slept almost twenty-four of the last thirty-six hours, she still seemed beat—not that anyone could blame her. Her sunburned skin had to be painful, and Dev didn't know how she was up and walking around after her ordeal. It had probably taken her a good thirty minutes in the shower to scrub the dirt, sand, and blood from her body, after the doctors had cleaned her bullet wound and rehydrated her with IV fluids. They knew she'd been debriefed yesterday and would probably be going through more today. Last they checked, Anderson was recovering here on the base, while McCoy had been flown to Germany where the doctors were going to try and save his leg.

She approached, her sharp gaze on Ian. "Yes, Lieutenant?"

Using his foot, Ian pushed out the empty chair across from him. "Sit."

"Sit, sir?" Her eyes narrowed in uncertainty, and a few smiles appeared around the table. They knew what was probably going through her head. It was almost unheard of for an Army grunt to be invited to sit with the elite Navy SEALs. It was like being back in high school, and the nerd was being invited to hang out at the jock table.

Ian pointed to the chair. "Yes, Michaels. Sitting is

something you should have been taught how to do as a rug rat. You know, do a squat and stop when your ass hits the chair."

"Um, yes, sir." She took the seat between Prichard and Marco, then scanned everyone's faces. "I want to thank you again for coming through for us. I don't think we would have survived the night."

Ian crossed his arms on the table and leaned forward. "Thanks aren't necessary, Michaels. I'm just glad we found you when we did. I spoke to Anderson in the infirmary yesterday. He told me how you stepped up and did what needed to be done. Says they may not have made it out of there alive without you."

"I don't know about that, sir."

"Well, I do. So do the men you were with and a lot of other people around here. And the name is Ian or Sawyer during downtime, Michaels."

He went around the table and introduced her to everyone. She nodded at each man and eyed them as if she were committing their names, nicknames, and faces to her memory banks. "Everyone calls me 'Mic.'"

Dev studied her, and she stared back in confusion. "Something wrong?"

He shook his head. Ian was the only one who'd witnessed what had gone down in Azizi's hut during the interrogation, and no one on the team had questioned him about it. They knew better. But they'd still heard the Iraqi's screams of pain, then his begging to die, and had wondered how the petite woman in front of him now had been able to do whatever she'd done. "Don't take this the wrong way, Mic, but you're a tiny, little thing. I guess I'm just having a hard time imagining you anywhere out of high school. You impressed a hell of a lot of people, and that's not because you're a woman or anything. It's because you and your men survived for two days out there with only a few supplies and no comms. How the hell did you know what to do out there without any real combat experience? From what we were told, up until a few months ago, you were sitting behind a desk."

"You're not the first person to say that in the past twenty-four hours. Just remember, dynamite comes in small packages. I pay attention and learn fast, and I've been following a lot of the activity." She shrugged. "Learned a lot from listening to you all and the other units. That, and I've been reading a bunch of officer training books. I know I have a few ranks to go, but my recruiter told me it was never too soon to start studying."

"Smart man. I wouldn't be surprised if you started flying up the ranks over the next few years."

As she reached for the salt, Devon slid the rest of the condiments her way—she would need them. "Thanks. By the way, I forgot to find out. Did you get Khatib?"

"Yeah, but not alive. Went down shooting. Five of his faithful followers went down, too."

Mic fell silent, and he knew she was thinking about the good men who'd been killed during the convoy's ambush and how it had been for nothing. If Khatib had been captured, the information they could have tortured out of him would have been invaluable to the US and allied troops.

Knowing she was going to be living with that for a long time, Dev changed the subject. "Well, if you ever need a job when you opt out, you can come work for Ian and me. We're going to be opening a security agency in Tampa next year, if we can ever think of a fucking name for it."

A few more names were tossed around the table, but none of them sounded right, and the group fell silent as everyone wracked their brains. Mic took a swig of her water. "What about—" When they all looked at her, she shook her head. "Never mind. It's a stupid suggestion."

"Tell us," Ian said. When she hesitated, he added, "Come on, it can't be any worse than Egghead's suggestion of 'Spank Me Security.'"

She rolled her eyes. "It's definitely not worse than that. Well, you're all SEALs—why not call it Trident Security?" As the men all silently glanced at each other, she shrugged her shoulders. "Told you it was stupid."

Dev and his brother exchanged a look and started laughing. Ian slapped the table several times with his open palm, grinning like a loon. "Now why the fuck didn't any of us think of that? I fucking love it."

Extending his hand across the table for Mic to shake, Dev said, "Anytime you want to come work for Trident Security, the job is yours."

"Thanks, I'll keep that in mind." She stood, gathering her half-empty tray. "I have more debriefing to do. Catch you squids later. Watch your asses out there." Without another word, she spun on her heel and left the mess hall. Shoulders back and head high, you could almost see the attitude on her like a custom suit. There wasn't a single person in the camp who didn't fully respect the corporal at the moment. But at what price had it come?

7

Six months later . . .

Leaving the gates of National Ground Intelligence Center—NGIC—behind, I hit the interstate heading north. Even though the air was cold, I had the top down on my Jeep. I loved the fresh air slapping me in the face. My usually unruly hair was contained under my cover, which, for once, came in handy. My orders were to report to a small town in Pennsylvania, change into civilian clothes, and await contact. My CO either didn't have more information than that or refused to give it to me. Either way, I'd find out soon enough.

Following the ambush in Iraq, I had been sent stateside and awarded both a Purple Heart and Silver Star for bravery and excellence in combat. The shiny pink scar on my bicep was my only wound. McCoy had ended up losing his leg. I'd given him my medal—since he was really an undercover CIA agent he wouldn't receive one—and left my Silver Star on Montez's grave in Arlington National Cemetery. I wanted no part of either one. I had the memories, which were plenty.

Crossing the border into Pennsylvania, I glanced down—my speedometer had me at eighty-five. Shit, the sign I just passed had said fifty-five. I'd no sooner noticed my speed when flashing blue and red lights appeared in my rearview mirror.

"Fuck me. This is not what I need," I muttered to myself. I slowed and flipped my blinker on, pulling over onto the shoulder. *Maybe I'll get lucky, and he'll let me off.* My BDUs were wrinkled as hell, but at least I was in uniform.

Turning off the engine, I kept my hands at ten and two on the wheel, well within sight, and waited for the state trooper to come up to the door.

"Afternoon, ma'am." He was huge, his gray uniform emphasizing his six-foot-six frame. He probably topped the scales at 250 or so. With a strong jaw and black hair, he was very intimidating. Well, to most people.

"Sir." I respectfully nodded.

"Can I see your license and registration, please? And since you're in uniform, I need your military ID as well."

"Yes, sir. They're in my glovebox. And before I reach for them, I just want you to know that I'm carrying a firearm."

"Where is it, ma'am?" His stance was casual but alert. I knew if I made a wrong move he'd have me out of the car and on the pavement in seconds.

"It's in the center console. It's loaded, and I have a permit."

"Well, in that case, get your papers and step out of the car, so I can secure your weapon, please."

"Yes, sir." With my left hand remaining on the steering wheel, I slowly and carefully reached into my glove box and found the little plastic thing with my registration and insurance card. I handed it to him. "My IDs are in my wallet, which is in my left cargo pocket."

"Go ahead and step out and get them." When he stepped back, I opened the door and climbed out, then moved to the front of my vehicle, away from the busy interstate with cars and tractor trailers whizzing past us. I retrieved my IDs and handed them over, standing near the hood of the Jeep. I kept my hands in sight and remained still.

"Do I have your permission to enter your vehicle and retrieve your weapon, since this is just routine?"

I knew how fast this could go from routine to not routine. Without probable cause that I had committed a crime or a warrant, he needed my okay, unless this was an emergency and lives were in danger. I had nothing to hide, so I shrugged. "Go ahead."

He leaned in through the driver's door of the Jeep and pulled my M9 from the console. He glared at me with a strange expression on his face. "This is your issued weapon, not a personal piece?"

"Yes, sir, it is." I took a second and read his name tag, *Sgt. Gaines*, as he popped the magazine out, made sure the safety was on, and set both the pistol and its magazine on the hood.

"Where were you headed today, ma'am. If you were on leave, you wouldn't be in uniform."

"With all due respect, Sergeant, that information is classified."

"Is that so, *Corporal* Michaels?" Stressing my rank, he raised an eyebrow at me, probably thinking he was smelling bullshit.

"It is, yes, Sergeant. Go run my ID and plates. You'll have your answer." I crossed my arms under my breasts and leaned my ass on the bumper—content to wait. Without another word, he headed back to his cruiser.

Boy, was he in for a surprise. He'd get some sort of error message on his computer, telling him to cease and desist with any further inquiries without military authorization and that my Army service number was classified. There would be no information available to him.

He came back a few minutes later, looking slightly perturbed. I couldn't help but chuckle.

"I stand corrected, Corporal. Your plate came back as unfounded. And when I called in your civilian license, it came back restricted. I did three tours with the Cavalry in Iraq. I'm not an idiot. You're military intelligence."

It wasn't a question, so I didn't say anything, just gave him a blank stare.

"I wasn't going to give you a ticket anyway, unless you were a zoomie, that is. Those fuckers in the Air Force have it too easy." He handed my documents back and tipped his hat. "Have a good day, Corporal, or whoever you are. Slow the fuck down on my highways, though."

"Yes, sir. Be safe." I shook his hand and watched him walk away.

As he drove by me, I reloaded my weapon and stowed it back in the center console. *Restricted, huh? That's a first.* My gut was a hard knot. My orders had been mysterious enough, which wasn't that unusual, but now I was beginning to think there was much more at play here than I knew. Only one way to find out. I had about three more hours of driving before I got to the small town in the middle of bum-fuck Pennsylvania, but with my lead foot, I'd make it in two.

Stomping on the gas, I hit eighty-five easily once more. Fuck, I loved this Jeep. Blasting the radio, "How's it Gonna Be" by Third Eye Blind filled the Jeep. I tapped my fingers on the gear shift and sang along.

Sergeant Gaines had pulled into one of those emergency vehicle turnaround places in the middle of the highway. I waved and honked the horn as I passed him. I slipped my sunglasses on against the setting sun as it flared red and orange against a darkening sky.

Forty-five more songs on my playlist later, I pulled into the parking lot of a small motel—it had maybe six rooms, tops. It was a little run-down, which wasn't all that surprising considering the town I'd just driven through. I'd seen a post office, church, bar, and not much else.

Shutting off the Jeep, I stepped out into the cool night air. We were nearing the end of spring and soon the nights would be sweltering.

Entering the brightly lit office, I was greeted by a gray-haired old lady, who was about four feet tall, using a twisted wooden cane to walk.

"Evening, dear. What can I help you with?" She looked and sounded like a classic grandma, the kind that baked cookies and knitted you scarves.

"I need a room, ma'am. At least two nights, please."

"Rooms are sixty a night, ice machine is between rooms four and five, and I don't allow smoking." She flipped a book around, so I could sign in. I hesitated a moment, unsure if I should use my real name or not. I had several aliases, along with corresponding IDs in my duffel, but I didn't think a false name was necessary here. Anyway, I was still in my uniform with Michaels on the right breast and U.S. Army on the left.

I handed her the cash, paying for both nights. She promptly handed me sixty dollars back. "No soldier for my country will pay full price. You get a free night. Thank you for your service, dear."

"Ma'am, thank you, but that's really not necessary. I can pay."

"Nonsense. I won't hear of it. I lost my boy in the damn jungle of Vietnam, and my father fought the Nazis. I won't hear another word about it, young lady. My name is Harriet, and if you need anything, you let me know."

"Of course, ma'am. Thank you." I took the old key she handed me for room number two. Leaving the well-lit office behind, I headed back out into the darkness.

Opening the door to my room, I was greeted by beige walls and green bedding. It was outdated, but like the rest of the hotel, it was clean and smelled fresh. Leaving my duffel on the bed, I stripped and stepped into the small shower stall. The water felt amazing washing off the gritty feel from traveling.

The shiny pink scar on my bicep was a reminder of Iraq. It had been six months, but it felt more like six days. It didn't take much to send me back to that dirty roadway . . . to see Montez's body jerking with each bullet that slammed into him.

Shaking the water from my eyes and the memories from my head, I got out and dressed. Jeans and a long-sleeved, black shirt, paired with my boots suited me just fine. I wasn't exactly going to a five-star joint—it was an Irish pub in the middle of nowhere. Unless I walked in there naked, I don't think I'd garner much notice.

My orders were to report there by 1900 hours and await contact. It was 1845 now—time to get going and see what the future held. I hoped I was getting a new assignment. I couldn't stand being on base anymore. Something had changed within me after that ambush. Riding a desk was torture for me now. If I couldn't be in the field, when my tour of duty was up, I was done with the Army.

8

S ipping his beer, Carter's gaze darted furtively around the large room of Finnegan's bar. The place was near what would be the new compound for Steel Corps, the elite and secret military team being formed by the man sitting to his right, who was also keeping an eye on all the patrons. Master Sergeant Fisher Jackson and Carter had met several times in Abu Ghraib. Jackson had been assigned there, and the black-ops spy had flown in on occasion whenever an al Qaeda prisoner with information he needed wasn't too willing to divulge said information. In other words—the prisoner had to be tortured. Carter wasn't thrilled with some of the things he had to do to gather intel to protect the citizens of the United States, but he was good at it. Damn, fucking good at it.

When he'd heard Jackson was putting together a new covert team, he'd contacted him with one person in mind. The man had been shocked when he'd been handed the file on US Army Corporal Bea "Mic" Michaels, but as he read through the paperwork, he began to see what Carter had— the woman was a natural leader. Despite starting off in intelligence, Michaels had ended up in a combat situation from Hell. Six Humvees and one cargo truck, filled with US military personnel and the huge weapons and intel cache that'd been found in a bunker, had been hightailing it back to base from a small Iraqi village where she'd interrogated an important source. Mic's Humvee, along with a second one, had been about five or ten minutes behind the others. Hers was the only one with survivors after an ambush. And it was because of her, they had survived after the initial assault had killed several troops, leaving her as the ranking NCO on scene. She'd led her ragtag and injured group to safety and received several commendations as a result.

The only thing Carter found in her file that might be a problem was her aunt, Beatrice Grant. Jackson's group would have to be off grid, meaning their lives as they knew them would be over. What little family they had, if any, would be told they'd died in combat. They would be wiped off the face of the earth. Carter was all too familiar with how that was done.

The front door to the establishment opened, and the woman in question strode in. Carter gave a subtle nod to the redneck he'd spoken to earlier. For $300 cash, the man had agreed to make a strong pass at her, sight unseen. Carter wanted to see how she would handle herself. He knew she would need a lot of training to get to where Jackson needed her to be. But she was intelligent and had responded favorably in a situation where many soldiers in the same position would have frozen and peed their pants.

He and Jackson watched as she scanned the room, looking for someone who fit the military image she had in her head. All she knew was to come here and wait to be contacted by a superior for a potential new assignment. They had been told she'd been curious about the secrecy but had followed the orders and traveled the four hours from where she was currently based. She eyed them both before moving on to another group of men. Carter and Jackson appeared as scruffy as all the rednecks in the place, with three-day-old beards, and the former's hair long enough for a ponytail. He would have been surprised if she'd picked either of them out as her contact. While she knew Carter by his code number from when he'd called her office for intelligence occasionally, they'd never met in person.

As she took a seat at the bar and ordered a drink, he studied her. She was five foot four, about one hundred twenty pounds with short, curly, blonde hair, and hazel eyes —a far cry from the black-ops soldier they wanted to turn her into. And that was part of the reason he'd recommended her to Jackson, especially after talking to Ian about the interrogation she'd done, followed by the convoy ambush. Looks could be deceiving. Carter knew under her long-sleeve, black T-shirt there were several tattoos and toned muscles, which gave away her training—at least to an experienced eye, which the redneck approaching her did not have.

Carter took another sip of his beer. Neither he nor Jackson had said a word since Michaels had walked in. There were about two dozen other patrons in the dimly lit bar, but no one else would be a problem they couldn't handle if things got out of hand within the next few minutes. He couldn't hear what the redneck was saying, as he invaded Michaels's personal space, but her body language was clear —*back off, asshole*. Even the bartender was giving the guy a warning glower, which was ignored. He saw Michaels's shoulders tense then loosen—*oh yeah, this is going to be fucking good*.

I SAT on the hard stool and ordered a Guinness—hard to find a bar that has it on tap anywhere, especially down by me. The cold, smooth creaminess slid down my throat. I scanned the bar again, not seeing anyone who fit the bill for my contact. I'd wait. If he was here, he'd come to me.

Propping my elbows next to my glass, I settled in. I felt more than heard someone walk up behind me. Glancing to the left, my muscles tensed. Some local asswipe was gonna have a go at me. Canting to the side, I tried to tell him with my body alone to fuck off. The idiot didn't get the message.

"Hey, darlin', can I buy you a drink?" He switched his wad of chew from one cheek to the other, spitting into a cup clutched in his hand. *Yum . . . so attractive.*

"No. Got one already." I waved my nearly full pint at him.

"You're not from around here, are ya?" The bold redneck sat on the stool beside me. Glancing down the length of the maple bar, I saw a few people watching our exchange. The bartender walked toward us, thinking he was going to come to my rescue, no doubt. I was no damsel, and the horribly scarred bartender was no knight.

"Listen, pal, I'm here waiting for someone. Go away before I make you." I pushed my beer further back on the bar, well out of reach.

"I'm better than any man you're going to meet here, baby." He put his hand on my waist, trying to pull me in against his body. I gritted my teeth and took a breath, relaxing my shoulders.

Reaching around, I grabbed his hand, twisting it backward and to the side. His yelps of pain only pushed me on. Turning my body around, I pulled up on his hand and arm, bending him forward at the waist. He was stomping his feet and making a pitiful, whiny noise. *Too fucking bad.*

I gripped his greasy hair with my other hand and smacked his forehead off the bar. Catching movement on my left, I saw the bartender rounding the end of the maple bar. Anticipating trouble, I tapped the redneck's head on the wood again, hoping I'd knock some sense into him.

"Listen here, fuck face," I hissed in his ear. "I was ready to be polite, then you put your fucking paw on me. Keep your slimy hands to yourself, got it?"

Sweat covered his reddened face, highlighting the giant lump forming on his forehead. "Ye . . . yes, ma'am. I'm s-so sorry." He stuttered and quaked in a combination of pain and fear. I let go of his arm and used his hair as a handle to throw him backward onto the floor. He scrambled away like a crab as fast as his boots could move. I wiped the hand that had been in his hair on my pants in disgust.

"Well, luv, I see ya got this under control just fine." The bartender's thick Irish accent threw me for a moment as he walked back behind the bar.

"Apparently so." I sat down again and took a long drink of my beer. Smacking my lips, I eyed the bartender. Studying him closely now, I noticed that scars covered one side of his face and neck, down under his shirt and over his arm. They highlighted his looks, instead of ruining them. Slick and pebbled at the same time, the white scars rippled, showing clearly the path the fire took when he received them. I didn't try to hide the fact I was staring—he knew they were there, and the scars were worth a glance.

"If you'd like a private showing, I can arrange that, luv." He smirked and walked away, a swagger in his step. *His jeans sure do fit nice . . .*

My line of thought was broken by the approach of a very scruffy looking guy. Tall as fuck—my guess was about six foot four and two hundred pounds easily. With long, blond hair pulled back into a small ponytail at the nape of his neck and classic good looks, I'm sure he had women everywhere throwing their panties at him. It takes more than a pretty face to get me, though, and he was wasting his time.

Rolling my eyes as he stopped next to me, I thought, *here we go again*. "Don't even think about hitting on me, unless you want to go the way of that asshole over there." I hitched a thumb toward the guy currently holding his arm and hanging his head in embarrassment as his buddies pretended not to know him when they saw us looking.

"I wouldn't dream of it." His voice was low enough that I was the only one who heard him. He held his hand out for me to shake. "Allow me to introduce myself, Corporal Michaels. The name's Carter, but you'll know me as 009-859SRU."

Holy. Fucking. Shit. I was stunned but refused to give him the satisfaction of knowing he'd shocked me as I ignored his extended hand. "About fucking time. Why didn't you say something when I first came in, huh? Was that show entertaining for you?"

He dropped his hand, and his grin lit up his handsome face as his blue eyes danced in amusement. "Oh, very much so, sweetheart. Come, bring your beer."

THAT HAD BEEN MUCH MORE enjoyable than Carter had expected. Michaels hadn't hesitated to put the two-hundred-fifty-pound man in his place. The redneck's arm and pride were hurting, but the cash in his pocket more than made up for it. Striding back to the table with Michaels on his heels, Carter took his seat once more with his back to the wall. He knew she was about to blast him for the "sweetheart" comment, so he cut her off at the pass. "Corporal Michaels, this is your contact, Master Sergeant Jackson. Take a seat."

"Pleased to meet you, sir," she said to Jackson as she pulled out a chair and sat.

Instead of returning her greeting, Jackson glared at her. "Rule number one of special operations, Michaels, is never sit with your back to a room. It can have deadly results."

The corners of Carter's mouth ticked upward as the meaning of the man's words became clear to the female soldier. Her eyes widened as she scooted her chair closer to Jackson's, so she could see as much of the bar as possible. She was a fast learner. *Good, she needed to be.*

She stared at Jackson in a mix of confusion and disbelief. She lowered her voice as if afraid to be overheard, which was an unnecessary worry. There was no one within fifteen feet of the trio, and the music from the jukebox muted their voices to the others in the bar. "Forgive me, sir, but special ops?"

Pulling out her file he'd been sitting on, Jackson opened the manila folder and began rattling off her background, both before and after joining the military. Her jaw dropped, and Carter snorted before taking another sip of his beer. *Welcome to the world of black ops, Michaels.*

When Jackson was done with her background, he closed the folder and placed it on the table in front of him. "A new unit is being formed, Michaels, and Carter here thinks you have what it takes to be a part of it. However, I'm not convinced. Yes, your background is close to ideal, but aside from that one skirmish you were in, you have no real combat experience."

As Carter expected, rage filled her eyes. "With all due respect, sir, I'd hardly call what my men and I went through a skirmish. Many good men lost their lives that day. My fucking NCO, Staff Sergeant Montez, had a two-month-old son he never got to meet thanks to that 'skirmish,' as you call it. I call it a fucking Hell on Earth. If you disagree with that, *sir*, then you can go fuck yourself."

She stood quickly, sending her chair screeching back a foot or two. Jackson glared at her with hard eyes. "Sit down, Corporal, and can the fucking attitude. I'm a superior officer and you will treat me as such—even in this fucking dive."

Carter grinned, earning a dirty look from her. *Oh, yeah. She's going to be part of Steel Corps, as long as she doesn't piss Jackson off any more than she already has.*

Slowly, she took her seat once more, but her anger was still simmering under the surface. Jackson placed his forearms on the table and leaned forward. "Here's the deal, Michaels. Take it or fucking leave it. I don't care either way." Yeah, that was a lie. The man was definitely impressed with what he'd witnessed over the past five minutes—he wouldn't be about to make his offer if he hadn't been. "This new unit being formed is going to be so far off the grid, you will cease to exist. No contact with anyone from your life before the moment you become part of my team. They will all be told you died in combat. *Everyone.* Your life will be black ops and nothing else until you decide it's time to leave. You'll then get a new name, new life, and no further contact with me or any of your teammates. You will train . . . my way or the highway. You will give yourself a hundred-and-ten percent to your team and its missions. You fuck up, and it will be the worst day of your life . . . and maybe your last." He pulled out another folder he'd been sitting on. "This doesn't leave my sight. Sit there. Read it. Then give me your decision. Either you leave here tonight on my team, or you forget you ever saw either one of us and go back to your boring life in Intelligence."

As Michaels gaped at the master sergeant, Carter's cell phone silently buzzed on his hip. A message had been left on his voice mail. Very few people knew the number, and those who did were either his bosses or high up on the US government food chain. Hitting the button to connect to the voice mail, he put the phone to his ear. After listening for a moment, he hung up and stood. "I have to go, so I'll leave you two to hash this out. Jackson, great to see you again. Michaels . . . good luck, sweetheart." He winked at her and headed for the door.

9

Gripping the burner phone tightly in my hand, I stared at the slip of paper with Jackson's number on it, unblinking. I'd been glaring at it so long, the numbers were blurring together, even though I had long since memorized them. I'd told him I needed some time, in private, to decide, and he'd given me two hours—a gift really. I had to call him either way—he needed to know my decision. Was I going to do this? Really go through with this?

Aunt Beatrice's face flashed in my brain. My supposed death would break her heart. I don't know if I could do this to her. She was all I had left in the world and vice versa. But this was a unique opportunity—I would be given the chance to swiftly deal out justice for those most in need of it. Maybe I had a hero complex, I wasn't sure.

Besides the opportunity for justice, I would be able to disappear. The note from my father was burned into my mind. I still had no idea how'd he managed to contact me, in fucking Iraq of all places. I'd only been there for two weeks when the message arrived. A clerk was handing out mail, and I was surprised when my name was called—I very rarely got mail. Sitting in my bunk with veins full of ice, I opened the envelope.

Bea,

It took me more effort than I would like to find you. You really ran away good this time. But I'm your father, your blood, and blood will always ring true. I'm so angry with you. How could you have left like that? And after that goon of yours beat me up, I spent two days in the hospital with broken ribs. You need to leave the Army and come home where you belong. You know you're going to fail. You're nothing and no one. I'm the only one who cares about you. How could you leave me—I'm your father and you will do as you're told. If not, well, you know what will happen. Get your ass home, girl. Where you belong. You can never escape me. I'm all you've got and without me you'll be all alone in a world where everyone can see what a lying, little murdering bitch you are. Is that why you joined the Army? So you can keep killing people? Did you get a taste of it after you murdered your mother? Everyone is going to see who you are. They will hate you. They already do. Come home. Now.

Your Father.

This was my chance, my golden opportunity to get away. For good. I'd be dead and forever out of my father's reach. I wouldn't get another opportunity like this, and I knew being back in the states it would be only a matter of time until he showed up at my door. My heart broke for what I was about to put Aunt Beatrice through, but I knew if I had the chance to explain, she would understand. I couldn't go through all of that again. Not now, not after what I'd been through in Iraq. I didn't have it in me anymore. I was so far past done with him and my past.

Maybe I was a killer, after all, and he was right. I had killed my mother by being born. Deep down, I knew it wasn't my fault. How could it be? But years of being told I was to blame was hard to forget. Maybe Steel could be my fresh start, a chance at a new life free from the burdens of the past. It was this or I'd go home and slit that bastard's throat—after I made him beg for death. I'd show him just exactly what it was I had been doing in Iraq. But, no, death was too good for that fucker. He didn't deserve it. His punishment would be living and remembering what my mother had been to him and what he'd done to me. When his death finally arrived, his judgment would as well. He could spend eternity burning in the pit of hell, and it would be too good for him.

My silence and then alleged death would bring him plenty of pain. That part of my life was over—a new chapter was about to begin. I flipped the phone open and dialed the number before I gave myself a chance to think anymore.

The call was answered. "Jackson," he barked impatiently.

"I'm in." No other words were necessary. My stomach was in knots, and my sweaty palms slipped on the phone, nearly dropping it.

"I'm texting you directions. Meet me there at oh-nine-hundred tomorrow. Bring all the gear you have with you. Check out of the motel. Get rid of your phone before you arrive."

A click and dead air was followed by a beep announcing the text message. I quickly memorized the directions and turned off the phone before pulling out the battery and SIM card. I'd dispose of them in different locations along the way.

I needed some dinner, I hadn't eaten since my last stop for gas on the drive up. Pocketing my room key, I headed out. The only place I knew of to get something to eat at this hour was Finnegan's. I pulled my Jeep into the parking lot. Even though I'd been gone for a few hours, the lot was still full of vehicles—more than it had been earlier.

There was a band playing covers, and the dance floor was

packed. I shoved my way through the crowd, making a beeline for the last empty stool at the bar. The music was excellent, the lead singer killing it on "Dragula." I tapped my fingertips on my thigh to the beat, tapping my nails against the knife in my pocket.

The scarred bartender noticed me and ambled down the length of the bar, dropping off drinks on the way.

"Couldn't wait to see me again, huh, luv? What can I get ya?" His whiskey smooth voice had my inner-girl sitting up and noticing. Between his tone and the accent, he probably had women throwing themselves at him every night.

"A menu and a Pepsi."

"Kitchen's closed, sorry." He shrugged and pointed at the clock over his shoulder. It was now almost eleven. Dammit.

I gritted my teeth in frustration. Hunger pains twisted my stomach. "Listen, I haven't eaten in over ten hours. I'll pay double, just get me a burger and fries. Please."

"Aye." He winked at me. "Can't let a pretty lass starve in my pub, but you'll eat in the back. If I serve you, then everyone is going to want food."

Leaving the other bartender to take care of things, he walked over to where the little door was in the bar and waved me back. I followed him into a gleaming kitchen. There was a large worktable in the middle with a few stools pushed under the edge. He pulled one out, indicating for me to sit, then fired up the grill.

"I appreciate this," I said, taking the seat.

"Don't mention it, luv. I won't let a beautiful lass like you go hungry." He was pulling open the doors to several fridges, spreading out ingredients on the counter. He slapped a burger on the flat-top, pressing it down. "Onions?" He looked over his shoulder at me, quirking an eyebrow up in question.

"Grilled, yes. Not raw. And cheese, too. And knock off the

'beautiful lass' crap. I am many things, but beautiful is not one of them. Please." I remembered to be polite at the last minute. Spending months at a time with a bunch of rowdy soldiers tends to wear away your manners.

"It's my bloody bar, and I can say and think what I want. Yer a knockout. Take the compliment or don't, but I speak the truth."

"Okay then. Thanks for the sweet compliment," I added as much sarcasm as I could, throwing in an eye roll for extra measure.

"You're a sassy one then, aren't you?" Chuckling, he turned his back to me and began to prepare my meal in earnest.

Watching him cook was like watching a symphony of motion. His body flowed around the kitchen, step-by-step, assembling the food. The room was soon filled with mouth-watering smells . . . and sights for that matter. I lost all track of time watching him prepare my meal—it felt incredibly surreal. He was fit and strong, I kept catching glimpses of his back and stomach as he twisted and reached over the counter. He wasn't rock solid, but instead, he was real. My mouth was suddenly dying for a taste of something more than a burger.

"Here you go." He laid a plate piled high with a burger and fries on the table in front of me.

My attention snapped back to the present, my daydreams evaporating under his amber gaze. "Thank you, this looks fucking amazing."

Chuckling, he swiped a fry. "If there's anything else you need . . . or want—anything at all. You let me know." With a wink and crooked smile, he left me alone.

My face heated, knowing I'd been caught ogling him. I let his obvious offer linger in the back of my mind. Maybe it was something I'd explore later. Taking my first bite, the flavors exploded in my mouth. I knew I was hungry enough to choke down an MRE, but this was the best burger I'd ever had. If he did this so well, I wondered what else he was good at.

Once I was finished, I put my dirty plate in the sink and left forty dollars on the counter. Over the course of my meal, I decided I'd be back. That was for damn sure.

GRABBING MY DUFFEL, I stowed it in my Jeep and went to the office to check out. A bell sounded as I pushed open the door, and Harriet stood in greeting.

"Heading out then, dear?" Her arthritis-twisted hands rested on the counter, supporting her weight. I didn't see her cane.

"Yes, ma'am. All set." I laid the key on the counter and turned to leave. "Thank you for your kindness."

"You are most welcome. Kindness costs nothing, and I'm happy to give it. You stay safe, young lady. Whatever you're up to is dangerous, I can feel it."

"Thank you, ma'am, and have a great day." She was correct—what I was about to do was indeed dangerous and not just physically. I'll be leaving my current life behind and starting a new one. The only thing I would keep was my name, if only in the presence of my team. My memories were my own, offering up their own set of challenges. My hope was I would be so busy I wouldn't have a chance to dwell on the past—Iraq or my father . . . or Aunt Beatrice.

My Jeep started with a throaty rumble, and I headed down the road, following Jackson's instructions. I turned onto a narrow dirt road, and when I broke through the tree line, I found myself on a construction site.

Earth, churned into mud, was everywhere, with the

skeletons of buildings rising around the perimeter. Two small cabins were completed, with the concrete pads and framed walls of three more going up. I felt the Jeep's tires slip a bit when I climbed the last, small rise.

Yellow construction equipment filled the area, and there was a black Silverado parked in front of the only other completed building. If I had to guess from the outside alone, I'd say it was the mess hall.

I was grateful for my boots when I stepped down into the mud. Shouldering my bag, I strode inside. The half-finished interior smelled strongly of paint, lumber, and drywall dust. I could see what the building would be—kitchen towards the back, tables in the middle, and maybe a rec area to the side.

A wooden door in the back corner was ajar and drew my attention. As I approached, a deep, booming voice coming from inside to let me know I was it the right place.

"I don't care what your boss says, this is your fucking deadline, and if you can't meet it, I'll fucking find someone who can!" Jackson shouted at someone in a white hard hat—the foreman, no doubt. Slamming his hand on the table, the large Black man, who was now my superior, seemed to grow even bigger as his temper rose.

The foreman tried to placate him. "Sir, my men are doing the best they can. But the mud is making everything take longer. This is the way construction is, delays happen. I can't control the weather. We're expecting more rain tonight."

"Great, just fucking great. I need this place operational in three months. Are you going to be able to make that deadline, or do I need to hire a different company?" Jackson leaned across the makeshift table and glared at the other man.

"My team is the best. We'll get it done. If we have to work nights, it will be finished." The foreman was red-faced and sweating. It was hard to tell if he was intimidated or choking back his own temper.

"Fine. See that you do." Jackson waved his hand, dismissing him like he was brushing off a fly.

I moved to the side so the foreman could leave, waiting for Jackson to acknowledge me.

"Come in, Staff Sergeant." He plopped down in a wooden chair. It was covered in paint splatters, and no doubt belonged to the workers. He was dressed all in black, his tactical pants tucked into heavy boots, and in turn, his fitted, black T-shirt tucked into his pants.

"Excuse me, sir, but I'm a corporal."

"Not anymore. You said yes—you're now a staff sergeant and will lead this team. Happy fucking promotion day."

Holy fuck! I dropped my bag, taking a moment to rearrange my scrambled thoughts. I tried not to gape at him. "Thank you, sir. What team? When do they arrive?"

"I haven't picked the team yet. You're it, for now. First, we'll complete your training, then I'll recruit the rest of the team. I have some candidates in mind. I'll take your opinion into consideration, but the final decision is mine."

"Understood." I was rigid, at loose ends, and unsure of what happens next. "When does training start?"

"Oh-six-hundred. You get the cabin that's farthest away." He pointed to his left even though we couldn't see the other buildings from here. "The other is mine. Stow your gear, sleep if you need to—do whatever. But in the morning you report here, ready for a ruck. You'll find standard gear in your cabin. After training tomorrow, we'll go shopping for weapons. Dismissed."

I was not looking forward to a hike with full gear, but it was the name of the game when training.

Slopping back through the mud, I opened the door to what was going to be my home. The inside was finished and, surprisingly, painted a soft blue. There was a couch and coffee table in the living room, but nothing else. Toeing off my muddy boots at the front door, I then followed the open floor plan—shiny new appliances greeted me in the kitchen. An apartment-sized fridge still with the stickers on, a narrow, two-burner stove, and a coffee pot still in the box were the only amenities.

A standard bathroom, stocked with towels and everything else I'd need was next. At last, a bedroom was at the end of the short hallway. It had a plastic wrapped mattress and a queen-sized bed set still in its package. I had expected a cot or bunk—this was much nicer.

Dumping my bag on the floor, I ripped the plastic away and set myself to moving in. I'd need to do some shopping, but that could come later. Whatever training Jackson had in mind was sure to be more intense than anything I'd experienced before. I pulled out some running clothes, deciding to get a quick run in before it got too hot out. No time like the present, huh?

TAKING the secure elevator from under the White House up to the back entrance of the Oval Office, Carter ran a hand through his hair—nonexistent as it almost was now. He'd gotten a buzz cut this morning, as instructed by Larry Keon, the Deputy Director of the FBI. While Keon wasn't exactly his supervisor, Carter was on loan from his own covert unit, Deimos, for the next few months. Deimos was the Greek god of terror, which fit perfectly for the black-ops group whose war against terrorists of all kinds included torture and assassinations, if necessary. When the unit was being formed, though, one of the other operatives had jokingly suggested calling it SRU—Spies R Us. While that hadn't gone over well, as expected, the name had stuck among the agents. That was why the SRU letters were tacked onto their code numbers.

The elevator doors opened to reveal the two Marines he'd known would be there. They'd been expecting him as he wouldn't have been able to access the underground tunnels from off-site and then the elevator without jumping through a few hoops first. After his retina and palm had been scanned, he'd then had to recite the first line of Abraham Lincoln's famous speech into a voice recognition box. *Four score and seven years ago our fathers brought forth on this continent, a new nation, conceived in Liberty, and dedicated to the proposition that all men are created equal.* The current president, Nathaniel Garrett, was a big fan of his long-deceased predecessor.

With barely a nod at the two, stoic men, Carter made a right into the short hallway and knocked on the door at the far end. When a strong, baritone voice answered, "Enter," he opened the door and stepped into the president's lair. Garrett, Keon, FBI Director Bill Moran, and Alan Frankfort, the Secretary of Homeland Security, were gathered in the sitting area by the unlit fireplace, along with another man he had not expected to see. Liam Cooper was an agent from Britain's MI6, the equivalent of the CIA, and was as embedded in the world of black ops as his American counterpart.

Carter stepped over and shook everyone's hands, starting with the salt-and-pepper-haired Garrett. "Hello, Mr. President."

"I almost didn't recognize you, Carter. I don't think I've ever seen you clean cut before."

He chuckled and took a seat on the couch next to Keon. "It's definitely been a while, sir. I take it there's a reason for it, and it's not just because you got tired of my scruff."

Getting right to the point, Frankfort leaned over and

handed him an orange folder, which was the designated color for classified information. "Meet Hans Wexler."

Carter opened the thick file, and on the first page was a picture of a man in his forties, with a blond crewcut, cruel blue eyes, and a faint, one-inch scar on his left cheek. But what stood out the most was the uniform the man was wearing. It was the exact replica of ones worn by Hitler's SS organization. *Fuck.*

Tilting his head toward the man on his left, Frankfort continued. "Cooper has supplied us with some of the information in that file, which is why he's here. Since Wexler is on US soil, and Cooper wouldn't be considered a poster boy for a neo-Nazi organization, we're sending you in."

Grinning at the MI6 operative, Carter nodded. The Black man would stick out like a sore thumb among what Hitler had described as the perfect race—blond-haired, blue-eyed men and women. "I can understand that. Your British twang and tea fetish would give it away in a heartbeat."

"Go swivel, ya bastard." The Brit flashed him the finger.

Garrett and Carter both barked out a laugh as the latter pointed at Cooper. "It's been way too long, my friend."

"So it has."

Settling back on the couch, Secretary Frankfort took over the conversation again. "Wexler has been slowly gathering weapons, cash, and personnel under the radar for the past few years. While he hasn't left the US, that we know of, he has associate cells in the UK, France, and of course, Germany. MI6 came across some intel that leads them and us to believe major domestic terrorist attacks are being planned for the four countries. The problem is we haven't been able to get any info on how organized they are and how widespread the attacks are supposed to be. That's where you come in. Wexler's compound is located in South Dakota, but you'll have to work your way through the organization to get invited there." He handed Carter another folder—this one was blue, and he could take it with him. In it would be the information he needed to start worming his way into the organization. "We expect it will take you at least six months to do that. You'll be starting in the Colorado cell. Cooper will be an outside contact for you for any info his man trying to get in the UK cell can deliver. France and Germany are also trying to infiltrate their own cells. We'll provide you with any other support personnel you need. If you don't have any objections or concerns, the mission is yours."

Closing the orange file, Carter added the blue one to it and nodded his agreement—not that any of them had expected otherwise. Unlike the other covert agencies, he had his choice of assignments. This was what he excelled at though, and if it saved one American life, then to him, it was worth giving it his all. "Mr. President, do you mind if Liam and I have lunch somewhere in your house, privately? We have a mission to discuss and a psychotic bastard to take down."

10

I popped three Motrin and tried to stretch out my muscles after I was woken up from the pain and stiffness. Jackson was putting me through the ringer. He was nearly impossible to keep up with. Never mind that he had a significant more amount of training than I did, his stride was as long as my whole body. I had to run faster just to stay even with his jog.

Today, we'd gone weapon shopping after a rigorous hand-to-hand combat session. There was a guy in town, he'd given me the obviously fake name of John Friggin' Smith, who could order us whatever we wanted. I had been allowed to choose two rifles to start with and had selected a Colt M4 and a Heckler & Koch MP5. There were some new goodies coming out from both companies that I also ordered. I loved the idea that I could customize my weapons to suit me. Jackson had tried to get me to give up my M9 sidearm, but I couldn't. That weapon had saved my life in Iraq, and there was no way in hell I would part with it.

I needed some air and a change of scenery. Hopping in my Jeep, I drove off the compound and toward town. My mind flashed back to the bartender at Finnegan's. Although I had figured out he was also the owner, I didn't know what his name was. That was something I wanted to remedy. He might be just the thing I needed to relax after the day I'd had. Other than weapons shopping, it had been running, fighting, and crawling through the mud from dawn until well after sunset. The nap had refreshed me, and now I was wired. Jackson said we were working on something different tomorrow, so the day wasn't starting quite as early.

Parking the Jeep in the nearly empty lot, I climbed out and headed for the entrance. I pushed the heavy wooden door open. It was nearly two a.m., and the scarred bartender was yelling out "last call" as I quietly stepped inside. There were three people at the bar and a couple playing pool. The woman was using her pool cue to keep herself upright, and her boyfriend was stumbling and tripping over his feet.

The bartender lifted the little built-in shelf on the bar, walking around to the pool table. He spoke softly to them, slinging his arm around their shoulders, and smoothly collected their keys. He deposited them on stools and picked up the phone near the register. I stayed back in the shadows near the door, letting their deep safety keep me hidden until I was ready to be seen.

I took a moment to really look around, which I hadn't done when I was here a few days ago. So much had changed since then. My whole life was resetting like a clock after a power surge—blinking the time over and over, just waiting for instructions.

There was a large fireplace on the far wall, its mantle full of framed photos of Ireland and various people here in the bar. It was a nice touch and made you think he really cared about his patrons.

Warm, dark-colored wood and low lighting made the whole room feel inviting and relaxing. There weren't TVs in every corner or flashing beer signs. This was a pub, a home away from home for many.

I slid further along the wall, away from the door, but careful to stay in the deep shadows. I waited there as the few remaining people trickled out in ones or twos. The two drunks stumbled into a taxi that had pulled up to the door.

The bartender came out and began wiping down the tables and stacking the chairs on top. He was wearing a simple, white, cotton shirt and nice, broken-in blue jeans—the kind that have a few holes and fit just right. And fuck me, did they fit him nicely. The denim cupped his ass perfectly, hugging his strong legs and lean hips.

"Are ye going to stand there all night, or can I get ya something, luv?" His whiskey-amber eyes pierced the blanket of shadows I was hiding within. He must have been in the states just long enough for his accent to come and go. I wonder if strong emotions made it thicker? I looked forward to testing my theory.

Giving up my ruse, I stepped forward into the light. My own black cargo pants and fitted green shirt felt comfortable and good. For now.

"I don't know. Do you have what I came here for?" One careful step at a time, I advanced on him. He was loosely holding the cleaning rag in his hand, twisting the end back and forth around his scarred fingers.

Was he nervous?

"What do ye have in mind?" His voice was low and husky, sending shivers down my spine.

"You. I came for you." I didn't have the time or inclination to play games. I'd come here for one reason—I wanted this Irishman in my bed, or his bed, or on the fucking floor. I didn't much care, as long as I had him. I needed to blow off some steam and couldn't think of a better way.

"Aye." He dropped the rag on a table and glided the last

few feet to me, stopping close, almost but not quite touching me. "I think I might have a spot of what you're lookin' for." With just his knuckles, he traced his hand down my cheek, chin, and along my neck. Goosebumps raced along my skin in a tingling rush.

Surprising me, he grabbed my waist harshly with both hands, jerking me flush against him. His hardness pressed against me, spilling a groan from my lips.

"Name's Willie, and I'm happy to be of service to one such as you." His lips descended to mine, and my thoughts and reasons why this might not be a good idea fled. Our clothes fell away, landing in little piles on the barroom floor as he backed me up to the pool table.

Coming up for air, I managed to gasp out a few words. "I'm Mic. And this is just for fun."

"Oh, aye, fun indeed. That's just the start of it." He lifted me up and onto the felt covered top of the table, pushing me back until I was in the center. After climbing up after me, he propped himself up on his hands and looked down my body. His eyes tracing the tattoos over my shoulders and chest, down to the center of my torso. "You can come here anytime you'd like."

His hands and mouth grasped and pulled, licked, and sucked every inch of my sensitive skin. I knew torture, and this was it. He drew it out, content to taste and grasp every inch of me. My legs shook, and our bodies grew sticky with sweat.

I returned the favor. His scars were slick and just a little bumpy under my tongue. The salty sweetness of sweat and an earthy taste I couldn't explain exploded in my mouth. I sipped from Willie as if he were a delicate wine. He was sweet and spicy all at once as I explored every inch of him. The backs of his knees were very sensitive, and my kisses

NO WAY IN HELL

made him twist and groan. His hipbones were firm under my teeth.

When he flipped me over onto my stomach, jerking me up on my knees, and surging into me, I saw stars. My muscles screaming and burning with the delicious torment he inflicted. He rasped sweet words into my ear, sucking on my neck as he took me . . . no, took *us* higher.

"Fffffuck . . ." I screamed, thrashing against him as an intense orgasm crashed over me. His hand was buried in my hair, holding my head up and back as I shattered around him.

"Oh, aye." He groaned, his body jerking against me, finding his own release.

We filled the bar with our panting breaths and gasps. My heart was pounding in my chest, and sweat coated my body in a shiny film.

"Mic . . . have a drink . . . upstairs," Willie gasped between breaths. "I'm not . . . through with you, woman."

"Sure." I panted, laying my head down on the table. My knees ached from the slate, and my arms were shaking. "Water first. Then round two, yeah?"

"Aye . . . oh, sweet Mother Mary, aye." He kissed the side of my neck before sliding off the table and offering me his hand.

His palm was filled with a star-shaped burn. Just like an old-fashioned doorknob. I jerked my eyes back to his, their amber depths welcoming. I laid my hand in his and jumped down, following him, gathering our clothes as we passed them.

I was going to like it here.

AFTER TYING the lace-up crotch of his black leathers, Carter shut the door of the permanent locker he had in the private, elite, BDSM club in the heart of Washington D.C., then pulled on his open, leather vest. The security at Club X was top-notch, since it catered to a number of powerful people who enjoyed a little kink in their lives away from the prying eyes of the public.

He'd never known what the world of BDSM held in store before he'd gone undercover in a club in Russia, years ago. Not only had he gotten the information he'd needed from his target, but he'd found the lifestyle that suited him perfectly. In between, and sometimes during, missions, he had found time to learn and explore the Dominant/submissive lifestyle, training under some of the best Doms and Dommes in the United States and Europe. None of them had known exactly who he was and what he did for a living—they'd all bought his carefully cultivated cover as a playboy businessman in the import/export world.

It had taken him years to establish the alias of Carter Burke. To make sure he would answer when called by either name, he used his real last name as his first. Then he'd taken the name of a high school history teacher whose positive influence had set him on the path that had led him to where he was now. If it wasn't for Ashford Burke, Carter would have been either in jail or dead a very long time ago. As it was, he hadn't gone by his real first name since transferring to the third junior high school he'd attended, instead, going by T. Carter. When he'd been drafted for Deimos, his despised given name, which had caused him quite a bit of misery and bullying in his young childhood, had been eradicated from every possible record. In fact, T. Carter did not exist in any computer database or document in the world now, except maybe in speculation of who he really was.

Striding out to the main dungeon of the establishment, he let the sights and sounds soothe him. Music pulsated through the air, mixing with cries of pain, ecstasy, pleading, and sexual release. The pain was never induced without the submissive's consent—they had full control over the scene with a Dom, weird as it may sound. Some people were just wired that way—they got off on the pain.

He had memberships in some of the most private and elite BDSM clubs in the world, and each one had its own personality. This one in D.C., however, was always entertaining. The citizens of the United States would be shocked if they knew how many movers and shakers in the federal government and business world enjoyed various kinks which were outside the norms of society. But who set those norms? Usually, closed-minded people. Here, there were no closed minds, just open acceptance.

Stepping over to the crowded bar, he ordered a bottle of water. He wouldn't have any alcohol until he was done playing for the night. Dulling your senses before a scene could result in the submissive being hurt. He'd be heading out to Colorado in the morning, so tonight he was going to enjoy himself, in more ways than one.

"Carter, my love, it's wonderful to see you again. Although it's a pity you cut those long, luscious locks of yours. You really must stop in more often to let me admire what you won't let me have."

Turning his head, he smiled at the tall Domme who could pass for a supermodel if it weren't for the cock and balls under her sparkling, red sheath. "Only in your dreams, Mistress Trixie."

She fluttered her false eyelashes. Her throaty voice was whiskey-laced as she stroked the head of her nearly-naked, male submissive kneeling silently at her feet. "Oh, and what dreams they are, Master Studly. You've starred in many of my wet fantasies over the years. One of these days I'm going to convince you to take a walk on the wild side."

The spy chuckled—yeah, that was never going to happen. Not only was he not into men, or transgender women with male parts, but he also wasn't interested in submitting to anyone, especially a sadistic Domme. "Well, in the meantime, what talent is here for me this evening? I'm only in town for one night, so I want to make it memorable."

"From what I hear from the chatty subs, love, you make every night memorable for them. But there are a few new pretties in the stable. I suggest you negotiate with the busty redhead over there in the black teddy. She should be a good match for your—endowments." She practically purred that last word.

His gaze followed to where Trixie's well-manicured finger with red polish was pointing at a group of submissives consisting of three women and two men in various states of dress. "Very nice. Her name?"

"Lucy."

He studied the curves of the redhead. In a fashion magazine, her body would be considered plus-size, but he loved women of all shapes and proportions, and plus-size just meant there was more flesh to worship and a larger buttocks to spank. "Hmm. Now, why does *I Love Lucy* come to mind? Thanks, Trixie."

"You're very welcome, love. Join me for a drink later, if you're still up for it. Come along, Pet."

As Trixie sashayed away with her submissive in tow, Carter stared at the pretty sub. When she made eye contact with him, he crooked his finger at her, inviting her over. Her eyes widened a little, then even more when one of the other subs whispered in her ear—probably telling Lucy who he was. He wasn't arrogant, but he knew he had a favorable reputation among the subs, and he was proud of the fact he never left a submissive unsatisfied at the end of the evening. He took great pleasure in giving them what they wanted or needed before satisfying himself.

Lucy walked toward him, her eyes respectfully cast

downward. She stopped in front of him. "Yes, Sir?"

His gaze roamed over her lush body, spending a few extra moments on her partially exposed breasts. She was stunning, and he knew her creamy skin would feel smooth and velvety, and display the perfect shade of red when he spanked her ass. He was certain their limit lists would be compatible, since Trixie knew practically every member's hard and soft limits. Placing his fingers under Lucy's chin, he lifted it until her mesmerizing gaze met his. "Hello, little one, my name is Master Carter. Would you care to negotiate a scene with me?"

Her breath hitched, which made his cock twitch in response. "I would love to, Master Carter."

11

Three weeks later . . .

I waited in the war room for Jackson to arrive. He'd said to meet him here at 1700. I checked my watch again—it was now almost 1800, and he still wasn't here. What the fuck? After another grueling day, and little sleep, I wanted to eat and crash—in that order.

Not one to wait on ceremony, I reviewed the construction plans on the table, noticing a set marked "Compound Two." There was a large clearing in the middle of a densely forested area. Topographical maps showing elevations accompanied the basic plans. There was a standard close-combat course with moving panels—I'd seen similar setups at other bases.

The area that gave me pause was a blocked off concrete structure that was not fully planned. *I could do something with this . . .*

Digging through the papers, I found the blueprint that only had that building on it. Finding a pen and ruler in the mess, I added a maze—twists, turns, and tight spaces. A trap door went in also. I scribbled notes down the side, listing the need for a pressure switch, top-notch sound system, and an observation deck above the course. It wasn't pretty, but it was a start. I'd run it by Jackson and pass it on to the foreman. Writing in all caps on the top of the page, I added the name—*THE PANIC ROOM.*

Smiling, I allowed myself to consider the possibilities. Doing the course at night would be fun . . . add in some barbed wire and mud . . . sounded like a good fucking time to me.

I turned at the sound of the door opening. A tired looking Jackson came in with a man I didn't know. He was around five six, and a solid 180 pounds. Classically Italian in looks, with a scar bisecting his chin, he had the air of a man who'd seen much in life and wasn't impressed by any of it.

"Staff Sergeant, this is Reid Huntington." Gesturing to me with a giant hand, Jackson continued. "Reid, this is Staff Sergeant Bea Michaels. She goes by Mic."

Stepping forward, I shook his hand firmly. "Nice to meet you, sir." Jackson hadn't mentioned a rank.

"Reid's here on loan from MI6, sort of. He does a little bit of everything when it comes to top secret anything. He's also acquainted with Carter."

"Well, considering how Carter is, I'll reserve judgment for now."

Arching a dark eyebrow, Reid finally spoke. "Likewise Staff Sergeant. I've read your file and reviewed all the transcripts from the ambush. You showed remarkable leadership."

"If you say so, sir." I wasn't sure how to respond. Only three of us had lived, out of the entire convoy. I didn't like those numbers, even though I was one of them.

"I do say so."

"Let's go, Mic, time to see Compound Two." Jackson

opened the door and waited for us to pass in front of him. "There should be just enough daylight left for us to check it out."

Reid handed me a folded, laminated map and a flashlight. "To make your day a little more fun, here's a map. We're going to drive—have a good hike."

They left me standing there in the open, mess hall doorway, gaping after them. I watched Jackson's truck drive down the main road, the red taillights bright in the fading daylight. The sun was on its way down. I took a guess, estimating I had maybe an hour of light left.

Unfolding the map, I saw an area marked off in red—no doubt my destination. Studying the terrain closely, I figured I had roughly ten miles of heavily forested land to hike. Ten miles . . . in the near dark, and in an unfamiliar area. When they'd said black ops, this hadn't been what I expected.

MY FOOT TWISTED on a tree root hidden by the leaves on the forest floor. Catching myself on a nearby pine tree, I righted myself and kept on moving. Darkness surrounded me—the hour since sunset seemed to have sped by. The flashlight beam pointed into the distance and not at my feet. The night was alive around me with insects chirping and frogs from a small natural pond singing their hearts out. If I wasn't trying to navigate around said pond, a bog, and impenetrable brush, I might have appreciated it a lot more.

Branches snapping to my left had me whipping the flashlight toward the sound. A deer bounded past into the trees, a white tail pointed straight up as it ran.

I was so focused on the deer, I didn't hear a person step up behind me until it was too late. I didn't have a chance against their surprise and strength. The blow to the back of my head dropped me to my knees as my vision blurred, and pain radiated out from the back of my skull. I caught a glimpse of a shadowy figure standing over me, the face covered by a clown mask. With a trembling hand, I aimed my flashlight beam directly at the face. This was not just any mask—no happy circus clown. This evil visage was the stuff of nightmares—a white face with a cruel, cherry-red grin. Vivid green rimmed the eye sockets, which held dark, deep-set eyes. Vicious teeth shone from the insane smile, pointed and sharp enough to make any predator envious.

A second blow to my temple had a grunt of pain escaping from my lips, and I fell sideways onto the soft leaves and pine needles. The flashlight slipped from my fingers and rolled just out of reach, the trembling beam throwing strange shadows through the already dark and eerie forest. The ground was cold and wet beneath my cheek. The last thing I saw was a pair of large boots before darkness swallowed me, and my eyelids shut against my will.

———

BLINKING, I opened my eyes and discovered the action was in vain. Complete darkness—unrelenting and absolute surrounded me. I attempted to bring my arms forward, but the sharp edge of metal sank into my wrists, not cutting but close. Moving my feet produced similar results. One step at a time, I took stock of my body. My feet were bare and pressed flat to cold concrete. I was sitting on a hard chair, my hands bound behind me through the slats of the chairback, which I could brush with my fingertips. Wiggling my feet, I heard the chair creak as I pulled on my legs.

"Struggling is pointless. You aren't going anywhere until I say so."

My panting breaths were loud to my ears, almost as loud

as my pounding heart. I could feel sweat sliding down my face and spine, dampening my shirt, making it stick fast against my back and stomach.

"You have no concept of who you're fucking with. Let me go or die, and when I kill you, it won't be quick." My voice was cold and hard as anger burned through my fear.

Sounding like it spilled from Hell itself, laughter erupted throughout the room, bouncing off the walls. Goosebumps raced down my arms, tightening my muscles. I was tensed to resist, anxious to move . . . to fight. Adrenaline was shooting through my blood, sharpening my senses.

"Silly girl. The fun has only begun. You saw me, I'm a clown. Don't you know what clowns do?" More laughter laced with insanity filled my ears. "We have fun."

Pain and shock exploded throughout my face and body as he began to beat me with his fists. Blows, one after another, struck nearly every part of me. As I was wobbling on the brink of unconsciousness again, my head felt like it was floating. I spit blood from my ruined mouth, checking my teeth with my tongue. I felt the sharp pain of a chipped tooth in the front, but otherwise they were intact.

My chin fell to my chest, and as hard as I tried, I couldn't lift it. If the cable or wire, whatever he'd tied me up with, wasn't holding me to the chair, I would have slid to the floor in a bruised and bloody heap.

JACKSON STOOD in the corner and watched Reid work Mic over. The hollow thud of flesh striking flesh echoed throughout the room. The covert operative from Deimos was breathing heavily and shaking his hands between strikes, his knuckles already broken open and oozing blood. Jackson waited, patiently anticipating the moment when she would break—when she would scream, beg, and offer up everything to make the abuse stop. She didn't make a sound beyond a gasp or groan when Reid slammed another fist into her ribs.

The Master Sergeant crossed his arms over his chest, counting the blows. Her blood was black in the eerie green light of the goggles, her face covered with it. Turning her head slightly, she spit blood onto the floor. The blindfold hid much of her face, but the set of her jaw told him almost everything he needed to know. This woman was bullheaded and strong—she took the beating like she'd done it before. And she had. He knew that much from her recruiter.

Snapping his fingers, he signaled Reid to give her a break. He wanted her to take a breath, because soon enough, she wouldn't have any to spare.

NOT REALIZING I'd passed out again, I was awoken by the freezing shock of ice water hitting me in the face and chest. Gasping against the cold and spitting water from my mouth, I tried to rally what strength reserves I had. Whatever this bastard wanted, I refused to give him.

Hands jerked and pulled on my arms, cutting my hands and then my feet free. My arms fell uselessly to my sides, numb and aching. Stumbling forward, I was dragged a few feet and shoved onto the hard concrete. Unable to catch myself, I tried to fall on my side, unwilling to take another blow to the face unless I had to. My stomach rebelled against the movement, and I choked as bile burned up my throat. I vomited for what seemed like minutes, my ribs screaming in agony at the violence of it.

Turning over, I laid my head gently on the floor, the spinning slowed as I felt blood begin to pool under my head.

"Done already? And here I was just starting to have fun." I

ground the words out even though speaking made the agony so much worse. I refused to give him the satisfaction of shutting me up. I didn't have it in me to quit or to give in, and he needed to know that.

"Oh, I'm not even close to being done." His voice was thick and almost heavy sounding. It didn't seem natural—his speech pattern was strange. *Was he disguising his voice?*

My weakness sickened me as I tried to push to my knees. My arms trembled and ached with the effort.

"Look at you, trying to be so strong for someone so small. You're not, though—you're weak."

My body jerked as he ripped my shirt off, the fabric rending easily under his strength. I slapped at him, struggling to push him away. Unable to see, but still fighting. I reached up to my face, grabbing at the blindfold in an attempt to rip it away. An openhanded smack across my face sent me backward onto the floor, the impact radiating from my ribs up through my pounding head.

I was getting confused, the throbbing in my face and jaw overtaking my other senses. Mere seconds seemed to pass, and I was back in the chair, the air caressing my bare legs. My arms were jerked behind me and retied, followed by my feet.

When had he taken off my pants? How had I not noticed him doing that?

Footsteps approached me quickly, and I pointlessly jerked back as yet another bucket of ice water splashed over me. Chunks of ice gathered in my lap, freezing the very core of me. My hair was plastered to my head, bitter cold rivulets of water trailing down my hunched shoulders and breasts. The blindfold was soaked, the coarse, wet fabric irritating my skin.

"Thanks for the bath, but I already showered today." My teeth chattered as I spoke, painfully clacking together.

The man snorted in either disgust or disbelief. "Now that we're acquainted, I have some questions. You know how this works, Michaels. I ask questions, and you answer them to my satisfaction. If you don't, our fun continues."

My freezing limbs shook involuntarily as I felt my heart race. This time, my anger had seeped away, leaving behind the only thing I had remaining. Fear.

"Where can I find Jackson? Who is he? And what is Steel?" His odd-sounding voice filled the room, the pointed questions echoing in the space.

"Go shopping and find the biggest rubber dick you can, so you can fuck yourself with it." I spit near where I guessed his feet were. Agony piled onto pain as the beating resumed. There wasn't an inch of my body that didn't hurt. He stomped on my bare feet with his heavy boots until I felt toes break. I stopped trying to count my broken ribs. My nose had crunched long ago. My blood mingled with the drops of sweat flying off of him.

"Ready to talk, yet?" He was breathing heavily, and I hoped the bastard gave himself a coronary.

"Ready for that cock, yet?"

His answer came, not in words, but in sounds and motion. My scalp burned when he jerked my head back by my hair. Duct tape screeched as he tore some off a roll, then sealed my mouth. I choked on the blood in my broken nose as I tried to breathe. My body thrashed and jerked as my oxygen starved brain fought to live. My heart was beating so fast, I could hear it . . . feel it . . . the muscle working and pumping overtime, trying to keep me alive. My lungs burned, aching with the need for air. I tossed my head side-to-side in vain, not thinking anymore—sheer panic ruling my movements and thoughts. Senseless struggles only weakened me further, but I couldn't stop my body's instinctive reaction. *I need to breathe.*

Vicious heat flared as the tape was ripped from my face taking some of the skin off my lips, cheeks, and chin with it. I gasped for air, gulping and nearly choking on the oxygen that felt thick and nearly viscous. My lungs inflated, then deflated, over and over, as I sucked in as much vital oxygen as I could.

The blindfold was ripped off my face, and a narrow beam of light flooded my eyes, blinding me. I jerked back as someone grabbed my face hard. Thrashing my head and rolling my stomach, but I refused to be touched if I could help it.

"Hold the fuck still, you're making this harder than it needs to be, Mic." A penlight was being flashed in my eyes.

What the fuck? "J-Jackson?" Emotions I couldn't name roiled through me. Anger and relief competed with anxiety and hate.

"Yeah, it's me. Hold the fuck still, I need to check your eyes."

I was so confused. *How did he get here? When did he get here? And where the fuck was here?*

My breaths came faster and faster as panic gripped me. My heart was speeding, double-time, in my chest, banging hard against my broken ribs. My hands fell to my sides once again as they were released, followed quickly by my feet and legs.

"Wha' the fuck's goin' on?" My speech was slurred through my swollen mouth.

His face was now swimming in front of mine, in and out of focus. "You passed my test."

"W-what?" I stuttered. The pain was ratcheting up at an incredible pace as he helped me to my feet. I briefly spared a thought for my near nakedness but quickly dismissed it.

"I'll show you." Hand under my elbow, he supported me until I was more steady on my feet. I hadn't noticed Reid before, but he stood against the wall near the exit, only revealed by the narrow beam of Jackson's flashlight.

A light flicked on overhead and surprise had me struggling for air once again. I was standing in the construction debris that would soon be the panic room. I hadn't been there yet, but I recognized it from the blueprints. Reid opened the door ahead of me and cool night air blew in, making me shiver even more as it hit my already chilled skin.

Shoving away from Jackson, I stumbled, attempting to run for the door. My shoulder slammed into the jamb—I pushed off and fell headlong out the door, landing in the mud on my hands and knees. The impact drove pain through my sides like a metal spike. I lay there, breathless, the mud cold between my fingers.

"Let me help you up." Jackson reached down for me.

"Get the fuck away from me." I smacked at his hand, scrambling through the mud away from him.

"Mic, stop!"

I looked back, sheer stubbornness getting me up on my feet to see Reid standing next to him, the clown mask dangling from his fingers. "Motherfuckers! You sons of bitches!" My lips split open all over again, blood filling my mouth. I spat and gagged on the taste, repulsed by what I'd just experienced.

"It had to be done." Reid stepped closer, holding out his jacket for me, his knuckles split open and seeping blood.

"So does this." Summoning the little strength I had remaining, I punched him in the jaw with every ounce of rage and disgust I felt. He cursed and fell to one knee. The impact spun me around, onto my ass on the cold, wet ground. My hands slipped in the slick mud, and my head hit the earth.

This time, when my eyes closed, I didn't fight it. I welcomed the darkness and slipped gratefully away.

12

The warmth surrounding my body woke me first. I was no longer freezing and half-naked. Softness cradled my back and head, heavy comfort, which was distinctive to a well-made quilt, covered me. I blinked, bracing for harsh light, but a soft glow from the bedside lamp was easy on my eyes and aching head.

"It's okay—you're safe."

Jackson's gentle, deep voice spoke softly next to me. I cautiously turned toward the sound. My head swam as dizziness assaulted me. It was like being on the worst bender of your life, then getting on a roller coaster.

"Am I?" My voice was hoarse, my throat sore and dry.

"Yes."

"Water?" I waved my hand at my mouth, licking my lips and wincing when I found all the cuts.

"Sure, just a second." I could see him clearly enough to tell he was sitting in a chair next to my bed. He reached for a pitcher of water and a glass with a straw in it on the bedside table.

Accepting the glass with a shaking hand, I carefully closed my split lips on the straw, and painfully took a drink. I noticed the bandage circling my wrist and looked down to see my other wrist was also wrapped. "How long have I been out? Where am I?" I needed to get the facts first, then proceed from there. *One step at a time, Michaels.*

"Just over a day. You must not remember, but I've been waking you every hour or so, keeping an eye on your concussion." He crossed his arms over his chest, looking very unsure and defensive for the first time since I'd met him. "You're in a secure room of the local hospital. The doc here is an old friend—he's been taking care of you."

"I thought I was dead." Setting aside the glass, I struggled to sit up further. Jackson reached forward, propping the pillows up behind me. Hissing from the pain in my ribs, I settled back as slowly as possible. I gently explored my face, feeling each bump, bruise, and cut. My nose was packed with gauze and taped securely. The break felt properly set, very sore but not the sharp needlelike pain of a break. "How many ribs were broken?"

"Five. Plus two with minor fractures." His voice was gruff, filled with unspoken words.

"Why?" I didn't elaborate because I didn't need to.

"It was the only way. You're vetted now. I know that no matter what happens, you won't speak of Steel Corps, me, or your team. When we get the rest of the team, that is."

I was pissed the fuck off. Anger was a living, breathing—thriving—thing settling deep within me. "Provided I don't tell you to go fuck yourself and leave."

"True. You have that option, but I think we both know you're not going to do that." Retrieving something from the table, he handed me two folders—one orange, one a regular manila. I set the orange one aside—I knew top secret when I saw it. I'd save it for last. Instead, I opened the plain folder and began to read.

This was obviously the first candidate for my team. His name was Sergeant Gary Phillips. According to this file, he had advanced medical training and was a SEAL, ready to leave his team. His parents had been killed shortly before he graduated high school, and he had no living relatives. His career has been a good one. He was well-trained and capable of leading the team in my stead if necessary. The perfect candidate in every way. Dark and tall, with a serious face and five o'clock shadow, he was intimidating, which I would have to handle. I was already thinking ahead to when I would meet him and how I would have to deal with him.

I didn't notice Jackson leave the room until the door softly clicked shut. My mind was reeling. The possibilities were nearly endless. We could do so much good in this world. A team. Steel Corps. A band of men with a specialized skill set—ready to go anywhere in the world and do what needed to be done. No matter the cost. Led by me.

Jackson was right—I couldn't say no. Decision made, I opened the orange folder and began to read. The contents and details of the upcoming mission erasing any remaining doubts I held. This was not something I could walk away from, not and live with myself after.

MITCH SAWYER PULLED into the large compound on the outskirts of Tampa that his cousins, Ian and Devon, had just purchased at a federal auction. They were getting ready to open their new business, Trident Security, when their retirements came through in two and three months, respectively. Their teammates, Brody Evans, Jake Donovan, and Marco DeAngelis, would all be opting out of the Navy around the same time and joining the brothers in their new venture. Mitch hoped he could talk them into an additional one.

He eyed the stack of papers he'd brought with him. With his MBA, he'd been able to put together an impressive business proposal for a private BDSM club he'd dubbed, The Covenant, and he hoped his dominant cousins agreed.

Many years ago, it was Ian who had introduced Dev and Mitch to the lifestyle they'd both embraced with open arms. While Dev found the answers he'd needed to deal with the unwarranted guilt over his younger brother's death, Mitch discovered a community that suited his personality and where he felt he belonged. All three men had Alpha tendencies which had drawn them into the lifestyle like moths to a flame.

After parking his SUV, he grabbed the business proposal, then climbed out and glanced around. The property looked like an industrial park, which had been the former owner's intent. However, the import/export business had been a front for an illegal operation which had been funneling cash and drugs to and from Asia. The DEA had auctioned off the place after the billion-dollar operation had been shut down and the men who'd run it were either dead or in jail. When Ian and Dev's father, real estate mogul Charles Sawyer, had heard about it, he'd sent his boys down to check it out for their business.

The compound was already surrounded by a security fence and beyond that there were plenty of trees for privacy. The surrounding acres were all undeveloped land, and there was only one road in and out to the highway, which was about a half mile away from the front gate. Four warehouses sat in the middle of the property, and three of those would house the Trident offices, a gym, indoor shooting range, training area, and apartments, so the brothers could live on-site. They still hadn't decided what to do with the fourth building, and Mitch hoped he had the answer in his hand.

The door to the second warehouse was propped open, so he figured his cousins were in there. In addition to a rental vehicle, there was a large Ford pickup truck with "New Horizons Construction" decals on the rear and side panels. He knew they were meeting with the owner of the company, Parker Christiansen, to go over the renovation plans. It would be a huge undertaking, but Christiansen had come highly recommended. Since Mitch had lived in Tampa all his life, Ian had asked him to monitor the construction while he and Dev headed back to the base in Little Creek, Virginia to finish out their time.

He was glad they were getting out of the Navy—they'd done their time, and Ian had almost bought it two years ago over in that hellhole. An Iraqi police officer who had been invited to train at the base had actually been an al Qaeda plant. His plan had been to shoot as many members of the US military as he could. Ian, another SEAL, and two Marines had been hit before the tango was taken down by Marco. The two Marines had died, and the other SEAL had survived with a bullet wound to his upper arm, but Ian had been hit in the chest. He hadn't been wearing his body armor, or flack vest as they called it, coming out of the mess hall. It had been touch and go for a bit, with the round passing through his body a centimeter or two above his heart.

Mitch's Uncle Chuck and Aunt Marie were just as happy their boys were getting out. However, their youngest son, Nick, had just been selected to go through the same SEAL training his brothers had. They would be supportive, while worrying about his safety for more years to come.

NO WAY IN HELL

Stepping through the open door, he let his eyes adjust to the dim interior light. The three men looked up from the building plans they were going over at an abandoned work table. There was debris all over the place—it would take many dumpster loads to get rid of it all, and that was just in this one building. He was sure the others were just as bad.

"Hey, Mitch," Ian called out. "What's up?"

He strode over to them. "Thought I'd stop by with another business proposition for you, in addition to Trident."

"Yeah, what's that?"

Dropping the research he'd done on top the floor plans, he replied, "Take a look." He then held his breath as his cousins poured over his proposal.

CARTER SAT at the bar of Good Time Charlie's, a hole-in-the-wall in the tiny town of Westcliffe, Colorado, population under six hundred. Country music blared from the jukebox and cigarette smoke filled the room—apparently, the Colorado Clean Air Act wasn't enforced in Westcliffe.

He'd spent the past few weeks gathering intel to plan for his entry into the neo-Nazi compound about twenty minutes from town, in an unincorporated section of land. After going over things with Liam, Carter had done his own surveillance on the compound until he'd learned everything he could about the place, the people, and the timetables they kept. Now, his cover was that he was a transient just passing through, and with Liam's help, he was hoping to be invited into the fold of the organization they wanted to take down.

There was only a handful of Nazi sympathizers from the compound in the bar and even fewer local residents. This was probably as hopping as it got on a Friday night in this town. Party-city it was not. The only woman currently in the place was the bleached blonde owner/bartender, who was in her early fifties. It was evident from her rough skin and expression that time, cigarettes, and alcohol hadn't been kind to her. Her raspy voice had him thinking she'd be hacking up a lung someday soon.

Glancing at the Coors Light clock above the bar, he noted he had about another fifteen minutes before the Black "weary traveler in need of a stiff drink" would be walking in, prepared to get his ass kicked. The trick was, Carter needed to ensure he was the only one pounding on Liam so the Brit wasn't hurt more than necessary. There was a fine line between pulling your punches and making sure there was enough blood and bruising to make it realistic. Liam had planned to put a small capsule of fake but realistic blood in his nostril, so Carter would only need to punch him hard enough to break the capsule and not the poor guy's nose.

Ordering a second bottle of beer that he would nurse until Liam got there, he stood and took it with him to where the neo-Nazi bunch was playing pool on a table which desperately needed a new felt lining. Taking two quarters out of his pocket, he placed them on the scarred and cigarette-burnt edge of the table above the coin slots, indicating he wanted to play the winner. One member of the group eyed him while waiting for his opponent to miss a shot. Carter ignored him, pretending to be interested in only the game.

The guy was in his late twenties and had a shaved head, but the blond hair was just starting to sprout up from his scalp once more. The other men's hairstyles ranged from just as short to a basic crewcut. A dark T-shirt, tan, black, or camo cargo pants, and military-styled boots, seemed to be the uniform of the organization because all five of the group were dressed similarly. A variety of tattoos were either visible or partially hidden by the clothing. The ones in full view were innocuous, but he could make out the edges of swastikas and Nazi eagles peeking out from the necks and sleeves of their shirts.

There was no way Carter was putting a real tattoo anywhere on his body—they were too easy for people to remember, and in his business, it was wise not to stand out. So his other option had been to have a semipermanent one applied by a CIA disguise artist. The great minds at MIT had discovered an ink which could be tattooed on in the traditional sense, yet only require one simple laser treatment to remove without leaving any scars or trace ink. The process was new and not available to the public yet. The only colors available so far were black and dark brown, and it would last for as long as needed or desired.

Carter had met the CIA tech in Denver when he'd first arrived, and after warning the guy his life was over if there were any permanent marks, he'd sat for his very first tattoo —temporary though it was. Instead of the swastika, he'd opted for the Black Sun, also known as *Sonnenrad*, which was German for "Sun Wheel." It was a recognized but not as common symbol of the Nazi's under Hitler. Carter's stomach churned in disgust, knowing it was on his upper left arm for any length of time. Right now, it wasn't visible with his long-sleeved shirt on, but when he wore a T-shirt, half of it would be exposed, enough to be noticed and accepted for what it was—a symbol of hate.

"You're not from around here, are you?" the guy eyeing him asked while stating the obvious. Carter already knew his name was Brett Harmon, born and raised in Denver before being recruited by the New Order two years ago.

The urge to roll his eyes was strong, but he needed to befriend these assholes. Harmon wasn't the alpha of the group. That was the thirty-year-old man sitting at a pub table to Carter's left and the one he needed to impress—Michael Strauss. Bowing to this idiot staring at him would fail to do that. He looked the skinhead wannabe in the eyes. "Considering this podunk town isn't big enough for a traffic light, I figure the locals know everyone here. So you're correct. I'm just passing through."

Harmon nodded as if that made all the sense in the world, and Carter turned his attention back to the table, where another striped ball was sunk in the side pocket, while waiting for the next question. The guy didn't disappoint. "Got a name?"

"Yup."

There was a long pause as the idiot waited for more, but Carter needed to make these guys come to him, and not appear interested in anything other than a beer and a game of pool. "Well, what the fuck is it?"

"Carter."

With a huff, Harmon rolled his hand in the air. "That's it —you only got one fucking name?"

"Yup."

The guy shooting pool—Daniel Robisch—missed a shot. "Shut the fuck up, Brett, and play the damn game."

"Fuck you."

Robisch glared at Harmon as he lined up his shot and missed it. Two more balls were sunk, and Robisch won when the eight ball disappeared into the corner pocket. Without saying a word, the winner nodded for Carter to rack up a new game.

Dropping the quarters into their slots, he pushed them in, and the balls fell loudly into the end receptacle. The wooden, triangle shaped rack, held together by Duct tape, was hanging from a peg on the wall next to the selection of pool cues. He grabbed it, then selected the least warped cue stick he could find, which was a feat in itself. After he had racked the balls, he stepped back and watched Robisch send the solid white ball flying into the set of fifteen with a resounding smack. One solid and one striped fell into pockets—the man made a few quick calculations and chose solids. He sank three more balls before missing one. Carter circled the table and lined up his shots, sinking four balls before purposely missing the fifth.

"Where you from, Carter?"

The question had come from Robisch as he sank the seven ball. Carter noticed Strauss was paying attention to the answer. "Was born in bumfuck Nebraska. Left that shithole as soon as I was old enough to make it on my own. Since then, I've been bouncing all over the place. Just call me a rolling stone."

Robisch missed, and as Carter was planning his next shot, the front door to the bar opened and in strolled Liam Cooper, wearing dress pants, a polo shirt, and a nice pair of shoes—looking very preppy and out of place in the hick bar. *Perfect timing.*

Carter stared at the man and snarled. "What the fuck? Can't even enjoy a beer without some fucking spook ruining it."

He'd spoken loud enough for everyone to have heard him, and they all froze. If it wasn't for Blake Shelton's voice blaring from the jukebox, you could have heard a pin drop in the place. He saw Liam's shoulders tense, but then the Brit pretended to ignore the derogatory slur. Taking a seat at the bar, he ordered a beer and a menu. Carter was surprised when the bleached blonde shook her head. "We don't serve your kind here."

Jesus, talk about falling down the fucking rabbit hole and coming out five or six decades in the past.

"'My kind'?" Liam asked in the smooth East Coast accent

JB HAVENS & SAMANTHA A. COLE

he'd adopted for this charade. "What exactly do you mean, 'my kind'?"

Carter tossed his cue on the table and ambled closer to the bar. In his head, he was counting down. An undercover FBI agent, in a state trooper uniform and vehicle, was just outside of town and would be driving down Main Street in a few minutes. Carter needed to time it right, so he was throwing Liam's ass out of the bar just as the "trooper" was driving by. They couldn't trust the local sheriff, so that meant they had to improvise. Otherwise, Liam might end up seriously hurt or worse. "She means, go back to fucking Africa, boy."

Standing, Liam squared his shoulders and glared at Carter as everyone else gathered around. "First off, I'm not a fucking boy. And second, I've never been to Africa, so I can't exactly go back there. Now fuck off."

He turned his back to the group, and that was the moment Carter had been waiting for. Before anyone else could act, he stepped forward, lifted his leg, and literally kicked his buddy in the ass, sending him sprawling across the room. Liam flipped over and scrambled to his feet fast. The last thing they needed was him on the ground before Carter had declared this a one-on-one fight. "Fucking spook. Turning your back on me like your shit don't stink. Get the fuck out before I kick your ass."

"Fucking try it, asshole."

Harmon stepped forward. "I'll kick your ass, too!"

Lord, save me from arrogant asswipes who would piss their pants without backup. Carter smacked the back of his hand across Harmon's chest, stopping him short. "I didn't ask for your fucking help, and I don't need it. The day I can't kick a spook's ass on my own is the day they'll have to fucking bury me. Now back off."

He shoved the prick to the side, then took another step

toward Liam. The Brit moved into a standard, schoolyard fighting stance, and Carter almost laughed out loud. The guy knew numerous ways to fight dirty and kill someone, yet you'd never know it from looking at him now. Without hesitation or warning, Carter jabbed the agent in the nose, breaking the capsule inside. Liam's head snapped back as he stumbled, but he managed to stay on his feet. Wiping the "blood" from his face with the back of his hand, he glared at Carter, then came at him with full force. Fists were thrown, both men getting in good shots, as the bigoted bar crowd cheered for the white guy to win.

Liam feigned left, and Carter purposely followed, allowing the guy to punch him in the ribs. *Fuck! That one hurt.* But he needed some bruises on his body.

They were working up a sweat, and despite the pulled punches, they'd both be sore in the morning. Carter threw one more right cross, which connected with Liam's chin. It was just about time to move this farce outside. With a sweep of his foot, he knocked the Brit's legs out from under him, caught him by the shirt, and dragged him out the front door to the street, throwing him to the ground. If he hadn't been expecting it, the sharp whelp of a siren would have caught him off guard.

He stepped back as the "trooper" pulled up, jumped out of his vehicle, and pointed at him. "You! Put your hands on the front of my car and stay there."

Turning slightly, he rolled his eyes at the group that had followed him outside, then did as he'd been ordered. "No problem, sir. Just teaching the boy some manners."

"Shut it and spread 'em."

The guy gave him a quick frisk before slapping the cuffs on him. He then spun him around until Carter's back was to the hood. The whole time the locals were shouting for him not to be arrested—that they were all witnesses, and the

Black guy started it. The trooper ignored them and "called in for backup" on his radio. An off-site operative acknowledged him. She would now alert the sheriff to the situation. If all went well, Liam would be told to take his business to another town, and Carter would be released with no charges filed.

The trooper shoved him against the car. "Stay there."

"Yes, sir." As the man went to check on Liam, Carter rolled his eyes again at the group, and several of them chuckled. Strauss leaned closer to Robisch and said something that had the other man nodding his head.

There were a few more minutes of bullshit, with the trooper taking down the names of the witnesses and doing everything he could to make it all look legit. Carter was impressed. If he hadn't known the guy was a plant, he would have bought the act.

A marked unit with "Sheriff" emblazoned on the side pulled up, and a uniformed man with a narrow mustache and potbelly climbed out. Carter recognized Sheriff John Buford right away from the piles of intel the spy had gathered. The guy's name was ironic, since it reminded Carter of Sheriff Buford T. Justice of the old *Smokey and the Bandit* movies. However, he doubted that the Jackie Gleason look-alike here was as funny as his Hollywood counterpart had been in the movie.

The sheriff pulled his duty belt higher on his hips, but his gut prevented it from going any further. "What's going on here, Trooper?"

The undercover agent filled the useless excuse for a lawman in. As expected, Buford "convinced" the trooper there was no need to arrest anyone, and it would be best if Liam got into his vehicle and moved on to the next town. The "victim" did his part to protest a little, then finally gave in when it appeared no one was going to arrest Carter. After the Brit limped to his car and drove away, the handcuffs were removed from Carter's wrists. He assured the trooper and the sheriff he would stay out of trouble.

The bar crowd strolled back inside, leaving only Strauss and Robisch with him. The former eyed him a moment longer, then held out his hand. "Name's Mike Strauss. What'd you say your name was again?"

13

Two weeks later...

The bruising on my face was nearly gone, thankfully. I was still stiff and sore but able to get back to full duty, which is why I was in the now-completed war room waiting for Jackson to arrive. The walls were paneled in rich wood, giving the whole space a warmth and comfortable closeness without being oppressive. I paced near the long, wooden table in the center. There were expensive looking office chairs around it, still wrapped in plastic.

The door opened, and Jackson strode in, purpose in his every step. He had an orange folder in one hand and an unlit cigar in the other. Opening my mouth to speak, the words stuck in my throat as Sergeant Phillips came in a few steps behind our master sergeant.

"Staff Sergeant Michaels, this is Sergeant Phillips. Get acquainted." Jackson sat, opening the folder in front of him. Jackson and I had gotten used to each other over the past two weeks. Often either calling each other by our names alone, or just rank. I was really starting to love the informality.

Phillips didn't say a word. Instead, he was standing at attention near the door. I felt small next to him and hated it. He was not only taller than me, but he was also broad in the shoulders and chest. His dark hair was cut very short, and a scruff of whiskers covered his jaw and cheeks. I couldn't quite make out his eye color from where I stood.

I needed to assert myself as his commander right away, or this would never work. "You may be a big badass SEAL, but around here, I'm in charge. If you have a problem with that, there's the fucking door. Do we understand each other, Sergeant?"

"Yes, ma'am." His brows furrowed, but he didn't make eye contact.

"If the dick-measuring contest is over, mind if I brief you on your mission?" Jackson chewed on the end of his cigar, a coffee cup clutched in his other hand, and waited impatiently for us to take our seats in the plastic-wrapped chairs. They crinkled and rustled as we settled in.

"Yes, Master Sergeant. My only concern is Phillips just got here. We aren't mission ready." I felt like I was pointing out the obvious. I was willing to bet just about anything that the info Jackson was about to dole out was from the same top secret folder I'd read in the hospital a few weeks ago.

"Why, thank you, I hadn't realized that." The sarcasm in his voice was thick enough to be touchable. "This mission will be happening, but your part won't come into play for at least three months. That should be more than enough time for you two to train, shouldn't it?"

I didn't respond and neither did Phillips. With a stern glare at us both, Jackson continued. "There's a neo-Nazi militant camp in South Dakota." He handed us both satellite photos of the area. "What you're looking at is a well-organized group with deep pockets and a hatred of anything not white, straight, or Protestant." There were bunker type structures as well as long communal buildings and small cabins spread throughout the area. "One of those bunkers is suspected to be full of enough weapons and explosives to supply a third world country. We have a covert operative working on getting into the group. Once he does, Mic, you'll be his girlfriend, Phillips here will be your brother, and you'll go in and raze this fucking place to the ground."

"Which operative?" I had my suspicious and was curious if Jackson would confirm them.

"I think you already know the answer to that question. He's perfect for this, and you two already know each other. You'll be able to fake a relationship much easier than two strangers would be able to."

Ah, fuck. "That'll be fine, but I know how these fucking neo-Nazis are about women. We're less than second-class citizens, and they expect us to bow to the men. Just so long as I don't have to call him 'Sir' or 'Master.'"

Jackson choked on his coffee, coughing harshly. When he finally caught his breath again, he said, "Don't worry, Mic. He would never want you to call him 'Master,' I can promise you that."

Confused, I narrowed my eyes at him. "What's so funny?"

He was doing his best to contain his laughter but failed horribly. "I can't tell you, but I'm going to tell him, and you can expect to get a razzing out of it. Oh shit, is he going to love this." Slapping his chest, Jackson got himself under control.

Phillips had yet to say a word, just kept glancing back and forth between the two of us. I would have said Carter's name, but while I knew next to nothing about the spy, I knew he appreciated secrecy more than anything. When we began the mission, Phillips would be brought in on the US government's secret that was T. Carter.

"In the meantime, you two need to get your asses moving. I want you training every day, all day. You need to get to know each other well, or the ruse of you being siblings will never be believed. Good news is, the Panic Room should be finished in about a week. Start today. Dismissed."

Standing, I led the way out of the war room, racking my brain trying to decide where to begin. We not only had to become a team, but I also had to continue asserting myself as his officer.

"What are your orders, Staff Sergeant?" Phillips forced respect into his voice. My job was to make him feel the respect for real and never let on that this was my first time in command. Other than those two days in Iraq, anyway.

"Just call me Mic, everyone else does. This unit is different. While rank is observed—we're a bit more casual." It was a gorgeous day outside, warm and sunny with perfect blue skies. "Get your pack, we're doing a ruck. Pack provisions for at least two days."

Veering off from Phillips near his cabin, I entered my own. For now, we're storing our gear in our cabins, but once the large hangar is finished, we'd have lockers. They'd been delivered, and there were more than I had expected. I would have to ask Jackson who would be using them.

I grabbed my large ruck and checked its contents. Jackson had purchased these for us, but like most soldiers, I was particular about how it was packed and what it contained. I had four MREs, a decent first aid kit, water, entrenching tool, flashlight, and various other items for survival in the wilderness, including a radio. I already had my KA-BAR strapped to my hip, along with my M9 in a thigh holster.

After strapping on my flack vest with my adjustable MOLLE vest on top, I slipped my H&K MP5 over my head on its tactical sling. I adjusted a few straps and settled everything as comfortably as I was able. Patting my left cargo pocket, I double checked that I had my compass and map. I was ready to go.

Nearly forgetting, I pulled my new phone from my pocket and sent Jackson a text. I wasn't used to having the stupid thing yet.

Going for a ruck. Back in two days.

His reply pinged seconds later.

Copy that. Take a radio.

Rolling my eyes, I shut off the phone and stuck it back in my pocket. Shutting the door behind me firmly, and double-timing it out, I scanned the compound. Standing in the muddy field of what would soon be our training yard and track was a fully-geared up Phillips. He was dressed nearly identically to me, black, tactical cargo pants, snug, Under Armour T-shirt, and his pack snugly strapped on. The only difference I could see was the butt of a shotgun sticking up from the top of his pack.

"Ready, Phillips?"

He cradled his rifle carefully. When his eyes finally met mine, I noticed his were a startling, dark blue. Not waiting for his reply, I led the way toward the tree line. Stepping into the cool, dark forest, I didn't hear Phillips behind me. His training made him both silent and deadly, even in the woods with thick leaf litter on the ground.

We didn't speak, didn't really need to. The forest was full of sounds all around us. Birds, insects, and all manner of life rustled and called out.

"How much combat experience do you have?"

NO WAY IN HELL

The question startled me, and I almost didn't answer. "Enough." I paused, then figured "what the hell." I spilled my guts about Iraq and the two days I'd spent in the desert with my men, running and fighting.

As soon as I said SEAL Team Four, Phillips grunted in response. "Sawyer's a good man. I was in Team Eight. We've crossed paths a few times. I remember that mission now that you talk about it. I didn't realize that was you. If you earned the respect of Sawyer and his men in combat, that's good enough for me."

This time, when Phillips spoke, there was real respect in his voice. *Fuck, if I had known that story would earn me the respect I needed, we wouldn't be out here. Too late to go back now.*

The mountainside steadily rose, and with every mile that fell away beneath our boots, we gained a better understanding of one another. Not quite a friendship, but close. I could live with that.

PHILLIPS EYED the back of the woman in front of him. Sure-footed and quick, she climbed the mountain like it was a personal challenge to her. She didn't seem to do anything half-assed. It was all in your face, all the time. He hadn't lied to her when he said he remembered that mission. Word had spread like wildfire through the SEAL teams. For Sawyer to give kudos to a nobody army corporal from M.I. carried a lot of weight.

Her whole team had been slaughtered and here she was, itching to get back into the shit. Some men could live through something like that and come out unable to even hold a weapon, let alone go back in. She was one tough bitch. She'd earned his respect with her story, but she'd yet to earn his trust. That would come over the course of the next three

123

months. It grated on him that his NCO was a woman. He wasn't sexist—he'd known some fine sailors that were women, but being a SEAL taught him a lot—some of which was not just anyone could hack it with him. In his experience, women just didn't have the personality or physical strength to be Special Forces. He hoped she was going to prove him wrong.

Keeping on her heels through the woods, he decided to give her a chance and see what would shake loose. He had to have a little faith in his superiors. They wouldn't have put her in charge lightly—not a unit like this. He'd seen the fading bruises and lingering stiffness. Someone had worked her over a bit, yet she was still here. That had to stand for something.

Shrugging his shoulders to settle his ruck better, he took a sip from the straw hooked to his Camelbak canteen and followed her up the damn mountain.

Turning to look back at him, she said, "Hurry up, Phillips. We don't have all damn day."

"Copy that," he mumbled, picking up the pace. *How could someone so small be so damn fast?*

A FEW MINUTES before 1100 hours, the buzzer for the front gate sounded. Ian moved the mouse on his desk, then hit the computer icon which would slide open the gate and allow the government-issued sedan into the compound. Trident Security was unofficially open for business, but there was still much to do to secure the property. After letting several of their federal contacts know they were available for contract work, they would need the facility secure in case any mission, past or present, came back to bite them in the ass.

They also wanted the security for the future members of The Covenant. The club would be in the first building upon entering the compound, and the renovations of the existing warehouse were coming along nicely. They were already taking applications for what was being billed as the most elite, private BDSM club in the Tampa/St. Petersburg area. It was scheduled to open in five months. Mitch was doing an awesome job, handling all the things that had to do with the club, so Ian and Dev could concentrate on Trident.

The New Horizons Construction crew had completed the Trident offices first and were concentrating on getting Ian and Dev's apartments done next. In the meantime, the brothers were renting a small house nearby.

Standing, Ian exited his new office, passing Dev's on his way to the reception area. He stuck his head through his brother's open door. "They're here."

Dev finished the phone call he'd been on, then followed him out. Brody was still busy setting up his massive war-room—they were already kidding him that it looked like NASA in there. The former SEAL was one of the best hackers in the world and had turned down jobs with several federal and private agencies to work with his teammates. Leaving him to do his geek stuff, Ian asked their new secretary, Mrs. Lillian Kemple, to send a text to Jake and Marco, asking them to meet everyone in the conference room. The two were over in the multi-purpose building, arranging the newly-delivered gym equipment.

The front door swung open, and two completely opposite-looking men walked in. With his Irish heritage, Larry Keon, the Deputy Director of the FBI, had fair skin, reddish-blond hair with a touch of silver in spots, and hazel eyes. His five-foot-seven frame was dwarfed by Master Sergeant Fisher Jackson. The bald, Black man stood six foot six, three inches taller than both Ian and Devon, and his sharp, brown eyes didn't miss a thing.

Ian and then Dev shook both men's hands. Taking a step back, Ian swept his arm toward the conference room. "This way. There's coffee set up if you're interested. Mrs. Kemple, please hold all calls until we're done."

"Absolutely, Mr. Sawyer."

Biting back his grin, he shook his head. He'd been trying to get the gray-haired, older woman to call them all by their first names because he couldn't get used to being called *Mr. Sawyer*. That was his father. Since he was eighteen, Ian had been a rank, followed by Sawyer. It was just one more thing he found different being a civilian for the first time in sixteen years.

The newcomers made their coffee and by the time everyone was seated at the table, Jake and Marco had joined them, shutting the door on their way in. Keon opened his leather briefcase and slid orange folders over to each of them. "Gentlemen, Trident Security is officially on retainer with the FBI. You've more than earned your reputations as SEALs over the past several years, and Uncle Sam wants to continue to use the valuable resource we have in you.

"Open to page one and meet Hans Wexler, who considers himself to be the next Hitler. You'll be teaming up with Jackson's new covert team, Steel Corps, and be under his command for this mission. Your friend, Carter, has already infiltrated Wexler's organization, but it will take him a few months to get where he needs to be in order take down this entire cell. There are operatives in France, Germany, and the UK working their way in as well. This will have to be a coordinated op—all four parent cells must be taken down at the same time—before they unleash their planned attacks on their home countries. According to our sources, we have seven short months before that happens."

Ian flipped through the first few pages of the thick file. There was a ton of intel, but he was certain there was more to be found. He hit a button on the landline phone sitting in front of him and waited for his secretary to pick up. "Mrs. Kemple? Please tell Brody to join us with his laptop, and order lunch for everyone. Reschedule my afternoon appointments and everyone else's too. We'll be in this meeting for the rest of the day."

After she acknowledged him, he disconnected the call, then met Jackson's gaze. "Okay. Start breaking it down. How do we nail these fuckers?"

14

My feet pounded on the newly-built track. Phillips was just ahead of me, and we were on the final leg of our five-mile run. Having spent years in the military, we were so used to starting our days with PT—physical training—that it would throw us off all day if we didn't follow that routine.

I crossed the line moments after Phillips and slowed to a walk. It was as important to cool down as it was to warm up for runs. "You ready for today?"

"Sure. I guess. But I still hate that we need their help, Mic. I'd hoped we'd have our own team by now."

"I agree, but Jackson will be working on that while we're gone. And since Steel isn't big enough yet for this and neither is Trident—we have to work together this one time. This is going to be the only time we do this—I can assure you of that. By the time we get back, Jackson will have beaten the drum, and we'll have more team members to train."

"I told him to find us a sniper, a pilot, and an EOD guy. Those are musts."

It was times like this where I could sense my command

128

grated on Phillips's nerves. "I agree with you there, Sergeant." I stopped pacing and turned to face him. "Shower and get your gear. We leave for Tampa in an hour."

"Copy that. At least it'll be fun to see some of the guys again— if they don't kill me for being alive." He headed toward the large cabin, which he would soon be sharing with someone else.

I was anxious to get our team put together and trained. There was so much we could be doing. I strode to my own cabin and stripped as soon as I was in the door. My duffel and weapons bags were already packed and waiting by the door. Like Phillips, I was also looking forward to seeing Sawyer and the rest of Team Four again. It would be kick-ass to work with them on something where they weren't riding to my rescue.

I briefly flashed back to that narrow desert road where our convoy had been ambushed. And everything that came after. Shaking loose those thoughts, I showered and dressed quickly and hauled my bags over to the hangar. It was mostly completed, enough for a jet to be parked alongside it. The sleek, black aircraft had cost a shitload, but it was good to have around. If for nothing more than no headaches getting our weapons through security. Our own personal Black Hawk would be delivered soon as well.

The row of lockers had been installed, and in front of them was a long bench, similar to what you'd see in a gym. There were boxes of weights and exercise equipment in the back, waiting to be set up. I'd had Jackson order a boxing ring as well. Sparring was essential to getting to know your teammates' weaknesses and strengths. Plus, it was a damn good way to blow off some steam. I turned away from the open hangar and climbed the already lowered steps of the jet.

Inside was the most impressive setup I'd ever seen—and being in military intelligence, I'd seen some seriously badass tech. A bank of computers had replaced the couch halfway back. The entire aircraft was custom, from the standing room height to the soft, buttery leather on the oversized seats. In the back was a small galley-style kitchen, though I wasn't sure how much use it'd get. There were pairs of seats on either side of the aisle, with one set having a built-in table between them. It even smelled factory fresh, like a new car.

"Pretty, fucking impressive," Phillips spoke from behind me, tossing his own duffel on a chair.

"Fuck, yeah. I think it's great." I plopped down into the seat closest to the door.

"My only question is who's going to fly it? We don't have a pilot yet."

The floor trembled as someone climbed aboard. Turning toward the noise, I watched with interest as Jackson ducked in with a gray-haired man behind him.

"This is your pilot. He was a test pilot for the Air Force. Half of what he did for them is still classified. He has a name, but you'll call him Captain. He can fly anything, anywhere."

With a respectful nod, the captain ducked into the cockpit and slipped on the headset with practiced ease. He was flipping switches and turning knobs rapidly. Turning back and catching us staring, he said, "Better sit down. I'm going to take off in a few. Buckle up, kiddies, we've got a five-hour flight to Tampa."

Knowing when to follow orders, I strapped in and sat back as we taxied out with a roar. As we took off, my stomach hit my feet and my ears popped. We were on our way to Tampa, Florida to meet up with Trident Security. I would see Lieutenant Sawyer again, although he was now retired from the Navy. Just the thought of him brought back the smell of blood, and the feel of hot sand on my skin. I was both looking forward to this and dreading it. My first black ops mission was about to begin. *Hooah*!

CARTER WATCHED as the skinhead recruits ran the obstacle course. He'd been under for a few months now, and it was almost scary how well the organization was militarized. His solid cover had him fitting in perfectly with Colonel Michael Strauss and the other leaders of this sect of the New Order. As far as they knew, he was Timothy Carter, a Marine who'd gotten a dishonorable discharge, been court-marshaled, and did three years in the military prison in Leavenworth, Kansas. All for punching a Black superior officer several times in the face. When Strauss had asked him about it, his response had been he'd gotten tired of taking orders from someone who wasn't fit to tie his boots. That fake history, plus not having any obligations tying him down, was exactly the type of recruit they looked for here—in addition to being the right color to fit into Hitler's ideal race. The First Sergeant ranking on his fictional military file, and his alpha leadership ability had fast-tracked him to Strauss's inner circle. Now, he just had to wait until they moved to South Dakota and met up with the other two US divisions.

When the last recruit of the twelve-man squad he'd been put in charge of crossed the finish line, Carter barked, "Move out to the shooting range! You've got four minutes to get there and break down your weapons for inspection! Move your asses!"

As the men took off, Strauss approached him. "Lieutenant."

He snapped to attention even though it grated on him. "Yes, sir!"

"At ease. How are the new recruits doing?"

Spreading his legs shoulder-width apart, he placed his hands at the small of his back. "They need some work, but nothing that a few weeks of training can't fix."

Strauss nodded. He was about three inches shorter than Carter's six-foot-four frame and a little stockier. Like most of the men at the compound, his blond hair was closely cropped. A faint scar bisected his forehead—it had probably been from his youth and had required numerous stitches to close. "Well, try to shorten that time frame as much as possible. In ten days we're packing up and heading to the main compound in South Dakota. General Wexler wants everyone training together to get ready for the big day."

"You've mentioned this big day before, sir, but I still have no idea what you're referring to."

Pausing, Strauss studied him carefully with hard, pale blue eyes. "You'll find out when I think you deserve to find out, Lieutenant. For now, all you have to do is follow your orders."

"Yes, sir."

"Carry on."

The man turned on his heel and headed back to the main house on the compound. Mentally counting down from ten, Carter got himself under control, when what he really wanted to do was slit the bastard's throat. He could almost feel the fucker's hot blood spilling over his hands. The only things stopping him were it would blow his cover and the mission, and karma was a real bitch—Strauss would get what was coming to him in due time.

Jogging toward the shooting range, he thought about how to bring Mic and Phillips into a conversation with Strauss at some point. He'd already established he had wandered all over the United States since his release from prison. The planned cover story for Staff Sergeant Bea "Mic" Michaels and Sergeant Gary Phillips, aka Mikayla and Phillip Robins, was that they were redneck half siblings from Aberdeen, South Dakota. Purportedly, Carter had met Mikayla during his travels, and she and her half brother had the same warped hatred for the US government, so they were ideal people to bring in.

Another squad of recruits ran past him in sloppy military formation. There were a total of fifty-eight men and six women occupying the compound. Training consisted of standard boot camp drills and weapons exercises. The arsenal at this compound alone could be used to take down hundreds of people at a football stadium within minutes— and that didn't include the explosives in an ordinance bunker on the far side of the property. If the other two training facilities were equally equipped, then the casualties on the "big day" could rival the numbers from 9/11. And he'd be damned if he didn't do everything he could to make sure it never happened.

LEANING against the passenger side of the Suburban he'd driven to the small, local airport, Ian Sawyer watched the jet taxi from the end of the runway to the hangar he'd parked in front of. Steel Corps's aircraft was almost identical to the one Trident had recently purchased, which was currently stored inside the large building behind him. Not only was this private airport on the outskirts of Tampa, within fifteen minutes of the compound, but also the security on the property was top-notch due to the number of corporations and government agencies that used it.

He was curious to see who Jackson was bringing with him. All he knew was there were two Steel Corps team members who would be infiltrating the neo-Nazi compound in South Dakota and meeting up with Carter. The rest of the hired special ops contractors would be under Ian's command in the areas surrounding the compound for support. He knew Steel Corps was black ops, but even his high government security clearance had its limitations. Well, he'd find out soon enough who the secret agents were.

The jet stopped in front of the hangar, and the engines wound down to a halt. A few minutes passed before the cabin door opened, and a set of stairs was lowered. The first person off the jet was a male Caucasian, about six foot four and 225 pounds, wearing a military-green T-shirt and tan cargo pants. His dark hair was mostly covered by a tan baseball cap, while a scruffy beard and mustache hid his facial features. Dark sunglasses completed his attire. But there was something about the man that seemed familiar to Ian as he studied him descending the steps carrying a large, black duffel.

Striding across the tarmac, the operative stopped a few feet from Ian, set his bag on the ground, and pulled off his sunglasses. Shock, then fury flashed through Ian as he stared at a man he'd thought was dead—killed during an undercover op overseas. *What the fucking hell?* They had all gone to the SEAL's fucking funeral, for Christ's sake, and pounded their trident pins into the lid of his coffin!

Ian's fists clenched in rage as he took a threatening step forward. "What the fuck? We fucking buried you, Phillips! What the goddamn fuck?"

Phillips wisely stepped back and held his hands at shoulder height in surrender. Regret filled his eyes. "I know, Sawyer. I know, and I'm sorry, but it was mandatory."

"Mandatory? Fuck that shit! Does Team Eight know you're fucking alive? Because they were mourning with the rest of us, you son of a bitch."

"No, they don't." Ian hadn't noticed Jackson join them. The master sergeant removed his own sunglasses and stood tall with authority. "And it was my call on my team going dark—they had no say in the matter. The only people who know he's not six feet under are my handlers, his teammate,

Carter, and now you. And your team will know when we see them—and that's only because of your clearance level. To the rest of the world, he's dead."

Itching to hit someone, Ian put his hands on his hips and glared at Jackson. "So, this is why none of the contract operatives are former SEALs for this mission, other than my team. You took them from other special-ops teams to make sure no one would recognize him."

A single nod was his answer. Tilting his head back, Ian took several cleansing breaths and tried to get his anger under control. A count of ten would have to do because they needed to get the hell out of there and back to the compound. "Fuck. All right, who's the other team member? Who else did you fucking resurrect from the dead?"

Jackson silently hitched his thumb over his shoulder, and Ian was thrown for another loop as a petite, blonde woman approached them before dropping her military-style pack on the tarmac. His eyes grew wide with disbelief.

"Mic?" As he gaped at her, a small smile spread across the face of the intelligence interrogator who'd supposedly died during a classified mission in Afghanistan. "Fucking A! Well, now I don't feel bad we missed your fucking memorial service. No offense, Corporal."

"It's Staff Sergeant, now, and none taken, Sawyer. It's good to see you again."

She held out her hand and instead of shaking it, Ian pulled her into a welcoming embrace. "Congrats on the promotion, and despite my shock, I'm fucking glad you're still alive. But it's going to take some getting used to." He let her go, turned to Phillips, and gave him a man hug with some slaps to the back. "You, too, frog. Sorry I flipped, but I fucking hate surprises. Give me a little bit to get my head wrapped around this."

"No problem, and I hear ya," the big man replied with a grin.

Ian eyed Jackson with annoyance. "Can we go now, or is there anyone else on that jet who you brought back from the dead? Elvis, maybe? Jimmy Hoffa? Kurt Cobain? Personally, I wouldn't mind if you brought Kurt back."

"No, that's it. Our pilot has made his own arrangements and can be back here within thirty minutes if we need him."

"Good. Load up and let's get the hell out of here." He shoved his sunglasses on his face and rounded the hood of the SUV, still feeling like he'd just fallen down Alice's rabbit hole.

Driving back to the compound, the last of his ire faded. He knew all about black ops, having worked with several operatives in the past. Hell, Carter was one of them, and Ian's team knew very little about the man beyond what they'd learned from being on missions with him. Most operatives who go dark are chosen because they have little or no family, and wind up having an empty grave somewhere in a military cemetery where their unknowing friends can mourn them. It was a lonely life he couldn't comprehend, and he had to respect those who lived it.

He glanced at Jackson in the front passenger seat. "Any word from Carter?"

"Got a message from Liam Cooper when we landed. Carter thinks they'll be moving to South Dakota soon. Hopefully, he'll have a date and exact location for us within the next few days. Until then, we train and prepare. I'll fill everyone in with what we already know when we get to your place."

Turning off the highway to the road leading to the compound, Ian drove the half-mile to the manned front gate. The armed guard waved and let him through. All of the Trident buildings were now complete, and the Sawyer brothers had their own apartments in the fourth building. The second and third ones held the offices, bunk rooms, gym, indoor shooting range, storage, and a panic room, which had been a surprising find. The former property owners had been drug dealers and had apparently thought of everything. There was even an underground tunnel which led out into the woods from the panic room—hopefully, neither would ever have to be used, but it was nice they were there if needed.

The first building was still undergoing renovations and would be their BDSM club, The Covenant. The grand opening had been pushed back one month due to this op and the fact that some of the custom-made equipment hadn't been ready for delivery.

Ian pulled up to the new interior fence and rolled down his window to place his hand on the security scanner, which would slide open the gate. His brother Devon was just exiting the building that housed their security business. Meanwhile, Brody Evans, Marco DeAngelis, and Jake Donovan were sitting on a picnic table outside the second warehouse, and the latter had one of his sniper rifles stripped down for cleaning.

Parking and leaving the vehicle and AC running, Ian turned to Mic and Phillips in the back seat. "You two mind waiting in here a minute so I can fill them in? They're going to be as shocked as I was."

The both answered, "Understood."

Climbing out of the SUV, he tried to find the words to explain the resurrection of two dead people.

15

P acing himself at decent clip, Carter jogged through the woods to the west of the New Order's compound. The first few weeks he'd been there, someone had followed him on his daily run, but they eventually learned that he did six miles—three out and three back. He never took a run at the same time every day, so there was no pattern to them. No one had been able to keep up with him for the long distance, and when they realized that, they'd switched over to ATVs. Strauss must have finally accepted there was nothing sneaky about the runs—Carter never gave them a reason to think otherwise—because the minions no longer followed him.

Once the coast had been clear, and he'd been safely away from the compound's cell scanners—any calls or texts within a mile of the perimeter were intercepted—he'd sent a text message to Liam. Carter had only risked the one text, giving the Brit the coordinates to a distinctive boulder off the hiking trail where they now left info for each other. He took perverse pleasure knowing the other spy had to hike in from a nearby logging road, every morning before sunrise, a full mile uphill to access it. Couldn't have Liam getting too soft and complacent sitting in his four-star hotel in Pueblo, Colorado, an hour away.

Slowing as he reached his destination, the spy furtively checked the surrounding wooded landscape while wiping the sweat from his brow. It was actually quite beautiful there and reminded him of his private retreat in the wilderness of Montana. He had several safe houses all over the world, but that was his Eden. Somewhere he could go to relax and recharge. It was also within an hour's ATV ride through the rough terrain to the small town where his foster sister Vicki Sanders had settled with her son Justin. While it was very rare for black operatives who'd gone off the grid and "died" to have contact with anyone from their past life, Vicki had been the one person Carter hadn't been able to leave behind. Two years after finishing his training with Deimos, he'd tracked where the Witness Protection Program had her stashed away. He'd only wanted to check on her, but circumstances lead her to finding out he was alive. He, in turn, had found out he was an uncle. Carter would do anything for his nephew . . . he would sell his soul to the devil for Vicki and Justin to have healthy, normal lives. It was too bad he wasn't a blood type match for Justin because, somewhere down the road, it was very likely the kid would need a kidney transplant. But they'd cross that bridge if it ever came to that point. For now, Carter and Vicki were doing everything they could to prevent Justin from knowing who his real father was—a man who was currently serving life in prison.

Pushing the past from his mind, he focused on the here and now. Ninety-five percent certain there were no eyes on him, he wandered a few feet off the path to the boulder where he would leave his current intel for Liam. From his sweatshirt pocket, he pulled out a folded up paper wrapped in cellophane. It contained the schedule and routes the Colorado sect was planning on using to move everyone, the weapons, and explosives to the northern compound along with some other info. Palming the small square, he stood next to the huge rock, whipped out his dick and proceeded to take a piss. During the steady stream, he placed his hand on the boulder and shoved the paper into a discreetly marked crevice for his counterpart to retrieve. It wasn't how James Bond would have done it, but reality always differed from Hollywood.

Once he was certain the intel was secure, he tucked himself back into his sweatpants and started the three-mile journey back to the compound. He had to admit, he was looking forward to working with Mic. Throughout his career and travels all over the world, he'd met numerous kick-ass women, but there was something about the former Army intelligence operative that he found attractive. Not looks, although she had them in spades, but attitude . . . and something else he couldn't quite zero in on. The woman was an enigma . . . one he wouldn't mind unraveling and exploring. Maybe there would be some time to mix business with pleasure . . . after all, they were supposed to be hot for each other. At least he didn't have to fake that. Well, he'd know soon enough. If all went well, she would be in his bed in a little more than six days.

JAKE DONOVAN LED a steady pace through the terrain of the wooded area west of the fenced in Trident compound. On his heels were his teammates, Devon, Brody, and Marco, with Mic and Phillips from Steel mixed in there too. Ian and Jackson were back at the office chatting with the Pentagon and MI6 on a video conference call. Hopefully, they'd have an update of when the team was heading out on this mission. But in the meantime, training was in order. After a ten-mile cruise through the woods, they'd be heading to the firing range. After that, they were having a Skype meeting with Boomer Michaelson, who would be giving them a rundown on the explosives and ordinance list they'd received from the go-between agent assigned to Carter in Colorado. Their Team Four EOD specialist was currently stateside in Little Creek and would go over all the dos and don'ts for each compound and device on the list. Like them, he understood this was classified and was sworn to secrecy as if it were a SEAL mission.

Thinking about what these bastards had planned for the country Jake loved and fought for had his gut churning. Having been a SEAL, he was no stranger to war and death, but that had been on foreign soil. It was a whole different mindset to bring that war and death to the country you were born and raised in. To idolize one of the biggest psychos in history was beyond Jake's comprehension. Yeah, Hitler had been intelligent and had almost gotten away with winning the war, but thankfully that hadn't happened. Jake could see other countries hating America for the freedoms they enjoyed, but for its own citizens to destroy those freedoms was something he would never understand.

But he didn't need to understand it. All he had to do was fight against it, with his team at his side, and save as many innocent lives as possible. He didn't do it for the recognition or praise, because there wouldn't be any. What they did, how they did it, and whether they succeeded or failed would never be made public. He couldn't even shove it into his bigoted sperm donor's face. That bastard had stopped being Jake's father the moment he'd began beating his then seventeen-year-old son after finding out that Jake was gay. The younger Donovan still bore the scars from the belt buckle that had cut into his back with every swing of the old man's arm. It had taken him weeks to recover, since Sean Donovan had refused to let his wife take their son to the doctor for treatment. The day Jake graduated from high school, he'd told his father to shove the football scholarship to Rutgers up his ass, then joined the Navy and never looked back. While he still saw and spoke to his mother and brother, Jake had barely said more than a dozen words to his father in the years since.

The squad reached the banks of a lake with a running path splitting the water into two parts. Culverts under the dry land joined the halves. Taking the path leading to the other side of the lake, Jake glanced over his shoulder when Brody nudged him from behind. The geek's voice was low, so only Jake could hear him. "Slow up and let them pass."

"Them" being Mic and Phillips. When the two Steel Corps members took the lead, Brody raised his voice again. "Y'all might want to pick up the pace here."

"Why?" the petite woman asked warily, looking back over her shoulder at them.

"Because the top speed of alligators on land is thirty-five miles per hour."

"What! Are you shitting me?" Mic started doing double time past the lake while Phillips scanned the area as he ran.

The Trident men burst out laughing, which earned them all a middle finger from Phillips and a "fuck you" from Mic. Slowing and turning, she jogged backward as she scowled at them. "Glad you all had a nice, fucking laugh. Just remember, dynamite comes in small packages and revenge is so fucking sweet."

"Uh-uh, darlin'," Brody drawled. "That was my revenge for you two making us think y'all were dead. Now we're even."

When the rest of them caught up to their temporary

teammates, Jake grinned at Mic. "Welcome to Florida. And by the way, Egghead wasn't kidding." He pointed at what looked like a log not far from the shoreline. "That's a gator right there. But don't worry, they tend to stay away from people on land unless they feel threatened—it's in the water that you have to watch out for them."

Mic smirked. "Good thing I'm not planning on going swimming. And Evans, if that gives you any ideas, I'll shoot you in both fucking kneecaps."

The rest of the run was pretty much uneventful, but Jake chuckled when he noticed Mic staying in the middle of the path past the lake on the return trip. She didn't show any signs of nervousness, but did keep a close eye on the banks on either side of her as she ran. Arriving back at the compound, they'd all hit the showers and were about to head to the indoor firing range when Ian sent out a mass text.

Conference room. Now.

They filed in and took seats around the table. The looks on Ian and Jackson's faces weren't good, and Jake had a sinking feeling in his gut that he was sure the others in the room were also experiencing.

Ian shut the conference room door, then sat at the head of the table. "We just got word from Germany. They know what's being targeted there, but no word on the date yet. If these bastards are hitting similar targets here, this shit storm is going to be worse than we thought."

In the seat next to Ian, Jackson hit a button on the laptop in front of him, which activated the large, flat monitor on the far wall of the room. Three pictures appeared, and there were several groans and "fucks" spilling from mouths around the table.

Using a laser pen, Jackson pointed to each picture in

succession. "Target number one—the Olympiastadion in Berlin. Target two—the Volksparkstadion in Hamburg. Target three—the Allianz Arena in Munich. Three of the largest football—or soccer—stadiums in the country. Combined seating capacity is over two-hundred-and-six thousand. That's not including the teams playing and the staff working there. Excuse the pun, but this is a whole new ballgame. We have to assume they will be hitting similar targets in France, the UK, and here in the States, however, until the infiltrating agents confirm that we're still up shit creek. But hopefully, not for long—Liam Cooper just heard from Carter. The Colorado sect is moving to South Dakota in ten days, which means we're moving out tomorrow at oh-eight-hundred."

Jake ran a hand down his face as he stared at the screen, dumbstruck as everyone else. *Fuck a damn duck.*

PHILLIPS and I were smashed together in narrow coach seats on a full plane bound for the small South Dakota city of Aberdeen. With a population of only 27,000, how they called it a city was beyond me. But as a result, it had been out of the question to take the jet because there was no way a black, multimillion-dollar aircraft would go unnoticed. We were supposed to be half siblings, going back home for a visit. Arriving by private jet was a risk we couldn't take.

Coach was as expected, cramped as all hell with too many children, and nothing but stale, dry crackers and saltless pretzels—at least they still had gluten in them. I rolled my eyes at the thought. My colleague was about to lose his shit on the seven-year-old kicking the back of his seat. His jaw was tight while his hands gripped the arm rests, and I probably had less than ten seconds to diffuse the situation before he snapped.

Leaning close, I whispered, "Don't do it. We can't get arrested because you lost your temper with a kid."

"Are we fucking there yet?" he snarled as he was thrown forward by a kick followed by an ear-splitting scream —again.

"Shouldn't be much longer. Just wait until we get out of this tin can, then you can make the kid piss his pants in fear. Okay?"

"Sure. I'll just sit tight and dream up ways to get back at the little bastard. Think there's any napalm I can buy in duty-free?"

I almost felt bad for the little tyke. But any drop of sympathy was erased by yet another scream and more kicking, this time on my seatback. Growling under my breath, I unbuckled, stood, and knelt on my seat, looking over the back at the kid. His mother was passed out cold with shiny pink earbuds in her diamond-clad ears. The little boy was red-haired with the eyes of a demon as he stared at me.

"Listen here you little punk, you kick these seats again, and I'll stuff you in the cargo hold. But first I'll gag you so no one can hear your screams. Your mommy will wake up and leave without you. You'll be all alone in the dark," I growled, completely losing my temper, but being careful to keep my voice down—the last thing I needed was to catch the attention of a flight attendant or air marshal. The freckle-faced little imp paled and swallowed hard. "Do you understand me?"

"Y-yes," he stuttered and tears formed in his eyes. A big fat one rolled down his red cheek, falling onto his Ninja Turtle shirt, but I felt no sympathy. This kid had no idea what it was like to be truly afraid—he was just a spoiled brat.

I sat back down and calmly buckled my seat belt, feeling much better.

Phillips crossed his arms over his chest and glared at me. "What, so you can yell at him and make him cry, but I can't?"

"It was a spur of the moment decision."

"So I see. You probably just scarred him for life, you know that, right?"

I shrugged. "*Eh*, maybe. Bet he'll be good on airplanes from now on though."

The overhead lights came on, and a bell dinged, the flight attendant stood and made the announcement for everyone to fasten their belts and put their tray tables back up. The aircraft slowly descended and prepared to land in Aberdeen. Thank fuck, because I needed to get out of this sardine can.

THE RENTED Ford sedan Phillips was driving was new enough to still be nice, but crappy enough for him to hate it. *Do people actually buy these fucking things?*

Mic was asleep in the passenger seat. It was a short ride to their hotel, but she'd passed out as soon as they were out of the lot.

They were meeting Liam something-or-other, he could never remember the Brits last name. Cooper—that was it. Liam Cooper, the British spy and their contact outside the militant compound. They had yet to meet him but had seen his file. What hadn't been redacted read pretty well. Moved up quickly through, SAS—Britain's Special Forces—to intelligence, then went black as a spy with MI6. On paper, he looked like he was going to be a great asset to their team. But Phillips was reserving judgment until they actually met the guy.

His stomach growled with hunger. The disgusting snacks

that passed for food on planes these days had been just this side of edible and did nothing to ease his desire for real food.

An image of a red-haired girl on a brightly lit sign was up ahead. Indicting a turn, he pulled into the parking lot and joined a few cars in the drive-through lane. The smell of hot oil and fries slapped him in the face, making his gut growl again in response.

"Yo, wake up." Touching Mic's shoulder carefully, he tried to wake her up. She jerked forward suddenly and grabbed his wrist, painfully twisting it backward. "Fuck! Dammit, woman, it's me! It's Phillips!" Stomping on the brakes before he rear-ended the mini-van in front of him, he needed to get control—immediately. She wasn't in the car, not mentally at least. Her eyes were open, but she didn't see him. She lunged at him, going for the throat.

Keeping his foot down on the brake and ignoring the honking horns behind him, Phillips blocked her strike with his forearm, the blow a loud *smack* in the small car. "Mic! Fucking snap out of it!"

She froze, confusion crossing her face. "W-what's going on? The fuck?"

Letting him go, she fumbled for the handle on her right, flung open the door, and stomped out into the night, slamming the door behind her.

"Dammit. Fucking shit," he mumbled. Slamming the gearshift into drive, he whipped the wheel to the right, drove over a small curb, and pulled into a parking spot. Mic was standing on the concrete divider separating this parking lot from the next one. Her hands were behind her head, and she was staring upward at the dark sky.

Leaving the car running, he stepped out and silently stood beside her. But not too close. Over the past few years, he'd known quite a few people with PTSD, some worse than others. Mic had classic symptoms, and he wondered

147

how often they popped up. And if Jackson was aware of them.

"Are you okay?" Other than her question, she didn't acknowledge his presence at all. She stood perfectly still, her only movement was her chest rising and falling rapidly.

He snorted in disbelief. "Really? Like that could ever happen. No, you didn't hurt me. I could bench you with one arm. Give me a little fucking credit, okay?"

"Arrogant fuck."

"Yeah, I guess so. You gonna tell me what that was?"

She dropped her arms to her sides. "Don't fucking touch me to wake me up. *Ever*. I'm sorry about that, but I have no control over it."

"How long have you been that way? Since Iraq?" he asked, trying to keep his tone calm and sympathetic.

Turning her head, she looked in his direction. Her eyes were shrouded in darkness, deep, black pools in her otherwise narrow face. The effect was eerie, like something you'd see in a horror flick.

"Long before Iraq, my friend. Long before. Let's get some food. I'm starving."

Leading the way, she strode purposefully into the brightly lit restaurant. He noticed her steps were hurried, as if she was anxious to get into the light. He decided he'd leave it alone for now but made a mental note to mention it to Carter and/or Liam when he could. Carter for sure needed to know, since he'd be sharing her bed.

He reached through the open car window, shutting it off and pocketing the keys. He followed Mic into the fast food joint, forcing his thoughts from her freak-out to a sweet and juicy heart attack on a bun.

16

I scanned the parking lot of the run-down motel. The neon sign announcing vacancies was blinking sporadically. This did not look good for us. There were a few big rigs and mini-vans in the lot, but no way to tell which belonged to our contact.

"Let's go check in, I guess. If he's here, we need to let him know we are." Opening my door, I grabbed my bag from the back seat and led the way into the office. The dingy windows blocked the view of the equally shabby lobby. A bell dinged when I opened the door, and a man of indeterminable age was behind the chipped Formica topped desk.

"Can I help yas?" the manager croaked in the voice of a heavy, long-time smoker.

"Yeah, we've got a reservation." Phillips stepped up to the counter, playing the role of the boyfriend or husband.

"Name?" Flipping open a book, the man held a pen at the ready. No fancy computer systems here.

"Phillip and Mikayla Robins."

"Paid in advance, I see. Here's your key. Room seven. End

of the line." Sliding an honest to goodness key across the desk, he turned his back on us and went behind a curtain.

"Real welcoming fellow we've got here." Gingerly picking up the dirty key by the red tag, I led the way out of the office. "I'll check the room, if you wanna bring the car down?"

With a nod, Phillips got in the sedan. I strode down the concrete walkway, swatting at bugs drawn in by the yellow security lights at each door. Moths large enough to carry away a small child flew around my head. *It's just a bug . . . keep walking . . . if you scream like a bitch you'll never live it down.*

I reached room number seven and unlocked the door as quickly as I was able. A musty, hot smell wafted out. "Fuck . . . this place needs fumigating. Whoever booked us here is gonna get their ass kicked."

"Good luck with that, luv."

I spun toward the voice and drew my concealed sidearm in one motion. A somewhat skinny and completely nonchalant Black man was standing in the doorway of the adjoining room next door.

"Who the ever loving hell are you?" Advancing, I kept my weapon trained on his center mass, ready to blow a hole through him at any second. His hands were tucked in the pockets of dress slacks, an old-fashioned vest unbuttoned over a slate grey business shirt. He dressed too damn sharp to be your average neighborhood gangbanger.

"What, Sawyer didn't show ya my picture?"

Now that my adrenaline was calming, I took notice of his thick English accent.

"I take it you're Liam then?"

"Yeah, and you must be Mic. Sawyer and Jackson did tell me you'd probably pull a gun on me. You Americans, so ready to shoot first."

"Yeah, me and Han Solo." I tucked the M9 back in its

holster and extended my hand for him to shake just as the door was opening behind me.

Phillips dropped our bags and closed the door behind him. "Making friends already, eh?"

"You must be Phillips." Liam stepped fully into the room, making the already small space, that much smaller.

"Who else would I be?" he gruffly replied.

"All right then. We wait here until Carter calls with instructions. Could be in ten minutes, could be ten hours. No idea, mates."

THE RED DIGITAL display on the cheap bedside alarm read 2:00 a.m., and we couldn't sleep. The hotel room was small and tastefully decorated—if you liked pink in every shade. Even the fucking polyester drapes were a sickening shade of Pepto-pink. The window was open against the stifling heat. Open for this window meant a mere three inches. It was the first of October, which in South Dakota may as well mean early winter, cold enough to have the heat on. Unfortunately for us, it was stuck on high and no amount of pounding and begging would shut it the fuck off. Calls to the front desk went unanswered at that hour.

Sweat ran down my temple, soaking my hair further. I was stripped down to a tank top and shorts, Liam and Phillips, in similar stages of undress, were in just shorts. Lucky for them they didn't have to wear a bra and top, giving stickiness a great place to gather.

"When is he going to call? I can't take this much longer." Phillips draped a cold, soaking wet towel around his shoulders, water running down his back in tiny rivulets. If he weren't my team member, I would have taken more notice of how tasty his skin looked when wet.

151

"He'll call when he calls," Liam said from the bathroom behind me. He was running cold water into the ice filled sink, preparing to soak his own small towel in it.

I sat on the floor near the heater, ignoring the blast of hot air hitting me in the face. This fucking thing was about to die. I'd had enough. "Phillips, you got a multi-tool?"

"Sure, hang on." Rooting through his pants, which were neatly folded on the chair, he pulled it from its holder and handed it me. "What's your plan?"

Looking closely at the screws holding the cover on, I flipped out the flat-head screwdriver and got to work taking the cover off. "This thing is wired in or something, I'm going to try and break the fucker." The cover came off easily, I dropped it quickly, sucking on my burned fingers.

Dust and dirt blew out into the room in a disgusting cloud. "Holy fuck, can you say fire hazard?" Phillips waved a hand in front of his face.

"Get me a wet towel." I was trying and failing to see the wiring setup inside. It was so caked in dust I couldn't make sense of it.

"Here." Phillips and Liam each handed me theirs. I stuffed one into the vent, temporarily stopping the hot air. I used the other to wipe out the inside of the heater.

"I feel sort of superfluous. Aren't men supposed to be the handy ones?" Liam spoke from behind me.

"Dude, shut the fuck up." I wiped sweat and dirt from my face and finally located the thermostat inside the guts of the archaic heater. The bubble was stuck, keeping the heat turned on all the time. Switching the screwdriver for wire cutters, I cut the lead going from the thermostat to the motor. The whirring stopped instantly. *Just like a car.*

"Thank Christ. Mic, you're a genius."

"*Duh*, tell me something I don't know, Sergeant." Standing up and wiping my filthy hands on the towel I tossed it on the growing pile near the door. "I fixed it, which means I get the first cold shower." Handing Phillips back his multi-tool, I grabbed clean clothes from my bag.

"No argument here. I feel like a fucking idiot that I didn't think of that three hours ago."

"It's because women have better brains than men, yours was mostly cooked, but I had reserves." Smirking, I shut the bathroom door and peeled off my disgusting clothes.

CARTER CLIMBED into the passenger seat of the box truck as Strauss took the driver's seat and started the engine. They were leading the first convoy heading to South Dakota. Two others were taking different routes. Following the box truck would be an old school bus filled with recruits, a few vans, and a tractor trailer hauling the ingredients for a nitrate bomb. Separate they were stable, but combine them together and it would be Oklahoma City all over again.

The other convoys were more of the same, plus a large cache of illegally obtained firearms. Those had been at the compound before Carter had worked his way undercover, and so far he had no leads for ATF to figure out where the military-grade guns had come from. They might never know, and right now it was a loose end Carter needed to leave hanging.

"So, what's the name of this town we're headed to, again?" he asked as he settled in for the long trip.

Strauss steered them out of the compound, glancing in the side view mirrors to make sure the others were following. "Clarksville. Tiny, little shit town, just like Westcliffe."

"Never heard of it. I wonder if it's anywhere near

Aberdeen." Carter put his sunglasses on and waited for the man to ask "why?"

"Why's that?"

These assholes never disappointed him. "Passed through there about a year ago and met this hot thing named Mikayla. *Ooh-wee*! That girl fucking rocked my world. She could blow me for an hour without getting lockjaw."

Strauss roared out a laugh. It was the first time Carter had seen him relax. Maybe he should have brought up some tail before this. "Damn, dude! It's been forever since I've had a chick like that. None of the pussy around here is worth more than a five-minute dip."

There was no way Carter was touching any of the pussy from the camp—he didn't want or need sex bad enough to risk getting crabs or the clap. "Oh, she's definitely worth a lot more than that. I wonder if she's still up in Aberdeen. Her brother's a cool dude too. A little bit psychotic though. Couldn't get past the exams for the military, so he went into private security, which is scary."

"Really? Why?"

Carter shrugged. "That boy's got a hair trigger. Surprised he's not in the hole somewhere doing life."

"Huh." Strauss merged onto the interstate headed north. Their little convoy followed. "Think he'd be interested in signing up?"

Eyeing the other man like the thought hadn't crossed his mind, Carter said, "I don't know. Hell, it's been a year since I've seen him. I don't know if he's in the hole or six feet under."

"Call him. Or call his sister. I wouldn't mind giving her a ride. Clarksville's about an hour from Aberdeen."

"Seriously?" Carter shook his head. "Maybe I should wait until I meet the general. I wouldn't want to piss him off by inviting someone he doesn't know."

"Fuck that shit. General Wexler trusts my judgement. You've been a good addition to the New Order. You keep these fuckheads in line. If you think this guy's got what it takes, call him. I'll okay it with the general. You still got her number?"

Carter leered and grabbed his crotch. "Oh yeah. There was no way I was losing that honey's phone number."

As Strauss laughed, Carter pulled out his cell phone and scrolled through the contacts. Most of them were to the Deimos call center where they had a list of all the people "Tim" Carter knew. If anyone called any of the numbers with varying area codes in his phone, they'd end up talking to one of "Tim's" friends and contacts around the country. Some would say he owed them money, but others would want to know when he was coming back to party with them. A few were "former employers" of cash-under-the-table jobs. He found the one listed as Mikayla Robins. It had been programmed in before he'd embedded himself into the New Order.

He pushed send and waited for Mic to pick it up. She should already be in South Dakota with Phillips and the rest of the team. Liam had taken off for the northern state as soon as Carter had given him the name of the town they were headed for.

The call connected. "Hello?"

"Hey, sweetheart," he crooned. "Remember me?"

He could imagine her fighting the urge to yell at him for the endearment. "Carter? Is that you?"

"It's me, babe. I'm going to be coming through your area in a day or two. Was wondering if we could hook up. I missed you." He looked at Strauss and laughed silently, which had the other man grinning. Just a guy, laying it on thick to get some tail.

"I don't hear from you for a year, and all of a sudden you

find my number again and expect me to be at your beck and call. Fuck you, Carter." She was doing well. They had no idea if anyone had tapped his phone or if there was a device in the truck that could intercept the cell signal.

"*Aw*, sweetheart, don't be like that. You know you missed me. We had some good times together."

"And then you left. Why are you in Aberdeen?" She was starting to sound interested in seeing him again. He hoped she was this convincing in person.

"Well, I'm not there yet, but I've hooked up with a good deal. Thought maybe Phil would want to get in on it, and then you and I could get reacquainted. Is your brother still around?"

"Yeah, he's still in town. What deal?"

She knew he wasn't going to tell her. That wasn't part of the plan. She was a chick, and chicks were low on the New Order totem pole. "Tell your brother to give me a call. I'll fill him in. In the meantime, why don't you go out and find something black and lacy to wear, and get that pussy waxed for me?"

There was the slightest of pauses, and he knew there was a blush on her face and steam coming from her ears. Yeah, she was going to ream him the first chance she got. "As long as you get some little, blue pills, babe. I remember the last time we were together you had a hard time keeping it up."

He bit back a bark of laughter. Shit, she was going to be fun to work with. "Don't you worry about that, sweetheart. Carter's going to take really good care of you. I'll see you in a few days. Tell your brother to call me. All right?"

"Yeah, all right. See you soon."

Carter said goodbye and disconnected the call. He grinned at Strauss whose eyebrows were raised. "Drive fast, dude. I'm getting laid as soon as we get there."

17

Following Carter's directions, Phillips downshifted the beat-up Chevy pickup that Liam had provided. The damn thing was mostly rust—how it was even running, I had no idea. We turned onto a dirt road that cut through some trees. Up ahead there were some blind turns— very appropriate.

"Stay cool," I prompted my teammate. "We're going to be stopped at some point. And remember, I'm Mikayla Robins and you're Phillip Robins, my half brother. We're from Aberdeen. We share a father." I recited the backstories we'd been given from memory.

"I got it, Mic." Phillips was exasperated at the reminder. "Don't forget, I'm a SEAL, this is a cakewalk for me. Don't take your nerves out on me."

"Copy that." I hated even thinking about admitting I was nervous. Give me a weapon and some tangos to kill and I'm happy. This undercover, subterfuge shit is new. If I fucked up, we were all dead and the mission was a failure. More than just my life was riding on my ability to keep my shit together.

The truck bumped further down the road, making another blind turn. Phillips slammed on the brakes, and the truck stuttered then stalled. There was a metal gate blocking the road, but that wasn't the problem—four heavily armed men guarding it were. Armed with what looked like M16s and M4s, they had their rifles trained on the cab of the truck. Phillips's knuckles were white on the wheel, and I kept my hands on the dash.

"You! You have no business here. Turn around or be shot!" One of the guards shouted, advancing on the truck.

"Keep your mouth shut. They won't like a woman questioning them," Phillips hissed.

The guard was at Phillips's window, motioning for him to roll it down.

"I told you, turn the fuck around, boy." The man was gray-haired and soft around the middle, but the unwavering barrel of his rifle didn't care about that.

"We were told to come here. Lieutenant Carter invited us. We're expected, sir." Phillips forced respect into his voice, when I knew very well he wanted to feed that twat his weapon.

"Were ya now? I'm gonna call on up to verify that, and if you're lying, consider yourself dead."

"Yes, sir."

The man trotted away, grabbing a handheld radio from the guard closest to the gate. We couldn't hear his words, but his entire expression and body language changed as Carter sauntered to the gate.

"Is that him?" Phillips whispered.

"Yeah, that's T. Carter. Don't ask what the T really stands for—I have no fucking idea."

Waving at the gate, the undercover spy motioned for us to get out of the truck. Opening my door with a squeal of rusted metal, I jumped down. My black boots made prints in the soft, dry dirt. I strode towards the gate where Carter stood. My stomach was flipping with nerves, but outwardly I was calm, which is all that mattered anyways.

"Search their truck," the head guard ordered.

"That's not necessary. They're with me, I vouched for them." Carter's voice was icy and firm. His rigid posture showing his superiority as easily as his commanding tone.

"Sorry, sir, no exceptions." Two of the guards took the cab, while the third checked the truck bed. Finding it empty, he slid underneath. What he expected to find, I had no idea.

"This is ridiculous," I snapped.

"Shut your mouth, Mikayla." Carter snaked a hand around my waist and jerked me against his chest. I saw the intent in his sky-blue eyes. I opened my mouth to say no, but it was too late. His lips pressed against my own, warm and soft. He tasted fruity, like he'd been drinking something sweet. His tongue slipped past my lips, and I clamped down on it with my teeth. His hands gripped my waist tighter, his fingers digging into my flesh as a warning.

I released his tongue and waited for him to move back—to break the kiss first. Holding the embrace a few moments longer, he finally let me go.

"It's so nice to see you again, little one."

"That was quite the welcome. I can't wait to do it again." I winked at him, earning a glare in response.

"I'm sure." Keeping his arm around my waist, he reached out his other hand toward Phillips. "Good to see you, brother."

Shaking his hand, Phillips gruffly responded, "Good to see you too, buddy."

"The truck is clean," one of the minions reported. "Well, not clean, it's dirty as fuck, but no wires, bombs, or any other nasty shit they aren't allowed to have."

"Told ya so," I said, mocking the head guard.

"Mikayla, keep your snarky mouth in check, or I'll do it for you. He's following orders."

"Yeah, whatever. Can we go now?" I was pouring the bitch on pretty heavily, I'd have to remember to ask Carter if I needed to tone it down a bit.

"Yeah, get in. I'll drive you up."

Stuffing the three of us in the cab of that truck was a feat in and of itself. I should have just sat on someone's lap. As it was, I had the shifter between my legs. When Carter changed gears, the back of his hand bumped between my legs. I glared at him, and he just shrugged and winked. As he shifted into second and bumped against my crotch again, I took this as his revenge for biting his tongue. *Bastard.*

───────

CARTER STOPPED the truck in a small parking area off to the side of the main compound. It was an impressive setup. Similar to the Colorado compound, it sat on about twenty acres surrounded by hills and a forest. He'd found out some fanatical cult had owned the place prior to disbanding after its leader was sentenced to life in prison for sexually assaulting several minors and arranging "marriages" between older men and preteen girls. He remembered hearing about the case a few years ago and knew the men were now getting what they deserved by being someone else's bitch in a cell block.

A huge meeting hall doubled as the dining room and could hold up to 150 people at once. The main house had been the cult leader's and now housed Wexler, his wife, and two young sons. Carter hoped once their father was in prison, the boys didn't follow in his footsteps.

The rest of the compound was dotted with a few multi-bedroom cabins, some bunk houses, and storage facilities.

There was a shooting range, obstacle course, and a combination gym and game room. He knew where all the weapons, ammo, and explosives were stored, but still hadn't gained access to Wexler's inner lair—the locked office in the main house. That was where the doomsday plans had to be and without on-site backup, breaking in hadn't been a risk he could take. With Mic and Phillips here, they would be able to run interference for him.

Purposely dragging his hand across Mic's thigh, Carter winked at her again. He couldn't help it. He didn't know if it was because she was an operative on his side that he could relax with for a moment, or if it was the woman herself that had him in the mood to tease her. A brief flash of annoyance appeared on her face, but disappeared when he said, "It's show time."

Throwing the truck into park, he turned off the ignition and opened the door to climb out. He grabbed Mic's wrist and stopped her from exiting behind Phillips through the passenger door. Dragging her across the seat, he took hold of her hips and pulled her out of the vehicle, letting her slide down his torso. He stared at her face and was pleased to see a mask of indifference with a bit of sexy attitude tossed in, which was perfect for her cover. *Good girl.*

Footsteps approached and he turned to see Strauss, Robisch, and Harmon walking toward them. Phillips came around the hood and stopped next to Carter, dropping his and Mic's duffels on the ground.

"Lieutenant Carter." Strauss eyed Phillips and then Mic. "Are these the new recruits?"

"Yes, sir. This is Phil Robins and his sister Mikayla. Phil this is Colonel Strauss, Major Robisch, and Sergeant Harmon."

The men shook hands with Phillips and engaged in light conversation, while barely sparing Mic a glance—except for

Harmon. The dirtbag was eyeing her like she was tonight's main course, but Carter didn't need to worry. Harmon was a scumbag and any moves he tried to put on Mic would result in the guy's balls ending up in his throat. Mic would have no trouble handling him, if it came down to that, but it would be best if Carter laid his claim.

He waited for a break in the conversation and then clapped Phillips on the back. "Phil, Sergeant Harmon will show you to the bunkhouse you'll be staying in. Mic's sleeping with me, and right now, if it's all right with you, Colonel, it's been awhile since I've seen my lady, and I'd like to get reacquainted."

Strauss leered and nodded. Picking up Mic's duffel, Carter put his arm around her shoulders and turned her toward his cabin. While she followed willingly, he could feel the tension in her body. Leaning down to whisper in her ear, he tried to get her to relax. "Easy, Mic. I'm not going to attack you. We're just going to talk."

She snorted, but at least her shoulders relaxed. "I'm not worried about you attacking me. Care to explain how we're supposed to talk in your room? Liam said it was wired for sound."

"Trust me. It'll be fine. We're going to take a shower together."

"What?" she hissed. Her shoulders tensed again, but this time it was in anger. "You're fucking insane if you think I'm showering with you."

"Yes, you are, sweetheart . . . at least, whoever is listening in on our conversation will think that. The only bugs are in the main room. I'll check again before we start talking, though." Opening the cabin door, he let her go in first, then closed the door behind them. Gesturing to the left, he led her to his room. Once they were alone—as alone as they could be with people listening in—he let her bag drop gently on the floor. Her eyes were darting everywhere at once, taking it all in—probably trying to figure out where the bugs were, in addition to eyeing the single queen bed. He tapped her arm and rolled his eyes—a signal to play along. "Baby, have I missed you. But I need a shower before I fuck you for the next few hours. Why don't you take one with me? After you get my dick nice and clean, you can blow me."

Mic's eyes narrowed, and she made a gagging gesture with her finger and mouth. "Sure, babe. I've been thinking about you and your cock all day. But do you think you can keep up with me? I want you hard and fast."

Carter strangled a hearty guffaw. There was the Mic he knew, beneath the nervous woman on her first black-ops assignment. Grinning, he pointed to the bathroom, indicating they needed to go in there. "Oh, I'm sure of it, babe. When I'm done with you, you won't be able to walk."

They entered the small bathroom, and he shut the door. Holding up a finger, he pulled out his cell phone and ran the CIA app to search for listening devices. It looked like any standard app that came with a phone most people didn't bother using. The response was the same as the last time he checked—they were clear. Reaching into the shower, he turned on the water as Mic leaned against the sink and crossed her arms. "Okay . . . talk."

Adopting a similar stance, he propped his shoulder against the wall. "Nice to see you too, sweetheart. How's Steel coming along?"

She shrugged and let the endearment slide, which was good because there would be plenty more of them when others were in earshot. "It's coming. Phillips is the only one who's reported for duty so far, but Jackson and I have a few others we agreed upon. If they accept the offer, then they'll be at the compound by the time this gig is over."

"That's great. I know Liam went over a lot of stuff with

you, but there are a few things I wanted to be the one to tell you. First off, we need to be a convincing couple, which means there's going to be some kissing and grab-ass when other people are around. Problem?"

"Nope, just don't get carried away. Keep your tongue in your own mouth as much as possible."

A snort escaped him. "Well, I guess that answers another one of my questions."

"Which is?"

"Sex."

Her eyes narrowed. "If you think I'm fucking you for a cover, think again. We can have a fight or just have a lot of shower sex." She gestured toward the running water.

"Or . . ." *Damn, if looks could kill.* "Relax and hear me out. We can have a simulated sex session in there." He tilted his head toward the bedroom. "You know, lots of moaning and groaning, get the bed squeaking, and a few shouts of 'Oh my God' and 'Hallelujah.' I'll tape it and get a copy to Liam. He'll give it to our outside support team, and they can play around with it . . . make up a bunch of sex sessions. It'll come in handy if we need to be in two places at once."

She gaped at him, and his brow furrowed in confusion. "What?"

"That wasn't the answer I expected."

Running a hand through his short hair, he released a weary sigh. "Mic, I've done a lot of things in the line of duty, some of which I'm not thrilled about. While I wouldn't mind one bit taking you to bed, I would never demand it for a cover. Besides, you're not exactly my type."

"Fuck you. And here I thought anything with a pair of tits and a pussy fit the bill for you. I'm relieved to know you have standards." The sarcasm was hard to miss on her sharp tongue.

He rolled his eyes. "Okay, that came out wrong. What I

meant is I prefer to take charge in my sexual encounters, and with your alpha personality, I highly doubt you would submit to me."

"Submit?" A lightbulb seemed to go off in her head, and her eyes widened. "Holy shit. That's what Jackson was fucking laughing about when I said I refused to call you Master or Sir."

This time, he couldn't hold back a bark of amusement as a grin spread across his face. "And that's exactly why you're not my type, but if you ever want to give it a whirl, let me know. I'd be more than happy to show you the ropes, so to speak."

"I'll pass—thanks anyway."

"No problem. It's not for everyone." He checked his watch —they had to be in here for at least a ten-minute blowjob. "Now, speaking of your alpha personality, I need you to walk a fine line with that. There are a bunch of women here, and you're going to have to establish your place in the pecking order. I want you to be on top, which means going head-to-head with a chick named Brittany. She's the leader of the group and makes sure all the women know it. You're probably going to have a physical fight with her, so forget your training and channel your high school self. It's got to be a catfight—slapping, hair pulling, screeching, the works. Feel free to fight a little dirty, but try not to use any self-defense moves that will give away your training."

"Okay, that should be easy enough. What else?"

"This next one, I'm not thrilled with, but I think it's necessary." He took a deep breath and let it out slowly. With what he knew of her childhood, he really hated to do this and wouldn't suggest it if he could think of an alternative. But time was running short, and he needed every advantage he could get to show his allegiance to the New Order. "You have to smart mouth Wexler, or do something to piss me off in front of him, and then I need to hit you. Slap you across the face. It will show him I'm on his side and won't tolerate anyone mouthing off to him, regardless if it's my woman. I need you to be submissive to the men afterward. I'll try not to hit you too hard, but I have to give you something that will bruise a bit. We'll tell Phillips it's coming, and he's going to stand up for his 'sister.'" He made quotations with his fingers. "Then I have to put him in his place, as well. Did Liam tell Phillips to walk that fine line too? He needs to be a leader to the flunkies around here but a follower when it comes to Wexler, Strauss, me, and one or two others. Okay?"

"Phillips knows what he's supposed to do unless anything has changed since the last update Liam had. And it's not as if I've never been hit before. I think I can handle a slap. Where do you stand with Wexler now?"

"I think by the end of the week I'll be pulled into his inner circle. That's when I'll be able to find out the details of the attacks . . . I hope." Pushing off the wall, he pulled his shirt up and over his head.

Mic's eyes narrowed. "What the hell are you doing?"

"Not letting the hot water go to waste—and we both need wet hair when we leave here in a few." He dropped his shirt on the floor and stuck his hand under the water to test the temperature as he toed off his boots. "Either join me, sweetheart, or go unpack your duffel and take your shower after mine—and watch your mumbling about what a dick I am in there. Dinner is in about thirty minutes over in the mess hall. Oh, and one other thing, you'll be sleeping in my bed—and no, I won't be sleeping on the floor. I may be a guy, but I can control myself. Just don't freak out if I have morning wood. It's not something that can be helped—especially around a warm, female body that has all the guys drooling."

She opened her mouth to say something more, but a

raised eyebrow from him and his hands going to unzip his pants had her giving him the finger as she headed for the door. He chuckled as he finished stripping and stepped into the shower. She sure was a firecracker and would make an excellent Domme if she ever explored the lifestyle. He would love to meet the man who broke through the barriers she had around her heart. The guy would deserve a fucking medal—a big shiny one.

But Carter understood where she was coming from—his childhood had been as shitty as hers, albeit in a different setting. He didn't know his biological father and his mother had left him at a Walmart when he was six years old. After that, he'd been bounced from one foster family to another.

It had been a long time since he thought about his mother —what little he could remember about her. For years, he'd tried to figure out what he'd done to be discarded like yesterday's trash over and over, but those events and the ones during his late teenage years helped define the man he was today. He may be a lot of things most people would frown on, but that didn't matter to him. He was a man of integrity, loyalty, and honor, and those were the reasons he could hold his head up high every morning. The day that no longer happened was the day they would have to bury him.

18

Sitting on the edge of the bed, I clutched my head in my hands. The rushing of the shower was loud, even with the door closed. I wanted to scream and break things. A growl built up in my throat, but I swallowed it down.

I knew where Carter was coming from. And I agreed with him. I needed to curb my attitude and let him take the lead here. The role of the subservient woman, taking a slap and the humiliation that goes with it, was going to be much harder than I'd let on.

Memories that I'd fought hard to keep buried rose to the surface in my mind. I felt the angry blows, and the hard wooden floor under my knees where I'd fallen. I heard the deafening click of the closet door lock, and the hot, close stench invaded my nose. The closet was so tiny I couldn't stand or lay down, even as small as I was. It was a jail cell in more ways than one.

My hands were trembling against my scalp, my fingers curling into claws as I was assaulted by my past.

"You stupid bitch." Pain exploded across my cheek from his backhanded slap. *"You're a whore, just like your mother."*

I wasn't sure what I'd done this time—it never did matter. Anything could set him off, from dinner being late to the sound of my shoes on the floor.

His grip was strong, biting and pinching the skin of my arm as he dragged me down the hallway. Flinging open the closet door, he tried to throw me inside. I twisted and pulled against his grasp. The darkness was absolute in there, oppressive and hot. Each time he locked me in there, it seemed smaller, the walls closing in, stealing my air—crushing me.

I was breathing too fast, my head spinning as panic assaulted me. Fear was a heavy weight in the pit of my gut. Sweat was running down my face and into my eyes, blurring my vision.

"No! Please don't!" I was begging him, as much as I hated it, the words forced out against my will. I loathed giving him the satisfaction of knowing he scared me.

"Get your fucking ass in there or I'll kick you inside like a fucking soccer ball!" Spit landed on my face from where he was screaming, inches away. I barely noticed the next slap. Fear was a living, breathing thing inside me. He grabbed a fistful of my hair and flung me like a doll. I landed on the floor of the tiny space with a thud. The wood was rough under my hands, I dug my nails into the wood. Knowing that when he shut and locked the door . . . I would disappear.

"Mic!"

I was jerked back to the present with that one hissed word. Carter's hands were gripping my shoulders and shaking me. I touched my cheeks and found my face was slick with tears. Dark wet spots dotted my shirt. He leaned close, and I jerked back, not wanting to be touched, but he followed me down, and I found myself flat on my back on the bed with him on top of me. His mouth brushed against my ear.

"Whatever is going on in your head right now, it was long ago. Let it go. I've been there, sweetheart. Don't lose yourself in the past—especially when the present is so much nicer." Not giving me a chance to respond, he kissed me, his lips hard and demanding on mine.

I forgot everything for a moment and let it all go—who I was, where we were, and why it was a horrible idea. His weight pressed me down into the bed, and my hands clutched his bare shoulders. His skin was velvety and cool from his shower, and he tasted fresh and clean. Gone was the tight space of the closet and the painful slaps. In their place was the masculine smell of Carter's skin and the smoothness of his cheek against my own as he nuzzled my jawline.

"Carter . . ." What I wanted to say stuck in my throat and remained there. He was kissing my neck and palming my ass, pulling me tight against his hardness. His back was cool and firm with muscle, as I rubbed my palms down his skin. He felt amazing—it all felt amazing. The kiss was just what I'd needed to snap me out of the past and pull me back to the present, which I was sure had been his intent. I froze when my fingers reached the damp terrycloth of the towel at his waist.

"What, sweetheart?"

His hands were under my shirt and hot against the skin of my stomach. It felt incredible, and it would have felt so good to give into the moment, but reality crashed into me like a cold shower. I put my lips close to his ear, taking a small amount of pleasure in his shiver. "We can't. I-I can't. I'm sorry."

Placing his forehead against mine, he squeezed my waist one last time before pulling my shirt back down. He kissed my cheek and rolled to the side, flinging an arm over his eyes and taking gulps of oxygen into his lungs. I took advantage of the moment, eyeing every exposed inch of him I could. I wanted to know just exactly what I was missing. To say he was cut and in shape was an understatement. There wasn't an ounce of fat on him, and other than the foul, black tattoo on his upper arm, his skin was unblemished and perfect. I traced each well-defined abdominal muscle with my gaze, slowly working downward. The towel was falling off. His modesty, if he had any, was preserved by only a few scant centimeters of terrycloth.

He rolled back to his side, facing me. His blue eyes were full of more understanding than I expected. His lips were full and red from our kiss, the corners of his mouth pulled upward in a small, self-satisfied smirk. Snaking his arm around my waist, he pulled me tight against his chest. He was so much larger than me, I had to look up at him. My head was a few inches under his chin. My hands were again against his bare chest, the fine, blond hairs there tickling me.

Leaning down to speak into my ear, he forced me to tuck my head into his neck as he whispered, "I understand . . . probably better than you realize. I won't lie and say I'm not disappointed we can't go further, but I get it. If you want to talk when we don't have to worry about bugs, we can. But whatever was in your head just then needed to be shaken out. I hope you don't hold my method against me." I felt his mouth pull up in a grin. "After all, I can only use the tools I have available."

My laughter against his neck made him groan and pull me tighter against him. The impressive evidence of his arousal was back in full force—so to speak. "One day I might tell you. But not today. Did—do you think they heard me crying?" I gritted my teeth in frustration, hating that I had been so weak.

"No. You . . . you were completely silent. I came out, and you were just sitting here, tears running down your face, and you were pulling on your hair. I couldn't help myself—the

Dom in me won't stand for a woman in my care being so sad and hurt."

Despite myself, I couldn't resist cuddling closer to his side. "Is that what I am? A woman in your care?" This conversation was fast becoming as dangerous as the kiss had been. I honestly had no interest in Carter beyond the obvious physical attraction. It would take much more than my lady parts wanting a man to get me to compromise my professional integrity by sleeping with a teammate.

"Yes. I love women . . . always have. I like taking care of them and making them smile. From now on, I'm going to consider it my personal mission to get as many smiles from you as possible. If you're like me, and I know you are, you haven't had much reason to. I'm going to help change that."

Rolling my eyes, I scoffed. "Right. Anyway. Shouldn't we be fucking like bunnies right about now?"

His laughter brightened his whole face, his blue eyes sparkling with delight. We were on a mission, a potentially deadly one at that, and here we were lying in bed, laughing like lovers.

Not letting me go, he raised his voice again. "Oh yeah, baby. Just like that. Play with those gorgeous tits. Damn, I fucking missed you." He moaned dramatically, bouncing slightly so the bed would squeak. How his towel was staying on, I had no idea.

"Oh God, I love how you fuck me. Harder. Fuck me harder." I screamed and groaned in fake pleasure. This was way more fun than I'd thought it would be. I yelped in shock and surprise when Carter smacked my ass, fire spreading outward from his palm. He just arched a brow, waiting for my response. I felt a truly devious smile curve my lips upward. "Oh, yes, Sir. Please spank me. Do you want me to count?"

His face flushed red, and he groaned for real, knowing I

was only playing along. But then his eyes lit up. "Oh, pet, what you do to me. We don't have much time. Count to ten, that first one was just a warm-up."

What? I hadn't expected him to take advantage of that. I guess I deserved it for poking the bear. Or rather, the Dom. His palm landed again, not as hard, but he cupped his hand so the sound was the same. When I didn't respond, he lightly pinched my ass, and I remembered I was supposed to count. "One. Thank you, Sir."

His jaw was clenched tightly, the cords in his neck standing out in what I assumed was the effort to not do this for real. I had a moment of doubt—was screwing with a Dom such a good idea? I didn't know much about the lifestyle he was in, but every man had their breaking point, right? Where was his? Over and over, he fake-spanked me until I shouted ten. Carter was sweating, his restraint evident in his expression, and I was holding back my laughter by a thread.

I grinned widely and decided to pull out the stops. Moaning and screaming my pleasure. "Oh, yes! Can I come, Sir? Please, I can't . . . I need to." Panting loudly and groaning, I was bouncing on the bed—making the springs scream in protest.

"Now. Come for me now."

I screamed, long and loud. His fake shout of release joining mine.

I collapsed on the bed beside him, worn out as if we'd just done that for real. Turning my head, I glanced at him. His face was red, and sweat dotted his brow, which he wiped away with the back of his hand. His expression was a combination of amusement and pain, probably due to the hard-on he couldn't hide under the towel, which he re-tucked around his waist. My ass cheeks tingled, but I knew it was only a small fraction of it would feel like to be spanked by him for real.

"Woman, you're going to be the death of me." Climbing off the bed, he strode toward the bathroom, grabbing a clean pair of jeans and a shirt on the way. "I need another shower. Alone."

I clapped my hands over my mouth, desperate to contain my laughter. My mirth was brought short by the towel landing on my face. I jerked it away, only to get an eyeful of Carter's glorious ass before he shut the door.

RESTING his head against the closed door, Carter inhaled deeply, trying to slow his racing heart. Getting his aching hard-on under control was a different problem altogether. Holy shit, that was the last thing he'd expected to happen when he'd walked out of the shower earlier. He'd only meant to comfort her, snap her out of the past, but it had quickly escalated after her tantalizing body had ended up under his. Her responses had made it difficult to control his own. His lack of sex these past few months hadn't helped, and there was no way he was screwing one of the neo-Nazi bunnies hopping around the compound.

Something about Mic drew him in. It had to be the similarities in their pasts, and that neither one of them were prone to letting others see beneath the façade they showed in public. While there wasn't any romantic spark between them, the physical attraction made his blood boil. What he wouldn't give to be able to tie her to the bed and spank her ass for real. Only she would never be able to submit to him. What had happened in there had been purely human nature —to give solace, and in her case, to seek out someone who could make the memories disappear. But he'd been wise enough to understand that and the fact she would have regretted things if he'd pushed her a little more.

He'd gone that route once before, giving in to an evening of unrestrained passion with a teammate, and while the night itself was burned into his memory, the aftermath had blown up in his face. What made it worse was Jordyn Alvarez was not just a colleague—he'd trained her. Now, she hated his guts, and he didn't have a fucking clue why.

Needing to get rid of his hard-on, he reached into the shower and turned the water back on. If he just got dressed in his jeans again, not only would he be in pain, but there would be no way he could get away with saying he'd just had a blowjob *and* sex when they walked into the mess hall.

The water was still warm from before, and he stepped under the spray. Grabbing the soap, he lathered it up and then wrapped his hand around his throbbing erection. Leaning against the tiled wall, he closed his eyes and stroked himself. A seductive vision filled his head—not of Mic, but of Jordyn. What was it about that damn woman that held him in knots, refusing to let go?

The twenty-eight-year-old exotic beauty from Argentina had been an international jewel thief his boss at Deimos had crossed paths with on an assignment a little over thirty-six months ago. Jordyn had been given two choices—go to jail for a very long time, or join the covert agency and become a spy. It had been a no-brainer for her, and she had exceeded everyone's expectations, becoming one of the top assassins Uncle Sam would refuse to admit he had in his employ.

His mind drifted to their one night together. It had been this time last year during an op when the shit had hit the proverbial fan. They'd managed to escape and hide out in an agency's safe house. The adrenaline coursing through them probably had a lot to do with that initial kiss, but after that, for him, it had been all her. The sweet and salty taste of her skin, the intoxicating scent of her arousal, the passion flaring in her eyes, and the electricity shooting from her body to his.

For the first time since he'd discovered the BDSM lifestyle, none of the kink had entered his mind—well, it had, but he'd been able to override it for her. All he'd wanted . . . needed . . . was Jordyn. To lose himself in her. And he had, several times that night.

Pumping his hand faster and harder, he imagined it was her warm pussy surrounding him. Her moans of ecstasy resounded in his head as if she were right there with him in the shower. His balls drew up tight as a tingling started in his lower spine.

"Fuck me, Jordyn," he whispered. "Come for me."

Tightening his grip, he yanked hard and came even harder, shooting his cum into the shower spray. His legs shook with the release, threatening to drop him on his ass on the porcelain floor. Black dots and white lights flashed behind his eyelids as his lungs sighed in relief. When the last of his orgasm faded, he ducked his head under the water and grabbed the soap again. This time, to clean off.

Damn, he'd definitely needed that. Now he could get his mind back on the mission. Too many lives were at stake for them to fail.

19

I stared at the ceiling and waited my turn in the shower —now that one was necessary. I almost felt bad for Carter, but that's what he gets for kissing me. Not that I'll ever admit to him that I needed that kiss. He could have slapped me out of it, but that wasn't his way. I didn't get his lifestyle and didn't really need to. It was apparent, even to a novice like me, that his role as a Dom included compassion and care of his woman, submissive, or whatever she was called. I can't remember anyone ever taking care of me that way before, or any way for that matter, beyond Aunt Beatrice. Most men I've encountered were either my superiors, under my command, or completely discounted me. Carter felt like an equal, and I wouldn't ruin that by giving into what my body was urging me to do, which was to go into that shower and give him a hand.

We had to go out and have dinner with Nazis. *Wow, what a thought that is.* Having a sit-down, somewhat civilized, dinner with skin-head-master-race-wannabes. It was going to be a pleasure and a privilege to wipe those fuckers off the planet. Their narrow-minded, twisted beliefs were a disease, infecting everyone they could with intolerance and bigotry. Their hatred of those different than themselves was the cornerstone of centuries of unspeakable cruelties. They thought they could force their ideology onto the populace with violence. I was here to show them something entirely different. I would end their very existence. Even though I knew it would mean little in the long run, I relished the chance to put my boot on their throats, spit in their faces, and open the door to Hell.

Carter stepped out of the bathroom, tucking a clean T-shirt into his blue jeans. His muscular arms and torso extended and flexed with his movements. The short sleeve of the shirt partially covered that sickening tattoo of his. Liam had explained to me that it was real but easily removed, unlike traditional ink.

I bounced off the bed. "My turn. You better have left me some hot water too, lover."

"If I didn't, and you bitch about it, you'll get another spanking." He raised an eyebrow at me. The tone of his voice was different now . . . harder. Gone was the caring and teasing Dom from before, and in his place was a crueler man who was willingly following a neo-Nazi leader—at least, that's who he was pretending to be. "This one not quite so much fun. That is, for you, sweetheart."

Rolling my eyes, I grabbed my bag and shut the door. This game might just turn out to be too much for me to handle.

SIDE BY SIDE, they walked to the mess hall after Mic's shower. He almost felt sorry she'd run out of hot water halfway through but figured she deserved it for the hard-on she'd given him. Now that his mind was back in the game, he wasn't sure his earlier plan was a good one. It could backfire on them if he wasn't careful. Furtively checking to make sure no one was within earshot, he put his arm around Mic's shoulder as if they were an ordinary couple. "Listen, sweetheart. Forget about the slap thing. I'll think of something else. I don't want to put you through that."

Stopping in her tracks, she brought him to a halt as well and glared up at him. "No, we'll do it. I can handle it."

"But—"

"No 'buts,' dammit. I'm not a masochist, but you said yourself, it's necessary. I'll just psyche myself into thinking we're sparring. No big deal. Now drop it."

They started walking again, and Carter had to admit that Mic was at the top of a very short list of people he had the utmost respect for. "You're one hell of an operative, Mic, and one hell of a woman too. It's an honor to work with you."

She smiled up at him. "Thanks. Believe it or not, that means a lot to me." He squeezed her shoulder in response. "All right, so what's the plan in here?"

"You're going to make nice with the women. Remember, the top dog is Brittany, the rest are all followers. Don't rush into a fight with her, but if an opportunity comes up, then go with it. Just don't let her get the better of you. Channel the alpha bitch who made an appearance with that redneck a few months ago at Finnegan's."

Stopping short again, she poked him hard in the chest. "You fucking set me up, didn't you? Why didn't I realize that before?"

Twenty feet away, the door to the mess hall flew open, and several men filed out. Carter grabbed Mic's hips and yanked her flush against him, bending down to kiss her—hard. He swallowed her surprised gasp as he devoured her mouth. And, damn, if that didn't that have his dick twitching again. Easing up after the men were out of range, he brushed his lips against hers and murmured, "Because I wanted to make sure you had the balls it took for this job. If it hadn't ended the way it did, neither Jackson nor I would have ever approached you. Now, get back into character and stay there, my submissive little sweetheart."

Her cheeks blushed slightly at the chastisement, but this was her first rodeo, and she needed to remember to stay in character. If her cover was blown, then so was his, since he was the one who'd brought her here. Carter wasn't worried too much about Phillips— he was a former SEAL and had been undercover many times. While they hadn't crossed paths before today, the spy had heard good things about him and had even perused his classified record when Jackson had brought up the man's name as a potential Steel operative. Having top security clearance had its advantages, and Carter liked to know who was going to have his back.

Pulling away, he asked, "Ready?"

When she nodded, he tucked her under his arm again and headed for the door. Holding it open, he fought against his natural urge to let her walk in first—women came second to the men here. The hall was almost full, and he saw Strauss waving him over to Wexler's table. Pulling Mic along by the arm, he approached.

Stopping in front of the group, he raised his right hand straight out into the air, his stomach roiling at the archaic gesture. "*Heil* Hitler." Wexler stoically nodded his welcome, and Carter lowered his arm, placing it behind his back with the other one, in a standard military stance. "General, sir, I'd like you to meet Mikayla Robins. Mic, this is General Wexler."

Mic hesitated. *Fuck!* He'd forgotten to tell her about the fucking salute. But once again, she impressed him. Smacking her boots together, she lifted her arm as he'd done. "*Heil* Hitler." When Wexler nodded again, this time with approval, she adopted the same military stance and added, "It's a pleasure to meet you, General."

"For me as well, Mikayla. Tell me, where are you from?

"Aberdeen, sir."

Strauss spoke up. "Lieutenant Carter, I already introduced Mikayla's brother to the general. We've placed him in Major Robisch's squad. He could use an extra pair of eyes on some of the less experienced recruits."

Phillips's fictional background had him trying to join up with every branch of the military, and failing because couldn't pass the psych evaluations. His "bigotry" toward anyone non-Caucasian showed through each time. After exhausting all his options, he'd instead turned his attention to private security and the training they offered. He'd been able to do the type of work he felt like he was meant to, all while his bosses calmly overlooked his mental shortcomings. He had a keen intelligence, but he was a borderline psychopath—or so everyone here thought. Perfect for a neo-Nazi militant group.

"That's fine, sir, thank you," Carter replied. "He'll do a good job as long as he has exact orders." He was responding to Strauss but didn't like the way Wexler was eyeing Mic. Unfortunately, he couldn't say anything that would raise suspicions. Besides, he couldn't quite tell if the bastard was interested in screwing her or deciding where to use her in his diabolical plans to take over the world. A flash of an old *Looney Tunes* cartoon popped into his mind from out of nowhere, and Carter fought the urge to laugh out loud at the memory of Marvin the Martian scheming to take over the universe. At least he had a few fond memories from his youth, thanks to television.

Finally, the general shifted his scrutiny back to Carter. "Lieutenant, please get some dinner and join us. We have a few things to discuss. Mikayla can go introduce herself to the women in the kitchen."

This was the first time he'd been invited to sit at Wexler's table. He hoped like hell this meant he was in. He had to find out the intended targets and date of destruction before it was too late. Failure was not an option.

I GLANCED around the mess hall, which really wasn't that different than Steel's. Long tables with an industrial kitchen and a chow line, it was all very straightforward and functional. The tables were filled with men, most of whom were shaved bald and decked out in various pieces of camo and surplus BDUs. I'd bet Carter's left nut that not a single one of these fuckwads had ever served. Jail time maybe, but not their country.

"Babe, go see if the girls need some help. I need to talk to the men." Patting me on the ass and giving me a little shove, Carter pointed to the kitchen and sent me on my way.

What the fuck am I supposed to do in a kitchen? I can work a coffee pot and microwave, but that's the extent of my culinary training. Kitchens were gold mines of torture implements though . . .

I pushed open the double swinging door and stepped into chaos. A bleached-blonde bitch-face was screaming at a brunette with the largest breasts I'd ever seen. The triple-D princess was shouting back, stomping her foot. Her black tank top was stretched so tight I was sure it was going to give, her ample flesh would explode everywhere, killing us all. And wasn't that a disgusting thought?

"That is not how you fucking do it, cunt!"

"Who you calling a cunt, you whore?" The blonde threw a stainless ladle at the brunette, smacking her in the face.

"What the actual fuck is going on here?" I muttered under my breath as the brunette gasped in pain and backed down.

This pit of vipers clearly had excellent hearing because their heads rotated and they glared at me with the focus of a single unit. The blonde, who I was guessing was their leader, placed her fist on a popped out hip and stared me down with more confidence than I felt. This must be the woman Carter was talking about—Brittany. *Lucky me.*

"Who the fuck are you?" She raised her nose in the air a fraction, looking down at me like I was dirt on her shoe. She was around five ten or so and built. Cords of muscles tightened under her fitted T-shirt. *Great. I get to have a slap-fight with a girl-version of a Bradley tank.*

"Mikayla. I'm Carter's woman." I was trying to follow orders and keep my "alpha" shit under control.

"Oh, so you're the new whore he brought in. I'm Brittany, and I run this place. Do what I say and we won't have any problems. Got it, bitch?" She sneered, not worried at all, secure in her position.

"I said my name is Mikayla. Not bitch or whore. If you have to call me something, call me Mic." My fists clenched as I imagined all the ways I could kill her with my bare hands. So much for keeping my attitude in check.

"What did you say?" She strode closer to me, her hands tightening into fists.

Is she going to punch me? If she swings, then I can use fists too. Oh please let me use fists . . .

"You heard me, ya white trash twat."

Her face twisted with rage, flushing red. She ran straight at me, a rookie mistake, but one that I couldn't take advantage of. So I did what any untrained, mouthy upstart would do. I ran.

Smacking the swinging doors open with my palms, I skidded out into the mess hall, with the screaming banshee on my heels. I saw Carter, Strauss, and Wexler jump to their feet seconds before I was tackled from behind. We hit the floor—hard. Dammit, she was fucking heavy. My breath was knocked from my lungs, slowing my reaction.

I screamed with real pain as she took a fistful of my hair, pulling with everything she had. My advantage was the wetness and short length of the strands. Her grip slipped, and I wrenched out of her hold. Carter's words in the back of my mind kept me in character, so instead of throwing her, I reached up and slapped her across the face, then pushed her off me and onto the concrete floor. My palm burned, and I fought to keep from climbing onto her chest and beating her senseless.

Gaining my feet, I stood, letting her get up. She flew at me again, all scratching nails and slaps. She was strong but incredibly unskilled. I managed to latch onto her wrists and knee her in the gut. Once. Twice. She was doubled over now, coughing and gasping. I let her go and shoved her down as hard as I could. My palms connecting square on her clavicles. Unable to catch herself, she teetered backward, and her head cracked off the floor. She lay there, dazed, her bleached hair spread out on the concrete like a blonde fan. Her shirt was riding up and her low-rise jeans, falling down, revealing a red, lacy thong. Classy—a real Walmart queen.

"Mikayla!" Carter bellowed as he advanced. If I didn't know better, I'd say he was really fucking mad. His eyes flashed in anger, and I thanked God that I knew it was all a charade—at least, I hoped so.

"Brittany! Goddammit!" Colonel Strauss was at Carter's side, fury darkening his features.

Carter grabbed me by the back of the neck, jerking me to his side. "What the fuck is going on here?" He snarled in my face as he shook me. "Explain yourself, Mikayla!"

He was pressing on the back of my neck, forcing me to

look at the floor and hunch over. Blood was seeping out of a few scratches on my arms, and I felt the burn of a few more on my neck. *Dammit.*

"She called me bitch. I have a name." I whimpered for effect, doing my best to act contrite.

"You disrespected Colonel Strauss and me in front of the general!" he shouted, shoving me away. I saw the apology in his eyes seconds before his hand struck out, connecting with my cheek. Sharp pain exploded throughout my face, and I collapsed to the ground. I gritted my teeth, keeping my eyes down.

"Brittany." Strauss's voice was cold and hard. Peeking through my hair, I saw her go pale, and her hands were trembling.

Her voice wobbled and cracked with fear. "Y-yes, sir."

There was no warning, nor hesitation. He punched her in the face, throwing his entire body into the hit. She cried out, and blood flew from her mouth in an arc before she went down. Her body was limp, unconscious. He'd knocked her out cold with one hit. *Fuck. Me.*

"I will not fucking tolerate petty catfighting. Make sure your woman knows that, Carter. Get these two bitches out of my sight." Strauss turned sharply on his heel with military precision and left us there, marching over to join Wexler, who was watching us carefully.

Phillips appeared from nowhere with fire in his eyes, getting into Carter's face. For a split second, I was worried, since we hadn't had time to warn him about the slap. "What the fuck was that for? She was defending herself!"

Carter's mouth turned into a sneer as he grabbed the front of Phillips's shirt, twisting the material in his fist. "Check your fucking tone. She may be your sister, but she's my property, and I'll discipline her as I see fit. If you don't like it, you can have a turn under my hand. Do I make myself clear?"

Taking a step back, my "brother" growled but relented. "Whatever."

"That's not the correct response, and you fucking know it. Do I make myself fucking clear?"

"Yes, sir!" Phillips snapped to attention and raised his right arm in a Nazi salute.

Carter jerked me to my feet and shoved me into Phillips's arms. A flash of pain and regret appeared in his eyes before he blinked and fury tightened his face once more. "Get her the fuck out of here. Put her in my room." Pointing at me, he added, "And fucking stay there until I come get you. This isn't fucking over."

I got the message—there was going to be more yelling in his room for the sake of those listening. Gripping my arm, Phillips helped me step over Brittany's still prone form and marched me out of the mess hall. Keeping a tight hold on my arm, he leaned down and whispered in my ear. "I'll bring you some food later and ice for your cheek. Nice performance, although I'm not thrilled he had to hit you like that. How did you keep from kicking her ass?"

"No way in hell was I going to compromise us for that stupid twat." I jerked my arm from his grasp and entered Carter's cabin myself. Even though it was a charade, I still felt like a child who'd been chastised and sent to my room. *Better than a closet I guess.*

20

Under the moonlight, Carter jogged through the woods in silence with Mic at his side. After he'd returned to his room and yelled at her for the sake of the listening devices, he'd told her to get changed for a run. They had a meeting scheduled with Ian and Liam at a new rendezvous point the former had scouted out. He'd given the coordinates to Mic before she and Phillips had arrived at the compound. Carter had received a bullshit account update text from his "cell phone provider" a few hours ago. It'd actually been a coded message with the meeting time. As with his runs in Colorado, he made sure they were inconsistent. Sometimes he went into the woods in the early morning, other times before or after sunset.

The three miles out were a piece of cake for the two of them and neither one was breathing hard. The elevation here was much lower than Colorado and his lungs were grateful. Spotting the rock formation he assumed Ian had been referring to, Carter checked the longitude and latitude on his military watch to confirm it. He slowed to a walk, then stopped, and Mic did the same.

"This is it?"

He nodded as he glanced around. No one had followed him the first few days here, but he always made sure he hadn't picked up a tail. "Yeah. We're about ten minutes early."

Mic took off the lightweight backpack she'd worn and pulled out two bottles of water, offering one to him. He ignored it, instead studying her face. Her right cheek, where he'd backhanded her, was swollen and discolored, and he winced as his gut curled in guilt and disgust. He'd never hit a woman in anger or self-defense with the one exception of a female member of the Taliban several years ago. She'd been trying to kill him at the time, so he was sure no one else would have done anything differently. He'd sparred with several women agents, including Jordyn, and of course, there was the spanking or flogging involved with being in the lifestyle, but that had all been consensual. This, though . . . this he regretted more than anything.

Reaching out, he cupped her jaw, and turned her head toward the moonlight streaming through the trees, so he could see the bruise better. "I'm sorry, sweetheart. I hope it doesn't hurt too much."

"I'm fine. It's nothing."

Mic tried to pull away from him, but he wouldn't allow it —the Dom in him wouldn't allow it. He tightened his grip to hold her still and disregarded her scowl. The second before he'd hit her, he'd seen a flash of fear and then resignation in her eyes. He was sure it was the same look she'd had when she was young and her father had been beating on her. It would be kid's stuff to track the bastard down and slit his throat for what he'd done to Mic, but Carter suspected she would want that honor for herself—if her sperm donor was even worth it. "It's not nothing. You don't know how sorry I am I had to do this."

"Are you going to kiss her, jackass, or can we get on with the meeting?"

Slow grins spread across their faces at Ian's interruption. It wasn't surprising the former SEAL hadn't made a single sound on his approach. In fact, if he had, he probably would have been staring down both Mic and Carter's pistols, which were currently in their shoulder holsters. Most, if not all, of the New Order's members open carried in and around the compound, but the concealed-carry laws of the state prevented them from wearing them when they went anywhere else. The last thing Wexler wanted was to draw suspicion to them—little did he know it was too late for that.

Dropping his hand from Mic's face, Carter spun on his heels to find Sawyer in a ghillie suit designed to help him blend and disappear in the forest with ease. The former SEAL whistled like a bird, and moments later, Liam joined them, dressed in all black. Carter knew other members of the Trident team were spread out around them in the woods, and would alert them to any incoming interference from the compound, so it was safe to take care of business.

Sawyer stepped forward, and when he caught sight of Mic's bruised face, his eyes flared in anger. "What the fuck, Mic? Who the fuck am I going to kill for hitting you?"

The woman had a warped sense of humor because she just smirked and said one word, "Carter."

Before Ian could come after him—it wouldn't be a shock if he did—Carter used his hands to make a "T"—the universal sign for timeout. It was evident that while the man obviously respected Mic as a soldier and operative, he also viewed her as a kid sister of sorts, and his innate need to protect and defend had risen to the surface. "Dial the Dom down, Sawyer. It was necessary." When Ian's eyes narrowed, he added, "Yeah, I know all about you and your team being in the lifestyle. Takes a Dom to know a Dom."

Beside him, Mic's jaw dropped almost to the leaves at her feet. "What? Are you shitting me? Is everyone a fucking Dom these days?"

Holding up his hands, Liam shook his head. "Don't look at me, luv. I'm a romantic."

Ian grunted. "Yeah, there's an oxymoron—a romantic Brit. But getting back to my original question, Mic, tell me what the hell happened."

Before she could explain, Carter did. "An opportunity came up—Mic got involved in a fight with one of the women. I needed to show Wexler I was on his side and wouldn't let anyone sway my favor, including my woman. You don't know how much I hated to do it—at least I didn't knock her out like Strauss did to Brittany—but it seems to have worked." He hadn't had a chance to fill Mic in yet. "I've been invited to a meeting tomorrow morning with his trusted officers. Robisch told me he thinks they're going to promote me to Major, which means I'm in on the details of D-day. As for Mic here, don't worry, after this is all over, I'm going to let her kick my ass in retaliation."

The petite but mighty woman snorted loudly and crossed her arms over her chest as she glared at him. "*Let* me, pretty boy? I don't think so."

He'd known that would get a rise out of her and hoped it would get them back on an even keel again. Things had been a little off between them since he'd hit her. "Yes, sweetheart. *Let* you. I'm about a foot taller than you, eighty pounds heavier, and have been trained in numerous forms of self-defense and have lost track of how many ways I know how to kill someone. But my biggest advantage over you is, unlike a few stupid rednecks, I would never underestimate you. You may get one or two good hits in but that would be it."

Liam and Ian let out barks of laughter, and the latter said, "Oh, shit. Mic, let me know when you're going to take this jackass down . . . I want to sell tickets to the show. And if you ever want an introduction to the lifestyle, I'd be more than happy to show you the ropes. You would make an awesome Domme and have both the male and female subs drooling over you, whichever you're into."

"I know, right?" Carter countered with a chuckle. "I was thinking the same thing."

Mic rolled her eyes, clearly done with this conversation. Ignoring their amusement, she pulled out the seemingly blank papers Carter had stuffed in her backpack earlier. He'd written on them with a special pen, similar to the old invisible ink from the 1970s. But this stuff had been updated by the CIA. The only way to see it was with an infrared light, which Liam pulled out of his pocket and handed to Carter. They couldn't take the risk of the paper being discovered by anyone in the compound.

Lighting up the pages, the ink reappeared. It was a list of license plates to all the vehicles in the compound and to several trucks that'd made deliveries over the past few days. Another page was an updated map of the compound where Carter had filled in the info on the contents and uses of a few buildings that he hadn't been able to scout out immediately after his arrival. There were several ammunition dumps, and one large building housing over 12,000 pounds of ammonium nitrate fertilizer—two and a half times the amount Timothy McVeigh had used in the Oklahoma City Bombing in April 1995. And Carter suspected there was another delivery of the volatile stuff due any day now. If they didn't stop the domestic terrorists in time, a lot of people were going to die.

After going over the rest of the intel as quickly as possible, he glanced at his watch. "Mic and I have to head back. We'll keep in touch." Before they'd gotten twenty yards down the hiking path, their contacts had disappeared into the woods.

When they got back to the main compound, Phillips was sitting on the steps leading into Carter's cabin. The guy was acting casual, spending his time honing the blade of a Bowie knife on a sharpening stone while waiting for them—but they knew he was alert to everything going on around him. The sun had set a while ago, but the overhead moon was almost full, illuminating the night.

As they approached, Phillips spotted the duo and stood, sheathing the blade in leather. "Have a nice run?"

"Yup," Carter responded. While Mic wiped the sweat from her face, he studied Phillips staring back at him. Something was on the guy's mind, and it was clear he wasn't going to reveal it with his teammate present. "Mic, why don't you go take a shower? I've got to check on my men. They're on guard duty tonight."

She hadn't noticed the tension and headed for the door. "All right."

When she disappeared into the cabin, Carter cocked his head for Phillips to join him as he began strolling across the compound—the cool night air chilling his sweat-covered skin. His squad was actually off tonight and probably playing pool or darts in the rec hall. Wexler was smart—he trained the men hard but also made sure they enjoyed some downtime. Dissension in the ranks was never good.

Carter subtly made sure no one was in earshot. "All right, what's on your mind that you didn't want to say in front of Mic?"

Running a hand over his short hair, Phillips hesitated a moment. "Shit, how do I say this . . . I don't want you to think I'm ratting on her or putting her down, because I'm not. I wasn't thrilled to have a woman as my superior at first, but that was just because it'd never happened before. I like Mic a lot. She's earned my respect on the training front, but this is our first op . . ."

"Understood. Now spill it."

"From what I understand, you knew Mic prior to Steel. Do you know about her PTSD?"

A heavy sigh escaped Carter. He knew she had a few issues, but anyone with her past—both military and childhood—would have, at least, some post-traumatic symptoms. "What exactly happened?"

"She fell asleep in the car. I'd pulled over to grab some food and tried to wake her. I know better than to startle anyone who's served, so I just put my hand on her shoulder. Fuck, man. Thank God I wasn't doing 65 mph down the highway because we would have rolled ass over teakettle. After that, it was like she couldn't get into the bright lights of the restaurant fast enough. I asked her how long she's been like this—I figured it was from the ambush she'd been in—but she said it was from long before that. Anyway, I just wanted you to know, since you're sharing a bed."

Phillips knew there was nothing to the fact that the two operatives were sleeping together beyond their cover, but his concern was valid. Carter suspected Mic had more symptoms than the flashback she'd had earlier, he just hoped like hell he hadn't been wrong about her. If Jackson was aware of her screwed-up-childhood-induced PTSD then it was evident he didn't see it as a problem—*if* he was aware.

They'd been out walking long enough, and Carter steered them back toward his cabin. "I'll talk to her without telling her about this conversation. I wouldn't want her to think this was more than just concern for her and the team."

"I appreciate it . . . I really do like her. She can be badass when she needs to be."

Carter snorted. "You have no idea." His thoughts went back to the shack in the Iraqi desert. He hadn't been present, but he'd heard about it afterward—the woman from Steel had guts of steel, pun intended. "Anyway, Cooper and Sawyer are looking into some details for us. Keep your eyes and ears open. I've got a meeting with Wexler in the morning and from the sound of things, I'm getting that all important promotion and entry to his inner circle."

"Sounds good. I better go hang out and make nice with rednecks. Catch you tomorrow."

They bumped fists and separated, with Carter heading into his cabin and down to his room. He'd sleep on Mic's PTSD for tonight. Tomorrow he'd find out if it was going to be a problem and, if so, how much of one.

Opening the door to his room, he found Mic in a clean pair of cotton shorts and a T-shirt, towel-drying her hair. The bruise on her face was getting more pronounced as time passed and his gut clenched once more at the sight. He stepped inside and closed the door on the rest of the world. "Did you save me any hot water for my fourth shower of the day?"

She gave him a teasing sneer. "Of course I did."

Little brat. He shook his head as he grabbed a pair of lightweight sweatpants to sleep in and headed for the shower. When he finished, he came back out, shirtless and sockless, and opened the drawer to the nightstand, pulling out the book he was in the middle of reading. Mic was sitting at the small table by the room's window with her M9 broken down to individual parts, giving them a good cleaning. Her backup piece was within reach in case shit went down while her main weapon was unavailable—although he knew she could have it reassembled in the blink of an eye.

Propping his pillow against the wall, he sat on the bed and stretched his legs out, setting his own weapon on the night stand. He had three backup weapons hidden in various places around the room and one more in the bathroom in case his primary gun was compromised. His room didn't have a TV, so he flipped on the clock radio to the classic rock station he'd found. The Eagles' "Hotel California" came through the speaker.

Opening the book, he felt Mic's eyes on him and he glanced at her. She raised an eyebrow, causing him to chuckle. It wasn't his choice of music she was questioning, it was the book he was reading—*Mein Kampf*, an autobiography by none other than Adolf Hitler. The psychotic leader had written it while imprisoned for a failed coup against the German government in 1923. Following his release in 1924, he'd risen to power, and history had been made. Carter had read the book several years ago, but was rereading it now because the best way to learn how to take down your enemy was to get into his mind. The key to Wexler's demise was hopefully somewhere in the pages of his idol's book.

They continued in silence—him reading while Mic reassembled her M9 then repeated the whole cleaning process with her backup weapon. When that was done, she got up and started sorting through her clothes and other things. After watching her for about fifteen minutes, Carter couldn't stand it anymore. As she walked past him for the umpteenth time, his hand shot out. Grabbing her arm, he yanked, catching her off guard and tossing her over his body into the bed. Mindful of the listening devices in the room, she glared at him as she tried to scramble to her feet again, but that was not going to happen. He pulled her back down each time she tried to stand. His arms and legs were much longer than hers as he wrapped them around her, and he weighed a lot more. Since she couldn't do anything that might cause him severe harm or pain, her resistance was futile. She was trying to avoid the two of them being in bed together, and if either of them were going to get a good night's sleep, she had to get over it.

After a few moments of halfhearted struggling, Mic finally came to the conclusion she was in bed to stay . . . at least, for now. When she let out an exasperated sigh, Carter grinned at her. Rolling her onto her side, facing away from him, he placed his book on the night stand and shut off the radio and lamp. He then spooned behind her—nothing sexual, just a comforting embrace. Tucking her close to his chest, he whispered in her ear, "You're safe. Get some sleep."

And she did.

21

Phillips tried to contain his revulsion at the bastard's words. Harmon the Flunky was talking about a girl he'd physically and sexually assaulted in Chicago a few years ago.

"The black bitch was moaning for it by time I was done with her." Leering and grabbing his crotch, Harmon turned his attention back to the bottle of rye whiskey he was doing his best to empty.

It would be so easy to kill this fucker and blame it on a drunken mistake. He slipped and fell . . . No, sir, I don't know how that knife got in his throat . . . He was playing Russian Roulette and shot himself like the fucktard he is.

The expectant stares of Robisch and one of the many nameless lackeys snapped him back from his murder fantasies. "Sorry, man, what?"

Chortling, Harmon punched him in the shoulder. "You just can't help thinking of that piece of ass I had, *huh?* That's the only damn thing these darkies are good for. Taking shit I wouldn't do to a good, Christian white woman."

His stomach recoiled, and his hands clenched into fists.

"Listen, I got shit I gotta do. Later." Standing quickly, Phillips hurried from the room before he beat Harmon to fucking death.

The frigid air outside did little to clear his head. Pacing around, he tried to walk off his anger and frustration. This mission was going too slow. They should just break into Wexler's house and steal the files, then call in some zoomies to cluster bomb the fuck out of this house of horrors.

"Phil!"

Turning his head toward the voice, he came to a stop. Robisch was jogging toward him.

"Yes, sir?" He forced false respect into his voice—hating every second of it. He gave the sloppy excuse that passed for a salute around here. These taint-faces didn't know the meaning of service or patriotism.

"You need to chill the fuck out. I know Harmon is a dick and all, but you have to suck it up." Pulling a knit hat down over his shaven head, Robisch continued. "There'll be plenty of pussy to be had after D-day. No need to get so bent out of shape over some snatch you can't have."

"Yeah." Swallowing down bile brought up by the words he was about to speak. "I guess you're right. Maybe I'm just frustrated, I haven't gotten laid in weeks."

Robisch slung an arm over his shoulders in a bro hug. Phillips fought to keep from force feeding the arm to him. "You're a good one, Phil. Next chance we get with a black whore you'll get first dibs."

Faking a grin that scarred his soul, Phillips walked along with Robisch shooting the shit until he could escape into his assigned bunk house.

Flopping face down onto his bed, still fully clothed, he mentally shouted everything he'd wanted to say earlier and hadn't been able to, then replayed all the ways he wanted to kill these racists pricks. Over and over, he watched their blood and guts spill as screams poured from their throats. This mission couldn't be over soon enough.

———————

BRODY EVANS SAT on a picnic table outside the local deli on Main Street in Clarksville, pretending to read a book on the local history. The tiny town was something from out of his mother's and sisters' favorite Hallmark Movie Channel. A town square, complete with a park and gazebo was surrounded by little mom and pop businesses. Everyone waved when they walked by whether they knew each other or not. He'd had at least four people say hello to him within the last three minutes.

When he'd first drawn the short straw for this mission, he'd been annoyed. They needed someone in Clarksville who could blend in and keep an eye on things. As far as the people in town knew, the current owners and occupants of the New Order compound were just another religious cult they wanted nothing to do with. As long as the newcomers didn't bother anyone or break any obvious laws then the townspeople ignored and tolerated them.

The team had lucked out when a check of the CIA database had located Mrs. Martha Albertson, a widow and aunt to an agency research tech, Sandra Albertson. The woman had been more than willing to open her home to Brody under the pretense he was her cousin's son who was visiting while researching the family tree. While he hadn't been looking forward to his detail, he had to admit Martha was not only a nice old lady, but she was funny, smart, sarcastic, and a fast thinker when talking to her neighbors. Never once had she come close to blowing his cover story, nor had she questioned what he was doing for Uncle Sam. She was also a damn good cook, as he let his teammates know every time they checked in with him. As far as the locals knew, he was a nice, young man who owned a dot-com business which let him travel and work anywhere that had Wi-Fi. Over the past three days, he'd met quite a few of the 3500 residents, and some of the older biddies had tried to set him up with their daughters. One or two of them had actually been tempting, but the mission came first.

According to Carter's intel, every Thursday, the women from the New Order came into town to get supplies from the various shops—the grocery store, hardware, butcher, and farmer's market. That was probably the best reason why the townspeople didn't mind another cult in their mist —ironically, it was a moneymaker for many of the businesses.

Two white commercial vans pulled into the parking lot across the street from the deli, and six women poured out of them. One of the women he recognized right away, since he'd been training with her for the past several weeks. Mic was one cool chick. If he hadn't already been impressed with her from what had happened in Iraq, she would have gained his respect down in Tampa. While she was still new to this undercover shit, she never once backed down from a challenge. That, and being kick-ass and hot looking, made her a welcome addition to the team—at least, from his point of view.

The team had no problem having her on their six, and at some time since they'd found out she wasn't six feet under, she'd become a sister to them. And Lord help anyone who messed with the sister of any of the Trident men.

Brody came from a big family and was used to having sisters around—he had three of them, as well as three brothers, all living near their parents in Texas. And Marco's sister Nina was close to the teammates, but Jake, Devon, and Ian only had male siblings. That hadn't stopped them from accepting Mic into their extended family. It took a lot to impress them, and the woman had it in spades.

Stretching his blue jean-clad legs out in front of him, he eyed the little group making their way from one store to the next. Mic knew he was there, having made brief eye contact with him, but unless it became necessary, neither would acknowledge knowing the other one.

The women seemed to be separated into two groups. A trashy, blonde bimbo with a chip on her shoulder was the leader of the two chicks practically Velcroed to her ass, while Mic appeared to have won the allegiance of the other two women. From what Brody had heard, they were probably happy to have a new leader who wasn't a C-U-Next-Tuesday toward them. Brittany, the blonde, he wouldn't touch with a ten-foot pole.

Ian had filled him in about how and why Mic had gotten a black eye, and the fact that Carter was a Dom—go figure. Now that he knew, Brody could see the dominant nature in the other man, who he'd had dealings with on numerous missions. It had probably killed the guy to hit Mic, but sometimes you had to do things undercover for the greater good. That didn't mean you had to like it though. At least Carter hadn't knocked her out like Strauss had done to Brittany.

About a half hour after they'd arrived in town, Brody noticed Brittany and her two clingers run across the street about a half a block east of him. Mic followed with the others, clearly trying to figure out what was going on. It didn't take long before she and Brody got the picture. An attractive, young woman was walking down the street, and Brittany jumped in front of her. While he couldn't hear every vile thing the bitch was spitting out at her shocked victim, he did get the gist of the bigoted tirade. The woman's flawless, café au lait skin had made her a target for racist venom.

A flash of anger and then fear shot across the victim's face as the other bitches from the New Order joined in harassing her. Mic stood a half step back from the group and glanced over her shoulder at him. Brody immediately understood. There was no way Mic could defend the woman without giving away her cover, and she also couldn't stand by and let an innocent person get hurt. There were a few pedestrians on either side of the street, but everyone seemed afraid to get involved.

Brittany shoved the woman, and jumping to his feet, Brody ran over to the group. "Hey! What the hell do you think you're doing to my girlfriend!" He purposely pushed Mic out of the way before giving Brittany an even harder thrust to the side that made her land on her ass—and he didn't regret it one bit. Squatting, he looked the pretty but terrified woman in the eyes, silently encouraging her to play along. "Sweetheart, are you okay? I'm sorry I was late."

She swallowed hard, glanced at the women behind him, then back at his blond hair and brown eyes. Making a decision, she took his proffered hand. "I-I'm fine. And you weren't late. In fact, you're right on time."

Standing, Brody helped her up before turning and tucking her in behind him. Rage filled his eyes as he stared at Mic and Brittany, who had gotten back on her feet. He took a menacing stepped toward them. "Who the hell do you think you are?"

Mic crossed her arms and glared up at him—he had a good eight inches on her. If he hadn't known her, he would have missed the regret and warning in her eyes. "We belong here, her kind doesn't. And since you're in love with a n—"

Cutting her off, Brody got in her face and snarled. "Finish that sentence, bitch, and I'll throw your ass in the sewer where it belongs. That goes for the rest of you racists too. I see you within a hundred yards of my girlfriend, you'll regret the day you were born." He took another step forward, forcing Mic and the rest of them to back up. "Now get the hell out of here."

A whelp of a siren interrupted the retort on Mic's tongue. Brittany grabbed her arm and pulled her down the street with the others following. "Let's go. Strauss will be pissed if we get into trouble."

"Is there a problem, Evans? Julie?" The sheriff shut his patrol car's door and strode over to them, glowering at the six troublemakers who were running back to their vans. He'd met Mrs. Albertson's "relative" on Brody's first day in town.

Spinning around, Brody ignored the lawman's question for a moment, instead, addressing the woman who had quickly pulled herself together. "Hi. You're Mrs. Dawson's daughter, Julie, aren't you?" Surprised, she nodded, but before she could ask how he knew that, he continued with a smile to put her at ease. "I met your mom at the library yesterday when I was doing some research, and we started chatting. Your picture was on her desk. She's really very proud of you." The librarian had told him how her daughter and she had started a new life in the small town after Julie's father had been murdered on the streets of Chicago. Julie had recently graduated nursing school and was working as a pediatric nurse at a hospital closer to Aberdeen. "I'm Brody Evans, by the way."

She smiled, her gratitude evident even before she spoke. "Thanks for coming to my rescue. It's been a long time since I've had a run-in with people like that. Just never expected it here, and it caught me off guard."

"Never let it be said that Brody Evans doesn't come to the rescue of a pretty damsel in distress." He gave her a flirty wink.

Giggling, she glanced at the sheriff who was still waiting for an answer to his question. "Everything is fine, Sheriff

Fowler. Just some lowlifes from that cult pulling the race card. I'm fine, thanks to Brody here."

The older man let out a *harrumph*. "Looks like I'm going to have to go out there and talk to that Wexler feller again. They may bring their business to our shops, but that doesn't give them the right to harass our citizens."

Shit, Brody thought. The last thing Carter, Mic, and Phillips needed was some interference from the local law. But Julie shook her head. "You don't have to bother. I think they got Brody's message. If it happens again, I'll let you handle it, but I don't think it will."

"You're sure?"

Her soft, brown eyes flashed to Brody and then back to the sheriff. "Yes, I'm sure. Now if my knight in blue jean armor has nothing better to do, I'd like to buy him lunch as a thank you."

Brody grinned. Yup, it was turning into a beautiful day.

THE COMPOUND'S gym was empty with the exception of Carter. Dressed in a pair of black cargo pants and military boots, he yanked his T-shirt up and over his head, throwing it to the floor. Without taping his knuckles or putting on a pair of boxing gloves, he attacked a heavy punching bag with his bare fists. He imagined it was Wexler's face he was pounding and poured all his anger and frustration into the beating.

How? How could the human race continue to come up with ways to destroy itself? And for fucking what? What makes assholes like Wexler, Strauss, Robisch, and the others, think they're better than everyone else and it is up to them to "cleanse" the population?

The meeting with the leaders of the New Order had gone as he'd hoped—he was promoted to major and now knew the targets in the US and the date for D-day. But there was still information missing. The allied agencies had discovered the marks for Germany and the UK, but still had no idea what the targets were for France. Until they found out, the raids on the New Order were on hold.

His muscles rippled as sweat coated his skin. He was hitting the bag so hard, several of his knuckles had split open, but he ignored the pain and blood. Instead, he tried to formulate a plan. At the meeting, while Wexler hadn't named the targets in the other countries, there had been a manila folder for each sitting on his desk. But the only one Carter had been allowed to see was the one for the US. France was the one they needed the most information on. Interpol and the French authorities had failed to get someone far enough into the organization to find out where the main compound was. As a result, only one target was confirmed so far—the one an agent at a sub-site had been privy to.

The stadiums they were hitting this Sunday here in the states were Lambeau Field, home to the Green Bay Packers in Wisconsin, US Bank Stadium where the Minnesota Vikings played, and the Chicago Bear's Soldier Field. Total seating capacity of approximately 210,000 fans. That didn't include the employees of each stadium, security, the six teams playing against each other, and their training and management staff. Several bombs, bigger than the one used in the Oklahoma City and loaded with shrapnel, could kill thousands of people in each stadium. Then add in Wexler's minions picking off those running for safety with assault rifles, the loss of life in one day would be far greater than anything the United States had ever seen or feared.

He'd grit his teeth as Wexler, Strauss, Robisch, and two other radical assholes explained how they'd been gathering security and stadium employee uniforms for almost a year now, so those planting the bombs would easily fit in. Security badges had been obtained by people already planted on several jobs at the targeted locations. Two dozen box trucks had been painted to match the stadiums' delivery vehicles for food and supplies. Radio frequencies for the security and police units in each area had been programed into receivers. Those would all be rendered useless though, minutes before the attacks. Men had been assigned to blow up the nearby communications towers, so the first responders wouldn't be able to contact their dispatchers or each other. Wexler had thought of fucking everything and didn't give one goddamn fuck that he was about to slaughter thousands of innocent men, women, and children. All he wanted to do was play God—or Hitler, the jury was still out on that one.

A few jabs and punches landed on the hard, brown leather, and another knuckle split open. The door to the gym swung open and several men wandered in, heading straight to the weight bench after saluting Carter. The assholes had no idea you didn't salute an officer indoors unless you were reporting to him for a meeting, which they weren't. Carter was also out of uniform, so the salutes were inappropriate, but Wexler had a superiority complex and required all subordinates to salute the officers no matter what. It was just one more thing that annoyed the crap out of Carter, Mic, and Phillips.

One last punch and Carter let his bloody hands drop. Grabbing a nearby towel, he wiped the sweat from his torso, downed a bottle of water, and then picked up his discarded shirt. Mic should be back from the trip into town soon, and he needed to fill her in. Then they had to wait for an opportunity to get into Wexler's office to find out where the France New Order contingent was located and what targets they would be hitting this Sunday. God help the people of France if Carter and Mic failed.

22

"Hey, sweetheart, have a good trip to town?" Carter slung his big arm over my shoulder and guided me toward the munitions barn. It wasn't unusual for him to take me along on his routine checks of the buildings where the New Order's weapons and bomb-making materials were kept, as it was part of his duties as lieutenant. We stopped at a big, red barn and he inspected the lock.

"Just grand." Glancing around to make sure we were alone, I leaned my back against the building and filled him in before adding, "Brody was a master. He averted the beating that poor woman was facing while still preserving both of our covers."

He rested his shoulder against the door, facing me. "He's a professional, that's for sure."

His voice was low, his tone unlike anything I'd heard from him up until now. Something was off about him. While it was doubtful anyone else would notice anything different about the man, the tension rolling off him had the hair on the back of my neck standing up.

"What's going on? Normally you'd take this golden opportunity to be sucking face or something, you know, to preserve our cover." I poked him in the chest, trying for levity. He gripped my fingers, squeezing them and grinding my knuckles together. "Carter, ease up."

I tugged on my hand. Noticing his bloody knuckles, I raised my eyebrow in question. He shrugged in response and didn't comment about the injuries.

"Sorry, pet. I didn't mean that." Kissing my fingertips in apology, he began to tell me about his meeting with Wexler. The dull ache in my hands forgotten, my blood turned to ice, and I think my heart stuttered in fear. The New Order had the power to kill hundreds of thousands of people. "We have to stop them. Whatever it takes."

My body thrummed with energy and the desire to go take care of this now. Between Phillips, Carter, and I we could eighty-six all the leaders in minutes. But I knew we had to wait, no matter how much I hated it. "That goes without saying." I rolled my eyes, trying to ward off the sick feeling in my belly. "So, when can I gut this bastard? After today, I've about had it with these fuckwads."

Carter ran his thumb over his busted knuckles, smearing a drop of blood across his hand. "All in good time. We need to know the other targets in France."

"Or, how about this for a plan, sparky—I can waterboard him until he spills his guts, and if that doesn't work, there are always more creative options."

His mouth ticked up into a slight grin. "I don't think that'll be necessary, my bloodthirsty beauty. Everything we need is in those files—just need to get them."

"Okay, then, but I'm keeping it in reserve just in case."

"You know, you've come a long way from the corporal answering the phone when I needed info." Stepping closer, Carter turned and helped me hold up the wall with his back.

The long line of his body brushed mine from shoulder to hip. I ignored the tingling awareness his proximity raised. Now was not the time for my girly-parts to be up and about.

"Speaking of, why did you do it?" Tucking my hands into my armpits to keep them warm, I hunched my shoulders and waited for his response.

"Do what?" His voice was low and smooth—guarded.

"Don't be coy, it doesn't look good on you."

He shrugged. Like mine, his gaze was on our surroundings, making sure we were still alone. "Back in Iraq, I just had a gut feeling about you. I'm sure you figured out I was the one who recommended you for interrogation training. But I don't know that I would have if I'd known then what I know now."

My back stiffened in response. Anxiety sped my heart as uncertainty gripped me. *Was he talking about what I thought he was?* "Explain that. Pretend I'm dumb."

A snort escaped him. "That's impossible. Your intelligence is one of things I find most attractive about you. Among other things . . ." He ran the back of a bloodied knuckle across my breast—my black shirt not showing any transfer of deep red.

Knocking his hand away, I glared at him. "That's not going to work, *Sir.* Explain yourself. What is it you think you know?"

His chest rumbled with laughter before his eyes met mine. "Damn. 'Sir' sounds so odd, yet delicious, coming from your pretty mouth, *Mistress Bea.*" My continued stare had him sobering again. "Okay. You want to hear it? You have PTSD. Or some form of it."

It was not a question nor was it meant to be. "What makes you think that?"

"Now who's being coy? Hmm?" Moving to stand in front of me, he braced his forearms on the wall on either side of

JB HAVENS & SAMANTHA A. COLE

my head, trapping me within. "Phillips told me about you nearly killing him in the drive-thru."

Cursing under my breath, I met his gaze head on. I didn't find the judgement I expected. Instead, all I saw was compassion and understanding, mixed with a little bit of worry. "That's super awesome of Phillips to tell you. I'll have to have a discussion with him later. But what's your point here?"

"Don't take this out on Phillips—he's just looking out for you. I told him I'd find a way to talk to you without spilling that he told me. I blew that. Be pissed at me if you have to be mad at someone." With a heavy sigh, he continued. "He told me you said you've been like that since before Iraq."

"Is this necessary?"

I tried pushing him away, but it was like trying to move a Sherman tank—impossible, unless he allowed it. Carter had a way of looking through me and seeing the truth beneath the bullshit and ego. I didn't want to talk about this and he knew it—not that he cared. He saw some reason or need to hear this story and wouldn't give up until I told him. Instead of pliers and torches, he was torturing me with kindness—the bastard.

"Yes. If there's anyone in this fucked up excuse of a world who can understand fear in the pit of their gut at the sound of footsteps, it's me. You're not the only one who came out of their childhood broken."

"If you know already, then why are you asking?" My voice trembled, and I hated it.

"I don't know much, beyond the little your recruiter told me. He put your father in the hospital, if I remember correctly."

"Yes, and I paid for it," I spat while my gaze flicked to stare over his shoulder. I didn't want him to see what I kept hidden in my soul. "He found me later—not long before I left for Iraq. There was more than one reason for me to join Steel. It was my chance to die—to be safe from him for good."

Carter's face turned red with rage. "He hurt you again?" Growling, he gripped my shoulders, forcing me to look up at him.

"More like threatened. But it's fine. I'm 'dead' now, so it doesn't matter. I'm beyond his reach. Calm your titties, Mr. Dom. I'm not a little girl hiding in her closet anymore—I can take care of myself."

Barking a laugh, he cupped my cheeks gently in his palms and closed what little distance there was between us. "If we weren't on a mission, in the lifestyle or not, you'd be over my knee for that." Without warning, his mouth descended and met my own. Smiling into the kiss, I nibbled his lips and swiped my tongue against his. He groaned, but I could feel him holding back—just as I was. While it was a nice distraction, we wouldn't go any further than this sweet kiss.

Drawing back, the laughter melted from his face like wax. "Seriously, can you handle this? Do you get flashbacks often? How's your sleep?"

I rolled my eyes. The tender moment disappeared, pushed aside by yet more aggravation. "Dude, look, Phillips startled me. Woke me up from a nightmare, and I didn't know where I was. I have bad dreams and don't like people jerking me awake. I'm sure you don't either. I've got it under control, and if you don't believe me . . . well . . . too fucking bad. Suck it up, buttercup. You say you know me so well, then prove it. Have some faith in me and my abilities. We all have demons from our pasts, Mr. *T.* Carter, and I'll keep on handling mine just fine. The day my issues start to interfere with my missions is the day I'm out of Steel. Got it?" I dug my finger into his chest, pushing and forcing him back. The second I had enough space, I shoved him aside with my shoulder and stalked away.

IT HAD BEEN two days since "Major" Carter and I'd had our heart to heart—that title grated on him as much as it did me. We'd kept our heads down and waited for our chance to get into Wexler's office. The New Order's leader was guarded at all times, his entourage never far behind him, and spent much of his time in the main house.

Phillips and I were doing a run around the perimeter of the expansive property with the other good little Nazis. I struggled to keep pace with him, but we had established a rhythm over the course of our training at the Steel compound. He slowed slightly and I sped up—we were several yards ahead of the rest of them.

"This fucker isn't making it easy on us." I spoke between breaths.

"What? Did you think we'd be baking cookies and drinking tea? It's not supposed to be easy, Mic," Phillips growled back.

"Dude, really? You know what I mean. I'm ready for this to be over. I'm sick of sleeping with Carter."

"Oh, how you wound me, sweetheart." Out of nowhere, Carter appeared, running at my side. Rolling my eyes, I tried to ignore him. "But don't worry about our deadline. We're going to have our opportunity this afternoon at 1400. Everyone will be training on the firing range or obstacle course while Wexler is headed into town to put his wife and kids on a bus to her mother's—he doesn't want them around when this all goes down. Mic, you need to be the badass brat I love so much, and I'll haul you off to be punished. This side of the compound will be empty." His gaze flitted toward the main house we were currently passing. Wexler and Strauss were standing on the porch watching us flunkies run by. "You'll need to keep watch while I bust in and grab the files, so we can get them to Ian and Liam." For the past few days, the former SEAL had one of his men stationed not far from the compound waiting for the intel to be dropped off. The team rotated through the detail in shifts, so who was currently out there, I didn't know, but it didn't matter— whoever it was would be right where we knew to find them, completely concealed from anyone else's view within the woods.

"Of fucking course, any opportunity to punish me does it for you. I'll meet you there. Right now, I have breakfast duty. This time I might drown Brittany in the dirty dish washer. If that filthy twat runs into me one more time I'm going to strangle her with her own fucking extensions."

"Where will I be?" Phillips asked.

"With the others at the firing range," Carter responded. "If all three of us left the training, it would be suspicious."

"True."

Nudging Phillips to the side, I jogged around a mud puddle. A quick glance over my shoulder told me everyone else was still out of earshot. "Gee, I'm so glad you asked my opinion on this. What if I think your plan is shitty, Carter?"

"Then too bad," he retorted. "This is what we've got. Suck it up, buttercup."

"Better than sucking you, jackass."

Sprinting off, I caught Phillips's response. "She needs sleep. Will you leave her the hell alone for one night, dude?"

Carter's rumbling laughter backdropped the pounding of my boots on the dirt. Shaking my head, I ran toward our cabin to take a shower—alone. This mission may be my first covert op, but it was not my first time in the shit. Most firefights lasted less than thirty minutes, for spec ops, it can be upwards of an hour. It seems I was making a career of taking forever to kill my targets. Two days of fighting in Iraq, and now we've been here for weeks. Doubt ate at me like a cancer, but just like that disease, I had to exorcise it. Self-doubt would get me killed quicker than anything else. Any second of weakness would be preyed upon by these people. The pressure to succeed was immense, as if I was deep-sea diving without a submersible. My very bones might just crack under the weight of this operation.

With no choice, I choked down my fear. I let the stress settle onto my shoulders and held that shit up. One more day and we'd be out of this mess. I couldn't afford to slip up now. I didn't care overmuch for my own life, but the lives of hundreds of thousands were depending on us and our team. I needed to erase failure from my vocabulary.

A few hours later, I was at my corner of the firing range, squashing the urge to shoot everyone around me. I caught Carter's eye, making sure he was ready for the fireworks. Sneering at the skinhead next to me, who's name I hadn't bothered to learn, I let my pent-up anger fly—for once, not having to act or pretend.

"Is that the best you can do, asshole?" I pointed at his target with a shitty grouping. Half his rounds were five-inches or more off center. "My grandmother could shoot better than that. How do you expect to defend the Order with fucking piss-poor marksmanship?"

Stalking over, he jerked on my arm and shook me. Grabbing his thumb, I twisted it up and back, forcing a groan of pain from him.

"Mikayla!" Carter shouted, stomping toward me. "It's not your fucking place to talk to my men like that."

I sneered, curling my lip in genuine disgust, while applying more pressure to the bastard's hand. "Men? You mean girls, right? *I* have a bigger dick than this fucktard."

"Can the fucking attitude before I do it for you." He reprimanded me loud enough for everyone around us to hear and grabbed my upper arm, forcing me to release the man, his face an ugly shade of red.

"Let go of me, you fucking animal!" I jerked hard, slipping his hold. Before I could turn around, he'd seized me again.

"You'll show me some fucking respect." His face was inches from mine—if I didn't know better I'd think he was pissed for real. Carter was quite the actor. He'd missed his calling for the silver screen. It would have been much more glamorous than blood, torture, and government secrets. But then again, James Bond always seemed to be having fun. And he *always* got the girl.

"Or what?" I retorted. "What exactly is your candy ass going to do about it? You know, you may be a god in bed, but I'm getting really sick of your shit."

"Likewise." Growling, he dragged me behind him as I stumbled for real. "You're going to learn some fucking respect if I have to beat it into you."

As he pulled me along, there were calls from his men. "Show the bitch who's boss, Major!" "If you need help, I can give it to her good!" There were a bunch of other remarks, whistles, and offers to put me in my place. Brittany was standing among the soldiers, wiping her sweaty face with a towel and smirking. She didn't bother to try and disguise her pleasure in what she thought was my coming pain. Carter ignored all of them.

"Having fun yet?" I whispered to him.

Glancing at me over his shoulder, he continued to haul me across the compound. "No, I fucking hate this. I feel like I'm hurting you, and it sickens me."

Once we were out of everyone else's sight, he released me, rubbing the tender spot on my upper arm that would be showing a prominent bruise soon. "I'm sorry." Without waiting for a reply, he handed me an earpiece and mic before slipping on his own. Taking a few steps back, he spoke into the mic, "Testing . . ."

"Loud and clear."

He nodded, signaling I was coming through on his end. We were standing in a small copse of trees at the rear of the main house. Wexler was gone, and Strauss was occupied with the recruits. We didn't have long but who knew when we'd get another opportunity. "Work your way around to the front and keep watch while I find the files. I'll go out the back."

"Copy that." My bitchiness was gone—in its place was cool professionalism.

After a quick visual to confirm the coast was clear, Carter hurried toward the back porch steps and was inside within seconds. Moving swiftly, I made my way around to the front of the house, staying in the shadows of the trees. Crouching down so I couldn't be seen, I kept my gaze trained on the front door.

"Fuck, it stinks in here," Carter rumbled in my ear.

Pressing the mic on my collar, I responded, "Sure it's not just you?"

"Very funny. I did shower today, though, I assure you. There's food sitting out in the kitchen. Nasty ass fucker."

"Less talking, more sneaking. No idea how long the cocksucker will be gone. Move it."

Minutes passed. The radio crackled slightly. Tapping it as if that would help, I watched in horror as Strauss appeared, striding across the compound and heading straight for the main house. *Fuck!* He didn't appear to be in a hurry and wasn't wearing his sidearm, but I had no doubt he was armed.

"Walk away . . . come on, fucker . . . go the other fucking way." My murmured begging had no effect. Strauss bounded up the front stairs. "Carter, get the fuck out. Strauss is coming in." No response. "Carter?" Crackling and the buzzing of static was my only answer. "Fuck!"

Jumping up, I ran toward the house. Strauss was inside and had shut the door behind him before I was halfway to the house. I had no weapon beyond my KA-BAR, it would have to do. I hurried up the stairs, avoiding the center of the boards which, according to Carter, squeaked. Seeing it was clear through the side window, I opened the door, and shut it softly behind me. Listening carefully, I heard footsteps toward the back of the first floor where Wexler's office was located. Pulling my knife, I crept forward on silent feet. My heart was slamming around in my chest as dread and adrenaline shot through my system. Sweat dotted my brow, but my hands were steady.

I heard a muffled thump and feared the worst.

23

I t only took seconds for Carter to jimmy the lock to the backdoor of the house. For someone as wary as Wexler was, he didn't have the greatest security measures. There were no alarms or cameras Carter had to take care of. Then again, why would Wexler need an alarm in a house on a secure and heavily-guarded compound? The lock to the office was just as easy. It was one of those standard interior doorknobs that parents got to lock the kids out of their bedroom when they wanted a little nookie time alone. But when you didn't have one of the universal keys handy, a nail was good in a pinch.

Once inside the office, he hurried behind Wexler's desk. After their meeting the other day, Carter had watched as the leader put the manila files in the top left drawer. On that lock he had to use the pick set he'd brought with him, but as with the other two, it was a piece of cake. Retrieving the files, he laid them on the desk and pulled his cell phone out of his pocket. He'd added a memory card earlier to the device, so he could just drop it in the woods in a little while next to an inconspicuous operative masquerading as a pile of leaves.

A short pop of static sounded in his ear, and he froze. "Mic?" he whispered into the microphone hidden under the neckline of his shirt. There was no answer or further sounds. *Shit.* Wexler's system to monitor cell phone calls was probably interfering with the radio frequency he and Mic were using.

This was the only chance he might have, so he yanked out his earpiece, so he could use both ears to listen for anyone approaching. A brief scan of the UK and Germany files didn't reveal any intel they weren't already aware of. Opening the France folder, he quickly snapped photos of each page, some with text, and others with maps, before putting everything back the way he'd found it. Hurrying across the room, he glanced back to make sure he hadn't forgotten anything.

He heard the door open and whipped back around, but it was too late. Strauss swung a marble statue he'd grabbed from a hallway table at his head, and although Carter ducked, it still made contact, glancing off his temple and sending him crashing to the ground. *Fuck that hurt!* He'd been so wrapped up in the mission and worrying about Mic, he'd let his guard down.

Nausea rolled through his stomach, and his skull felt like it was splitting open. Black and white stars flashed in front of his eyes as Strauss dropped on top of him wrapping his hands around Carter's throat. He struggled against them, but the bastard was stronger than Carter had imagined he'd be. Red-faced and sweating, Strauss sneered as he put more pressure into his grip. "What are you? A fucking fed? ATF? Son of a bitch. Doesn't fucking matter. They'll never find your body."

Shit. That's usually my fucking line.

Getting a hand between them, Carter pushed up on the other man's chin, but the head injury and position he was in put him at a disadvantage. His lungs screamed for air, but between the hands around his throat and the crushing weight of Strauss body on his chest, they were denied the vital oxygen they needed. His fingers stretched, aiming for the evil eyes staring down at him.

Suddenly Strauss's head snapped back. The man's mouth became an "O" in silent shock and pain as his body seized. His hands left Carter's throat and tried to reach back for the KA-BAR Mic had shoved between his ribs to the left of the spine, but his attempts were in vain. She'd nailed the guy right in the heart—he'd be dead within a minute.

Carter's lungs drank in copious amounts of air. "Don't—" The word barely came out of his mouth in a hoarse whisper.

"I know, I know. I'm leaving it in there so he doesn't bleed like the stuck pig that he is. I'm just pulling it out enough so his fucking heart stops. I wish I could say nice knowing you, Strauss, but I hate racist assholes like you. Tell the fucking devil I said hello."

Moving from underneath a dying Strauss, Carter rolled to his knees and put a hand to his head. The room spun as Mic let go of her knife, and they both watched as the man died at her feet. While the blade in his back slowed the flow of blood, it had still darkened the man's white shirt. They had to get him out of here before he bled onto the floor, or Wexler or anyone else showed up. Carter's blood from the gash on his forehead had already dotted the oriental rug but had blended in nicely with the red, gold, and green colors. Unless someone was looking for it, the drops would be hard to spot.

Ignoring the throbbing pain in his skull, Carter stood, trying to get his shaky legs to hold his weight. "You saved my life, Mic. Thanks."

"Don't mention it—you'd do the same for me. Let's get this shit cleaned up. Did you get the fucking file at least?"

He chuckled, wiping the blood flowing down his

forehead to his left eye. "All business. Our mission was almost blown, I've probably got a skull fracture, we have to figure out how to explain Strauss is missing, and you're bossing me around—definitely a Domme. And yes, I found it. Took pictures of each page."

"Whatever. We'll pop open some champagne and celebrate later. Right now, we're running out of fucking time."

Carter reached for Strauss, and with Mic's help, a grunt, and a heave, he hefted the man's dead weight onto his shoulder and headed for the kitchen. "There's an old well out back. We'll dump him in there. Put the statue on the table in the hallway."

Mic relocked the office door and placed the marble, naked lady where she belonged, before pushing past Carter to open the backdoor for him, double checking to make sure they hadn't missed anything obvious. "The well works for me. Just be sure to tell Phillips not to drink the water."

After Mic recovered her KA-BAR, Carter pitched the body head first into the deep well with a grunt. A satisfying splash echoed up the stone walls. "Always the comedian, aren't you?"

"You love me and you know it." She wiped the blade on the grass and used some leaves to clean her hands as best she could. Carter's appearance wouldn't be so easily fixed. He now had Strauss's blood on one side of his shirt while his own blood covered the other side where it had flowed from his wound down his neck. Mic eyed him appreciatively as he pulled off his ruined, white T-shirt.

"Like what you see?" he asked with a smirk as he wiped the blood off his face and neck, then tossed the shirt into the well. The cut on his head was still seeping, but they could explain it as Mic having gotten one good shot in before he'd whipped her ass. "Let's go grab a shower and then get these photos to the contact."

"There you go, again. Trying to get me in the damn shower. Give it a rest already."

He chuckled. "It was worth a shot, sweetheart."

WEXLER WAS PISSED as he stared down into the well. His gaze was filled with rage as he turned to the man standing next to him. "How'd you find out he was a fed?"

Carter shrugged and crossed his arms over his chest. "I wasn't sure at first. I spotted him in the woods last night on my run, and he kept looking around like he was worried someone was going to see him, but I didn't see what he was up to. I didn't want to bring it to your attention until I was sure—I mean, he was your second-in-command."

Wexler's eyes narrowed at the subtle jab, but he didn't acknowledge that he might have screwed up appointing Strauss to the revered position.

"Anyway, while everyone was on the range before, he apparently told Robisch he needed to take care of something and headed up to the main house. I was coming out of my cabin after I put my woman in her place for her smart mouth again. I knew you weren't home yet, and again, Strauss was looking like he didn't want anyone seeing him. I followed him in and found him sneaking around your office. I know you're the only one with a key, so he must have picked it or something. He freaked when I confronted him. We fought." He pointed to the now clotted wound on his forehead as if that proved his statement. "Bastard pulled a knife on me, and I turned it on him. Tossed him in here, so no one would ask questions you didn't want to answer with the mission coming up. Figured you'd make up a story to cover it for now."

Carter retrieved a burner phone from his pocket. It was one of two he'd hidden in his room for emergencies—which this small cluster fuck qualified as. As soon as they'd gotten back to the room, he'd looked up the number for the Denver FBI office, then made a call to it. While he'd showered, Mic had taken care of dropping the memory card in the woods so Liam could pass on the information to the right agencies.

Showing the cell phone to the general, he said, "Found this in his room. Only one number on it, and it's to the Denver FBI office."

"Fuck," Wexler spat. "When was the last call he made?"

Carter shrugged like he hadn't thought to check and brought up the call log. "Right before I saw him enter the house, lasting three and a half minutes."

Scowling, Wexler ran a hand down his face while Carter waited like a good minion when what he really wanted to do was throw the bastard down with his second-in-command in the well. The sadistic leader paced back and forth.

"Should we postpone D-day?" Carter asked.

Wexler spun to face him. "No! Everything's already scheduled. Besides, Strauss didn't know everything. No one does except me. If the feds interfere with the plans, they won't be able to stop everything."

His blood running cold, Carter fought the urge to attack and torture the man. What had he missed? Each country had three stadiums as targets. They now knew where and when. So what weren't they aware of? He hadn't noticed anything in the files that he hadn't already learned or been told. *Shit!*

Following Wexler back to the main house, he ran the details of the D-day mission in his head. Bombs would be placed by the fake security officers and employees throughout the stadiums. When they went off at halftime, moments after the communication towers were taken out, New Order soldiers, pretending to be tailgaters in the parking lot, would be waiting to spray bullets into the crowds of people trying to escape. Using high capacity assault rifles, they would shoot as many innocent people as they could within two minutes before heading for the exits in the ensuing chaos.

But that's not where it ended. Vehicles packed with explosives would be left behind scattered around the parking lots. Cars, SUVs, and vans, were set to explode fifteen minutes later after scores of first responders were on the scene and most of those who'd survived the initial assaults thought they were safe. As Strauss had said a few days ago, it was going to be like shooting fish in a barrel.

"Major."

Carter came to attention in the very room he'd almost lost his life in earlier. Damn, he owed Mic big time. "Yes, sir."

"Find Robisch and tell him I want to see him. Then take two men you trust and make sure every building and the perimeters are secure. We're leaving first thing in the morning."

"A day early, sir?" Shit, this wasn't good. They now had less than eighteen hours to coordinate raids in four countries.

"Yes. Have the men finish loading the weapons and gear. I want each team at their assigned locations by tomorrow night. In the morning, I'll give everyone the GPS coordinates of where they'll hole up until it's time to head to the stadiums."

"Understood. Anything else, sir?"

Wexler shook his head. "Dismissed."

Since he had to remain visible, pretending to make sure everything was secure, Carter sent Phillips in his place to a scheduled meeting with Ian to pass on the revised information. The raid would now have to be at 0400 hours tomorrow morning. They didn't have to worry about this compound, as Jackson and Ian had approximately one hundred feds and special-ops men and women ready to converge onto the property at a moment's notice. The UK and Germany were also prepared for their raids. France was the one that would have to scramble to the main compound they'd just learned about. The other worry in his gut was that they were missing something—something vital—something that would put this mission in the failure column. *Fuck!*

WEXLER STARED at the door Major Carter had just walked through. His jaw clenched. How could he have missed Strauss being an undercover fed? And how many more had infiltrated his organization? Failure was not an option.

He'd planned this down to the last detail. Five years in the making, the New Order had grown, not just in the US but in the UK, France, and Germany. Hitler hadn't been wrong—he'd just been born in the wrong era. His brilliant mind would have excelled in this day and age and brought the rest of the world to its knees. Hitler was long deceased, though, but men like Wexler were more than willing to carry out the man's prophecy. The perfect race would rise again.

Pulling his phone from his pants pocket, he dialed the number for the man who he trusted above all else. When the call was picked up, he didn't wait for a greeting. "We may have a problem. I've moved up the timetable to get on the road. If anything happens, if you don't hear from me by noon tomorrow, I'm counting on you to get it done. *Heil* Hitler, my brother."

24

His internal clock hit 3:05 in the morning, and Carter awoke without moving a muscle. Mic was just as still, yet he knew she was awake too. In cotton shorts and a T-shirt, she was spooned against his bare chest and abs, as well as his groin and thighs, which were covered by his sweatpants, just as she had been practically every night they'd slept together. Weird as it may sound, this was the longest he'd ever shared a bed with a woman, not to mention that sleeping was all they'd done.

He picked his head up a few inches and whispered in her ear, "I'm going to miss this, waking up next to you. I kind of like it. You know, it's not too late to consummate this boyfriend/girlfriend relationship. We have a half hour or so to kill."

Shocking the shit out of him, she shifted her hips and ground her ass against his morning wood, which had him hardening further in an instant. His arm around her waist tightened. All hope was lost though, when he heard and felt her chuckle.

"Damn, woman. That was so wrong. I'm upgrading my

opinion of you. You're not just a Domme—you're a sadistic Domme."

"And don't you forget it."

Rolling onto his back, he sighed. They still had to worry about the listening bugs in the room, but stealth was something they were both accustomed to. Mic had gotten a hands-on lesson in that during this op and proved she was a fast learner. He'd spoken the truth moments ago. He was seriously going to miss her—not just in his bed but working with her. They'd developed more than a teammates or friends relationship during the op. It was something he couldn't explain. Maybe kinship was the word he was looking for. Whatever it was, Bea "Mic" Michaels would only have to snap her fingers in the future and Carter would move heaven and Earth—and even Hell—to run and cover her six.

By the time the digital clock on the nightstand read 3:25, they were dressed and geared up. Mic looked badass dressed in her black tactical clothing and armed to the teeth. She had a KA-BAR, three guns—on her hip, back, and ankle—and ammo in every available pocket. He was sure if he frisked her, he'd find a few more surprises just as he had on his own body.

He cocked an eyebrow in a silent question, and she nodded, confirming she was ready. Opening the door, he checked the hallway, found it clear, and gestured for Mic to follow him. Out in the compound, the air was cold, their breath evident in puffs of condensed droplets of liquid and ice, swirling around their faces. The moon was hidden behind dark clouds that promised rain or possibly snow within the coming hours. Winter was rapidly approaching the hills and valleys of South Dakota.

Phillips was right where he was supposed to be, behind the building that housed the gym, waiting for them in matching dress and similar weapons. Without needing to check, Carter knew that Trident, Jackson, the contracted special-ops teams, and the feds were gathered outside the compound's perimeter, waiting for the signal to blow this popsicle stand sky high. They would take as many members of the New Order as possible into custody, but also had clear orders to eliminate threats as necessary. Carter would prefer to bomb the place, but he didn't always get what he wanted.

With Mic and Phillips disappearing into the shadows, Carter strode out into the open, heading for the main gate. He'd made it a practice to conduct surprise inspections at all hours, first in Colorado, and then continuing here, so no one would think it was out of the ordinary for him to show up unannounced. As the front gate guards were being put out of commission, the perimeter security team would be shitting their pants as the special-ops guys snuck up and took them down in utter silence.

Two of the three guards tossed their cigarettes to the ground when they saw Carter approach and stood at attention. The detail's leader saluted. "Major, sir, all secure."

"Good," he responded with a nod, stopping right in front of the man. The others never saw Mic and Phillips come up behind them. Both men dropped after being choked into unconsciousness as Carter knocked his man out with one punch. Figures dressed in black emerged from the shadows, restrained the guards with zip ties, then dragged them into the darkness. In under two minutes, the front gate was under the control of the good guys.

Ian, Devon, and several other trained operatives met the three insiders on the dirt driveway leading back up to the compound. Marco and Brody were close by with their contingent, while Jake was in a tree somewhere with his scoped rifle, as were several other snipers. There was almost one operative for every New Order member in the camp, but there was sure to be some who wouldn't go down easily.

A glance at his watch told Carter that he, Phillips, and Mic had ninety seconds to hoof it to the main house. Wexler was theirs as the other teams prepared to raid the cabins and bunkhouses. With a thumbs up to the Sawyer brothers, the three began to jog past the meeting hall, weapons at the ready.

The shuffling of feet and a female giggling had them stopping short. Harmon and Brittany came stumbling around the corner of the building fixing their clothes. Of course, the horny trailer trash had picked tonight of all nights for some nookie.

Harmon spotted them first. A look of confusion was replaced with rage as he noticed the operatives swarming the compound in silence. He drew his sidearm and was about to sound the alarm, but his yell was cut short by the bullet from Phillips's gun that pierced his throat, the shot just louder than a *puff* through the silencer. Harmon fell to the ground in a heap, struggling to get air into his lungs but failing. Brittany's scream of horror was also halted before it could escape, but that was from Mic's fist making contact with her jaw. The bleached blonde's head snapped back, and she assplanted on the ground.

Mic smirked. "Damn, that felt good."

She squatted down, flipped her unworthy adversary onto her stomach, and crushed her face into the dirt as Phillips pulled out some more zip ties to restrain Brittany's arms. Certain Phillips had things under control, Carter and Mic double-timed it to the main house.

Slipping in the front door as easily as Carter had gotten in the backdoor yesterday afternoon, they crept upstairs and into Wexler's bedroom. The New Order leader was in his boxer shorts and snoring away in the king-sized bed, causing Mic to roll her eyes in disgust. The takedown was anticlimactic as Carter set his 9mm on Wexler's lips as a wakeup call.

The bastard awoke with a start then froze when he realized his predicament. An evil grin spread across Carter's face. "Good morning, sunshine. Welcome to your worst fucking nightmare. Mic and I will be your hosts for the next hour while you spill your guts. If you don't, we'll gladly do it for you."

My, oh my, how the tables have turned. I stared at the door to the kitchen. We were still in Wexler's house, and he was currently tied to a chair behind that door.

"Ready for this, sweetheart?" Carter asked from beside me, a large, black duffel resting near his boots.

"Yes." My palms were a little sweaty, and my heart was racing, but I was ready. The brass was waiting anxiously in the meeting hall for the information we needed to extract from this piece of crap. I wasn't sure if it was because they couldn't stomach what was about to happen or if they wanted plausible deniability, but either way they didn't want to watch. "Let's get it done."

"I like your 'can do' attitude." Picking up his bag of tricks, he followed as I opened the door. The Sawyer brothers, who'd been keeping watch over the neo-Nazi leader, just nodded and left. I knew, at least, Ian had the stomach for torture, so their excuse for leaving was probably so they could deny being part of it.

Wexler was slumped in the chair, bruises were already starting to show on his face where he'd "fallen" while in custody. We'd be doing a lot more damage than helping him down the stairs. Lifting his chin with a look of defiance, he spit in our general direction.

"Now, Wexler, that's just plain rude." I smiled prettily, not trying to hide my appreciation of this moment. "I could give you a speech about doing this the easy way or the hard way, but that's just clichéd as fuck. I've been looking forward to this moment since I walked onto your compound. Actually, that's a lie. I've been looking forward to this since I learned of your miserable existence."

"Go fuck yourself, you cunt," he snarled.

The crack of Carter's fist was loud and satisfying. "Oh, I've been waiting to do that for months now." Tilting his head to the side, he eyed the blood leaking from Wexler's mouth. "It felt so good, I think I'm going to do it again." Carter's fist shot out, smacking into Wexler's jaw with a thud. Groaning, the bastard spit red down the front of his shirt and then grinned at us with blood-stained teeth.

"You're going to have to do better than that, you bitches."

"Oh, goodie, Mic, he's going to make it fun for us. I fucking love when they do that." Dropping the duffel on the counter, Carter began pulling things out—setting them down well within Wexler's sight. Pliers, knives, chisels, and a few hammers of different weights slowly began to pile up. "See, we all have things we're good at. You . . ." He pointed at Wexler. ". . . for example, excel at being a level ten douchebag and racist. I have to hand it to you though, if I wanted to kill half a million people in one day, your plan would be brilliant. Only, you didn't count on me and my pretty associate here."

Adding an acetylene torch, bottles of different liquids, and a hefty wrench to the pile, Carter continued to speak as I watched, trying not to laugh. *Damn, we both have sick senses of humor.*

"See, this woman is not just some regular bitch—although she likes to bust my ass at times. She's a trained, government interrogator. As am I. This is what *we* excel at. Taking cock gobblers like you and making them sing."

"There's nothing you can do. There is no stopping what's coming. You can torture me all you want, if won't make a fucking bit of difference. I win. You lose."

Picking up the large plumber's wrench, Carter spoke again. "But I don't like to lose, and we can't just take your word for it now, can we? Ready?" Bringing the wrench down with speed, he smashed Wexler's knee. The crack of bone and Wexler's blood-curdling screams echoed through the house. Blood seeped through the fabric of his jeans, and his face was white with pain.

Tossing the wrench onto the table with a metal clang, Carter stepped back and waited for Wexler to recover from the initial shock. His knee was twisted sideways toward his other one. It almost turned my stomach—almost. Knowing what the bastard had planned to do to innocent people made it satisfying to see the damage.

"Wexler. You okay? I imagine that hurt a lot, but I can't have you passing out on us. I'll just pull out the smelling salts or ice water to wake your ass up." Crossing my arms over my chest, I did nothing to hide the delight I felt.

Groaning, he lifted his head. Blood, snot, and spit coated his chin. "Fuck off."

An evil grin spread across my face. "I was hoping you'd say that. My turn." I stepped forward and examined the implements on the counter. Pain might not be the way to go. "Carter, get a couple guys in here. I want this piece of shit on the table."

Understanding flashed in his blue eyes along with a bit of evil amusement. "Oh, sweetheart, I like the way you think, but I don't think our friend here will agree."

In moments, Wexler was transferred to the kitchen table, and ropes kept him in place. Duct tape across his forehead kept him from lifting his head. I held a thick towel in my hand, and Carter was filling buckets with water as Ian and Devon left the room again.

"Do you understand what's about to happen to you?" I asked our prisoner.

His only response was his broken record of "fuck off."

Ignoring his remark, I continued. "I'm about to put this towel over your face and pour water over your head. You'll feel like you're drowning, only you won't drown. Over and over, you'll feel like you're about to die. It'll be impossible to take a breath. Your chest will burn like fire with the need for air, only there will be none to be had." Bending down closer to his face, I spoke directly into his ear. "Before we're done with you, you'll be begging for death. Only I'm going to hold the reaper off for as long as I can. I'm going to use every bit of skill I've been taught to make you beg for death." Involuntary goosebumps spread over his neck and bare chest, and he couldn't hide his shudder of fear.

Without another word, we brought Hell to Earth and into that room with us. The Devil was getting his due. One bucket after another, we poured them over his face. To make it extra *fun* for the bastard, we alternated hot and cold water. We were careful to keep him in shock but not send him into cardiac arrest.

My boots were soaked—water covered the whole kitchen floor. I'd just poured the fourth bucket over Wexler. He was sputtering and gasping, the wet towel suctioning to his mouth, as his limbs struggled against their restraints. Carter let go of the ends of the towel he'd been pressing flat onto the table.

I surveyed Wexler's body. His broken knee canted unnaturally to the side, the pain forgotten under the stress of waterboarding.

"Give him a short break," Carter said from where he was

233

taking the man's pulse. "His heart rate is dangerously fast. Can't have him dying too soon."

Nodding, I stepped away and dropped the empty bucket in the sink. Needing a short break myself, I headed out to the hall only to find Ian holding up a wall and staring at me. His thick arms were crossed over his chest, and he said nothing.

"What? Got a fucking problem, Sawyer?" I was irritable and on edge. This was hard work, both physically and mentally. I pushed past him and strode into the living room as he followed.

"Nope. No problem. Just remembering Iraq and that hut in the desert. How you worked over that poor bastard. You scare me, woman." The last was said while the corners of his mouth ticked up in a slight grin, belying his statement. There was nothing but appreciation and respect in his gaze.

"Yeah, don't get on her bad side. Mic here is gaining a reputation for cold-bloodedness," Phillips chimed in.

The only person in the filled room who wasn't Trident or Steel was the Brit, who I'd come to like during this op. I glared at all of them. "Any other comments from the peanut gallery? Huh? Got something to say to me?" Silence. "Well, then, fuck you very much." Jackson smirked, and Liam was blank as a canvas. A few others hid their grins.

Pivoting, I left the jackasses behind me—break time was over. I smacked the kitchen door with my hand, sending it crashing open. "I'm done fucking around." Snapping on latex gloves before handing a pair to Carter, I selected a knife, and advanced on Wexler's limp body. "That was just foreplay— now the fucking starts."

Jerking the towel off his face I set the blade against his cheek. "Last chance, fuck face."

"Go—go to hell," he choked out.

"You first." As I dragged the blade down his cheek, it didn't take much for the sharp edge to slice it to the bone.

Wexler screamed long and loud. Blood soon coated the table around him—and me. It looked like I was wearing red gloves.

Carter stepped up to the table, a pair of pruning shears in his hand. "Come here, pin his hand. He doesn't need all his fingers anyway."

"Which one first?" I asked as I pinned Wexler's right hand flat against the table. He was trembling and jerking, but between the restraint at his wrist and being weak from pain, it took very little effort to hold him down.

"Let's ask him." Arching an eyebrow, Carter addressed the man who was finally nearing his breaking point—close but not quite. "Hey, buddy, is this your jerking off hand? I bet it is. Thumb or pinkie?"

Seconds passed with nothing coherent coming from his mouth. Mumbled prayers and begging could be heard, but nothing more.

"Thumb it is," my partner announced. I held the digit still by the end while Carter slid the blades of the pruners around it. "Count of three." I nodded as he began to count. "One . . ."

Snap! Blood spurted onto Carter's face. Wexler howled, kicking his good leg and thrashing as best he could in his restraints.

I gaped at Carter. "Did you fail math in school?"

An innocent expression came across his face. "What?"

"Who the hell taught you to count? The poor guy thought he had two more seconds to enjoy his thumb. Oh, well, guess he's not going to be spanking the hairless monkey anytime soon." I dropped the thumb onto Wexler's chest with my latex-clad fingers. I saw another scream building up in his chest and face before he even let it loose. Pain was one thing, but seeing your own severed finger sitting on your chest was horrifying in an indescribable way.

When the screaming stopped, and he passed out, I exchanged glances with Carter. Half his face was a mask of blood, his eyes a very bright blue against the red. It was almost artistic in its eeriness. He looked like he'd just walked off the set of a slasher film.

"We've got nineteen more fingers and toes. Fifty bucks says we get one more off before he starts talking." I smiled, trying to maintain a bit of humor in this horror show. He was one tough bastard. The trick with torture is being mentally stronger than your victim is physically. I knew the sight of the fucker's severed thumb resting like a savage offering on his chest was going to haunt me for a long time. But if what we were doing saved the lives of a quarter of a million people, I would gladly carry the scars.

"You're on. I think we're going to have to take all of them from this hand first."

"Let's hope not." Wexler was coming around, moaning and blinking rapidly. "Hey buddy, How ya doing?" I smacked his check with my palm. The exposed check bone felt warm and very slick under my hand. He was beyond screaming— he just moaned in agony.

Carter clicked the pruning shears open and closed, fiddling with the bloody blades. "Wexler, your index finger is next. I'm going keep cutting until I run out of fingers—then I'll start on your toes. Or you can talk and save me the trouble."

"O-okay. I'll t-tell you. Does-doesn't matter an-anyway. You'll never s-stop it in time."

Several minutes of Wexler spilling his guts nonstop passed. He told us everything we needed to know and more. The recording app on my phone came in handy—I didn't want to forget one syllable of what he said.

"Okay, Wexler. That's it." Pulling out my KA-BAR I laid the blade against his throat. Carter's hand on mine stopped me. Wexler closed his eyes and tipped his head back, welcoming death. Thinking it would be an end to his pain.

"Let me," Carter ordered.

"Fuck that! And you in the process. I'm doing it."

"You don't need the burden. I can handle it." Stubbornness tightened his jaw.

Not willing to argue, I elbowed Carter back and shoved the blade in deep. Wexler gurgled once and shuddered as his heart pumped his life away. Jerking the knife out, blood splattered our chests and arms.

"Stubborn ass. I can live with this easier than you." Spinning on his heel, Carter strode to the sink and began to wash the blood from his body. I joined him, dropping my knife into the sink. The water was dark red as it swirled down the drain.

"I'm not one of your girls who needs protecting. I'd think you'd know that by now, Carter. I finish what I start. Now, if we're done feeling our feelings, can we go and bag these mother fuckers before they ruin my country? Oh, and you owe me fifty bucks."

Five minutes later, Phillips, Carter, Jackson, and myself were jogging our way across the compound to an Air Force chopper we had standing by in a clearing. Ian and Trident would follow in a second bird. A dozen of the other special-ops guys were already en route to Kansas City and would set up a landing zone for our arrival. There was so little time, I tried to mentally prepare myself for the possibility that we wouldn't make it.

Liam was on the phone with MI6, his share of the mission complete. He'd be heading home on the first flight out. He needed to be on the ground to assist with the aftermath of the raids in Britain while Germany and France coordinated with Interpol to take care of the other cells in Europe.

25

They were flying as fast as the Air Force helicopters out of Ellsworth, South Dakota, could muster toward Kansas City, Missouri. Wexler's revelation that his stepbrother, Joel Kohring, had a backup team and plan for Arrowhead Stadium was the final piece of the puzzle they hadn't known was missing. While today was Saturday, and there was no pro football game scheduled, it was law enforcement, EMS, fire department, and military appreciation day at the stadium. The SLPD and SLFD football teams had combined to play against the visiting NYPD and FDNY united team. The event was a fundraiser to benefit the families of the cops, firemen, and EMTs killed during 9/11. The stadium wouldn't be completely filled, but thousands had been pouring into the parking lots since dawn for one huge tailgate party. Almost 10,000 tickets had been sold. Sounding an alarm to evacuate would only push Kohring to hit the remote control for the bombs earlier than planned.

Jackson tapped the microphone on his headset and spoke

to the pilot. "Captain? Patch me through to Ian Sawyer on the other bird and Alan Frankfort back at the compound."

"The Director of Homeland Security?"

"You know of any other Alan Frankfort I'd want to fucking talk to at a time like this?"

"Roger that." Seconds passed followed by buzzing static and then a beep. "You're on."

"And you're off," Jackson ordered then waited as the pilot flipped a switch, so he couldn't hear the ensuing conversation. "Sawyer?"

"Here."

"Director Frankfort? I'm on the line with Sawyer, Carter, and my team."

The director's voice came through loud and clear despite the roar of the choppers as they sped toward their destination. "What do you need?"

Jackson nodded to Carter who answered, "Sir, we'll need a SWAT team to take out the tangos assigned to blow up the communications tower closest to the stadium. I don't have an exact location, but it's probably within a two-mile radius of Arrowhead. Send someone to meet us at the landing zone with vehicles and about three dozen football jerseys—2X and 3X—so we'll blend in with the tailgaters. Oh, and one medium." He winked at Mic. "We'll need a second SWAT team to meet us at a secure location near the stadium, and we'll coordinate when we get there. Tell them nothing goes over the airwaves—we have no idea who's monitoring them."

"Consider it done," Frankfort declared. "Anything else?"

Carter glanced at the others who shook their heads. "Sawyer, anything?"

"Just a few prayers, sir," was Ian's response.

Carter agreed completely. "Amen."

A click came over the air as the director disconnected. Ian

was still on the line. "Egghead's busy on his computer working with the feds. We'll have a picture of Wexler's stepbrother and his known associates by the time we land."

Even though they were in some of the fastest military helicopters, their estimated flight time was an hour and forty-five minutes. Plenty of time for Kohring's men to get everything set—or for something to go horribly wrong. Carter's gut clenched, and it had nothing to do with the turbulence they just hit. He ran different scenarios through his head, planning for every contingency, but would it be enough?

He felt Mic's gaze on him. "What, sweetheart?" Her eyes narrowed at the endearment he'd gotten so used to calling her. While it hadn't been an issue undercover, they were now surrounded by men she demanded respect from. "Sorry, Mic. Habit."

Her shoulders relaxed a tad. "Did you believe Wexler when he said he didn't know where his brother was setting up his control center?"

"No. But it's got to be nearby for the types of remote detonators they're using." He pulled out his cell and sent Brody a message. "He could be in the stadium, but my bet is right outside the perimeter somewhere. It's going to be like a needle in the proverbial haystack. I'm having Egghead widen the search area radius by one mile."

Mic nodded. They were all thinking the same thing— failure was not an option. If they did, they might just be among the dead when the smoke cleared. Or wish they were. Living with a catastrophic failure this mission had the potential for being would be impossible.

When they finally landed at a small, municipal airport in a suburb of Kansas City, everyone was beyond anxious to get this over with. FBI agents met them with transportation, and as they were driven to the off-site command center, they changed into a variety of football jerseys over their bulletproof vests. Brody sent Kohring's picture to everyone's cell phones and tablets, along with his known associates. According to Wexler, Kohring was going to be the one pushing the detonator button for the bombs, so he was their main focus.

The command center was set up in the parking lot of the University of Kansas Hospital Training Complex less than a mile away from the stadium. There were agents from the FBI and ATF as well as KCPD Chief of Police, Mark Howard, and his subordinates. Some were in uniform or suits, while others had donned jerseys to blend in with the crowd.

Jackson then Carter and the Trident and Steel teams shook hands with Howard, SAC's from both federal agencies, and the head of the stadium's security team, Wayne Alexander. Everyone then stepped over to a table under a tent where maps of the surrounding area and floor plans for the stadium lay.

"I've got a lot of my men and women, and their families, over there," Howard said. "Tell me what we need to do to make sure I don't lose a single one of them."

Jackson began going through a list that he, Carter, Ian, and Mic had come up with during the flight. "We need at least two helicopters hovering overhead with laser heat seekers. With the crowds, we need pinpoint accuracy." His gaze sought and found Devon's. "You and DeAngelis are in the air. Aim the lasers at every truck, van, and building within the search zone—let the ground teams know if they have to take a better look at something. Chief, how many snipers do you have available?"

"With long range capabilities? Seven."

"Make that nine. Donovan here and another man on our

team will be joining them." Jackson eyed the head of stadium security. "Alexander, how do the snipers get to the top of the stadium facing the parking lots without anyone seeing them? We have no idea what jobs have been infiltrated."

The man pulled the map with the floor plans from under another map and set it on top. He pointed to a section on the north end of the stadium. "This is the stairwell for the count room, where all the money goes before it's picked up by the armored trucks. The room remains locked during the game, and the money bags are dropped into a deposit box. No one will be going up there until one hour before the game, so that gives us a little over an hour. The snipers can access the top from three flights above that. I'll give them a passkey. The only problem is the security cameras—they're being monitored in the main control room."

Brody stepped forward with his laptop. "I'll hack in from here and make them dark until the snipers are through."

Nodding, Jackson continued. "Good. The rest of the teams that are going into the stadium and lots will need to check every inch of it. I assume we have bomb dogs available?"

"Affirmative," Howard responded. "They're already on scene. Since the Oklahoma City bombing and 9/11, they're standard for every event. We already have them doing a routine patrol of the stadium. They've been advised to call here if they spot anything, but not sound any alarms, as you requested."

"According to our source, this shit is supposed to go down at halftime." Jackson crossed his arms over his chest. "Any sign of an evacuation will lead to an immediate detonation. That's why we didn't want you passing the info on to your off-duty people on scene. We're in a catch-22 here."

"Understood. We've located the communications tower. The SWAT team is ready to take out the two suspects there on your go."

"Have them hold off for now," Carter instructed. "If Kohring tries to communicate with them, and they don't answer, his trigger finger might get itchy. We have about two and a half hours until we get down to the wire. Alexander, delay the gates opening as long as possible but don't make it out of the ordinary. Chief, what do you have for communications?"

Howard signaled to a man dressed in black tactical gear who stepped forward with a box, setting it down on top of the maps. "Hand these out to your team. They're set for random frequencies. It's almost impossible for anyone without a specific receiver to intercept the comms transmissions."

Taking a combination earpiece and microphone from the box, Mic began handing them out to the team. "Anything else, or are we ready to go ice this fucker?"

Several men seemed startled at her question, or at least the venom in her voice, and Carter chuckled. "We don't let her out much. But Mic is right, let's do this. One of our team members will be assigned to each group of federal and local searchers. Anyone comes in contact with a suspect or bomb, they do nothing until Jackson or I are contacted. Let's go."

Fifteen minutes later, they were blending in with the tailgaters. Carter caught Mic's glance at a group of kids throwing a football back and forth. Her worry mirrored his own. Thousands of men, women, and children were in imminent danger, and the teams couldn't warn them. "We've got this," he told her.

She nodded but didn't verbally answer him.

As they checked every van or truck in their assigned

section with three other agents and cops, the snipers checked in after arriving at their posts. Three explosive devices had been spotted so far in the stadium but were ignored for now. It made everyone in the know even antsier, but it had to be done.

The two helicopters were hovering overhead, and Devon and Marco were giving coordinates to the teams below if they had something that needed a closer look. One minute turned into ten which then became thirty and still Kohring's hiding spot was still unknown.

Transmitting from high above the ground, Devon's voice came over the comms. "Carter? Mic?"

Pressing the transmit button, Mic answered for both of them. "Go, Devil Dog."

"Is that you near Row 9 in the J lot?"

She glanced up at a sign on a light pole twenty feet away. "Affirm. What do you have?"

"Solo heat signature coming from what's listed as a utility shack. Far end of row eleven, about two hundred yards west of the other side of I-70."

"Copy that."

Their five-person team started in that direction. As they approached the fence, Ian, Phillips, and two feds met them. They could just make out the green shack amid tall weeds and a few trees on the other side of the interstate. It looked like a double wide outhouse, but what caught their attention was the black van parked next to it.

Carter looked to his left and then right before spotting a chained gate in the fence. The group jogged toward it, and he took out the lock pic set he still had in a pocket of his cargo pants. As he worked, Ian spoke over the comms. "Snipers, can anyone get eyes on this shack?"

"Got it," Jake replied. "Not that it's any help. No windows on this side."

"Keep watch. Command center, this is Teams Four and Five, have another team approach from the west. We're coming in from the east."

"Command copies," a female voice responded. "Mobile Team Eight, you're closest. Approach from the west. Teams Four and Five are your leaders."

"Mobile Team Eight copies."

Once Carter had the lock open, the nine of them exited the perimeter and ran toward the interstate. Traffic was heavy, but slow enough that they were able to zigzag through the lanes of vehicles and get to the other side without getting hit.

"Why'd the chicken cross the road?" Mic asked with a smirk.

Ian laughed as they hurdled over the guardrail on the far side. "Because it fucking wanted to."

A member of Mobile Team Eight rattled off the license plate of the van. Seconds later, a KCPD dispatcher responded, "The plate comes back to a 2009 Ford Econoline, black, registered to a Joel Kohring from Joplin, Missouri."

"Bingo," Phillips said, stating the obvious and earning an eye roll from Mic.

As they approached the shack, Ian asked, "Mobile Eight, any windows?"

"Negative. The one door is the only way in and out. No signs of cameras either."

"Doesn't mean there aren't any. Use caution. Command, have the team at the tower take down their two suspects. Get ready to start a mass evacuation."

"Copy that."

Ten yards away from the shack Carter announced, "I'm first in."

Mic's gaze shot to his stoic face. "Why you?"

"You killed Strauss and Wexler. Phillips took out

Harmon. I've been on this detail longer than everyone and haven't killed anyone yet. I'm fucking due. If this piece of shit is going down hard, he's mine. Deal with it."

Ian, Phillips, and Mic all chuckled but let him have the lead. There were more cops, agents, and operatives than needed for one man in a tiny shack, so some stood back. Standing to the side of the door, weapon at the ready, Carter nodded at the cop holding a battering ram while waiting for the signal. The man swung the big, black door-buster back and then forward with all his might, before getting out of the way. The door crashed open, and Kohring was caught off guard as Carter pivoted around the doorjamb. Leaping from the chair he'd been sitting in, Kohring lunged for a device sitting on a milk crate that'd been turned on its side. But he wasn't fast enough. A .40 caliber bullet penetrated his skull and brain before exiting, splattering the wall behind him with blood and gray matter. He dropped like a rock.

Satisfied the bastard wasn't getting back up, Carter lowered his weapon. His ears were ringing from the gunfire, but he'd gladly take it. The alternative had been incomprehensible.

Standing behind him, Mic patted his shoulder. "Feel better, big guy?"

"Much."

Ian was already on the comms giving the go ahead for a full-fledged evacuation. Stepping over to the control board, Carter noted twelve switches, each with a letter written with a black marker taped above it. A piece of paper sticking out from underneath it had the locations of the other nine explosive devices they hadn't located yet. The bomb squads were going to be busy fuckers for the next few hours.

Teams started calling in the takedowns of several suspects who'd been spotted as word of the evacuation order spread throughout the parking lots. Carter's shoulders sagged with relief as his gaze met Mic's—they'd done it. The good guys had won this battle in the war against terror. It felt like they were in a movie, where the hero stops the timer with one second left. Sometimes life really does imitate fiction.

EPILOGUE

Three chauffeured, blacked-out SUVs pulled up to one of the hangars at a private airport outside Washington D.C. and parked. Doors opened, and the occupants poured out. A bitter wind blew over them as they retrieved their bags from the back ends. A cold front had swooped in, putting the East Coast into an early winter. Ian and the boys were anxious to get back to the warmer Floridian weather, and Carter couldn't blame them.

It'd been a week since the team members from Trident Security, Steel Corps, Deimos, the FBI, and the Department of Homeland Security had stopped the worst domestic terrorist attack on U.S. soil since the Oklahoma City bombing in 1995. With a huge international coordinated effort, the attacks in Britain, France, and Germany had also been prevented. The raids on the compounds in each country had resulted in all the major players being either killed or arrested. From what Carter knew, a few low-level scum had escaped in both Germany and France, but their identities were known and everyone in Europe was on the hunt for them.

With Wexler and Strauss dead, the rest of the U.S. infrastructure of the New Order had crumbled. Those arrested were all trying to cut deals to avoid life in prison. Carter, Mic, Jackson, and the rest of the main team had spent the last twelve days in debriefings with various agencies and committees, starting with the White House on down. They were finally done and heading home.

There were a bunch of back slaps, fist bumps, good-natured ribbing, and goodbyes all around as the Trident team got their gear loaded onto their private jet. Ian pulled the only woman among them into a brotherly hug. "You did good, Mic. We're damn proud of you. If you ever need us, we've got your six, no questions asked."

"Thanks, Ian. Same goes for me. I'll be there in a heartbeat."

A few more goodbyes from Brody, Devon, Marco, and Jake, and then the Trident jet was soon taxiing down the runway, leaving Carter, Mic, and Phillips on the tarmac as the government-issued SUVs pulled away. Jackson had to stick around for another day or two for meetings and briefings at the Pentagon, so his team was heading back north without him. At the moment, Steel Corps's pilot was doing his final flight checklist, and then Mic and Phillips would be ready to go.

Carter had another plane waiting for him. The vile tattoo had been lasered off his upper arm a few days ago, and although there was no visible trace of the symbol of hate, as promised, it still bothered him that it had been there at all. From here, he was planning on going to his retreat—the one place he could be alone and decompress. Once he had a few days to himself, he'd head to one of the kink clubs he belonged to and get what he needed there—the trust and submission of a woman who would soothe his soul—before taking a new assignment. An image of Jordyn Alvarez flashed through his head, and he pushed it right back out. She was a complication his mind didn't want to deal with at the moment, even if his body disagreed with that decision.

Turning to the big man next to him, Carter held out his hand. "Phillips, it was great working with you. Good luck with Steel. Jackson mentioned he's got a few new team members reporting for duty next week."

Phillips shook the proffered hand. "Yeah. They seem like a good group. I think he and Mic chose well. If you're ever in Pennsylvania, stop by for a few beers."

"You got it."

Carter faced Mic and silently stared at her. She stared at him. Looking back and forth between the two, Phillips got the picture and picked up his duffel. "Um. I'm just going to go check on the pilot. See you onboard, Mic."

When the other man left them alone, Carter took a step toward the petite blonde. Reaching out, he stroked her cheek with the back of his fingers. "I'm glad the last of the bruising is gone. I felt a kick in my gut every time I saw it."

She shrugged but didn't pull away or take her eyes off him. "Forget about it . . . it's over."

"So it is." He continued to caress the soft skin of her cheek, her jawline, and under her chin. They weren't made for each other—a fact he truly regretted—but there would always be a strong connection between them he couldn't explain to someone else if he tried. They were too much alike, and if they attempted to have a physical relationship, he knew in the end they would just wind up hurting and hating each other. He valued his newfound friendship with her too much to lose it. But that didn't mean he wasn't going to take the opportunity to give her a proper farewell. "If I walk away without kissing you goodbye, I'm going to regret it. This may be the last chance I ever have . . ."

His words trailed off as he cupped her chin, and his

mouth turned up in a somber smile. "Somewhere down the road, you're going to meet the guy who's going to win you over, sweetheart. You deserve to be happy, not just content with your life. Don't get so wrapped up in your career and missions that you don't reach out and grab him with both hands. Remember to live in the moment, not in the past, because if you blink, you may miss out on the one person who makes you complete."

She didn't answer him. Instead, she swallowed hard as she gazed at his mouth with sad yet hungry eyes. Taking that as consent, he leaned down and brushed his lips against hers. When her breath hitched, he did it again. Her hands flew to the back of his head as she crushed her mouth to his. They wouldn't . . . couldn't go any further than this, but kissing her goodbye was worth the painful hard-on he was now sporting. Drawing her up in his arms, he lifted her feet off the ground as the kiss deepened and rued the thick winter coats preventing him from having her body closer to his.

They clung to each other as if their lives depended on it . . . at least, as if their souls did. Their tongues danced to nature's music, which was as old as time. This wasn't the usual kiss he shared with a woman. Bea Michaels was his equal, in more ways than one, and they both gave and took as much as they could in that brief moment. In another lifetime, she could have been his—but not in this one.

In the hangar behind Mic, the whine of the Steel jet's engines started. It was time for her to go and for him to disappear once again. With great reluctance, Carter eased up and placed a few more pecks on her swollen, red lips before setting her down on her feet again. He took a step back as she straightened her jacket, which had risen up above her waistline. A wistful smile spread across his handsome face. "That was better than I'd hoped for." Picking up his duffel bag, he slung it over his shoulder. "I don't know when we'll see each other again, sweetheart, but you take care of yourself, you hear me? And if you ever need me . . . for any reason . . . even just to talk . . . you know how to get a hold of me."

"Same here." Her voice was raspy, and she cleared the same lust and desire he felt from her throat. "You take care of yourself too. The woman who's going to rope you in, so to speak, is out there, and I'm sure she's one hell of a badass. Don't let her go, my friend."

Bending, he gave her one last tender kiss on her formerly bruised cheek before turning and heading toward where his own pilot and jet were waiting for him a few hangars down. But before he got out of earshot, Mic shouted at him, "And stop fucking calling me 'sweetheart'!"

If you're following the best reading order of the Trident Security series, continue the adventure with T. Carter's story - *Absolving His Sins* - now available.

If you haven't start the Trident Security series, then get *Leather & Lace*.

If you haven't started the Steel Corp series, then get *Core of Steel*.

OTHER BOOKS BY J.B. HAVENS

Other Books by *samantha a. cole*

THE COLLECTIVE: SEASON TWO (WITH 7 OTHER AUTHORS!)

Angst: Book 7

SPECIAL PROJECTS

First Chapters: Foreplay Volume One

First Chapters: Foreplay Volume Two

First Chapters: Foreplay Volume Three

Trident Security Coloring Book

Shaded with Love Volume 5: Coloring Book for a Cause

Cooking with Love: Shaded with Love Volume 6

ABOUT THE AUTHORS

J.B. Havens lives in rural Pennsylvania, and is a wife and mother of three, a boy and twin girls. She has a love for a good cheesesteak and anything that involves coffee or chocolate. When she's not caring for her family, she is busy researching and writing her next novel.

Find JB on her website where you can find character bios and even a short story or two. She loves to hear from readers, so reach out and tell her what you think!

USA Today Bestselling Author and Award-Winning Author Samantha A. Cole is a retired policewoman and former paramedic. Using her life experiences and training, she strives to find the perfect mix of suspense and romance for her readers to enjoy.

Her standalone collection of short stories, *Scattered Moments in Time*, won the gold medal in the 2020 Readers' Favorite Awards in the Fiction Anthology genre. Her standalone novel, *The Road to Solace* (formerly *The Friar*), won the silver medal in the 2017 Readers' Favorite Awards in the Contemporary Romance genre.

Samantha has over thirty books published throughout several different series as well has a few standalone novels. A full list can be found on her website.

CONNECT WITH THE AUTHORS

J.B. Havens

Facebook
Steel Corps Stalkers Group
Twitter
Website

Samantha A. Cole

Facebook
Bookbub
Sexy Six-Pack's Sirens Group on Facebook
Website
Subscribe to my newsletter
All Author
Youtube
Instagram
Pinterest
Goodreads
Amazon

ACKNOWLEDGMENTS

As always, I want to thank my husband, Mike, for his unending support. Thank you for believing in me when I didn't even believe in myself.

Sam, I just gotta say, co-authoring a novel never entered in my mind. But as we've worked together on this project I've come to call you friend. Thanks for your help, guidance, and support. What are we going to write next? It's been so damn amazing that I don't want it to end!
Jules and Jess, you're more than beta readers, you're friends. Your love of Steel is just as great as my own. Thank you!

Brian Parker, thank you for your insight and for tearing us a new one and helping us get it right. We strive to entertain and you helped make sure we do it accurately. Mic and Carter thank you as well.

And to you dear reader, thank you for reading. I hope you love this collaboration as much as Sam and I do. It's EPIC I tell you! :D

Sincerely, J.B.

———

Oh, where to begin? There are so many people I need to thank!

My family and friends, of course, for supporting my exciting journey into the world of literature.

J.B., this has been the most fun I've had since I started the Trident Security series—and that's saying a lot because you know I much I love writing it. This collaboration started as a joke between new friends and fans of each other's stories. But then something clicked and I couldn't have asked for a better co-author. Just say the word, and Carter and the Sexy Six-Pack will be ready to work with Mic and the boys again.

Jess and Jules—Lucy & Ethel, Frick & Frack, Jekyll & Hyde, and whatever future nicknames we come up with for you two—without you this book would never have been written. It was because of you yelling at me to read *Core of Steel* that J.B. and I connected. You didn't steer me wrong, and I will be forever grateful. As J.B. said, you're beyond my beta readers, you are my friends, and I will never take that lightly.

Eve, you have been a godsend to me. Your editing and input helped make this book the best it could be (not to mention all my other books, lol). Thank you for everything and for meeting every deadline I've thrown at you.

To my beta readers and the Sexy Six-Pack Sirens, your continued support and encouragement means more to me than you'll ever know. I cannot say thank you enough. Your posts, messages, shout outs, and reviews are the highlight of my day, every day.

And last, but far from least, to my readers. Your love and loyalty has humbled me. I wish I could one day meet each and every one of you, just to thank you in person. I hope you enjoy *No Way in Hell* as much as we did while writing it. Stay beautiful and happy reading.

Sincerely, Sam